ORPHAN

The Fæ Prince
Of
Fir Manach

Copyright © 2013 K. R. Flanagan
All rights reserved.

Cover photo
by AlgolOnline

ISBN-13: 978-1481092715
ISBN-10: 1481092715

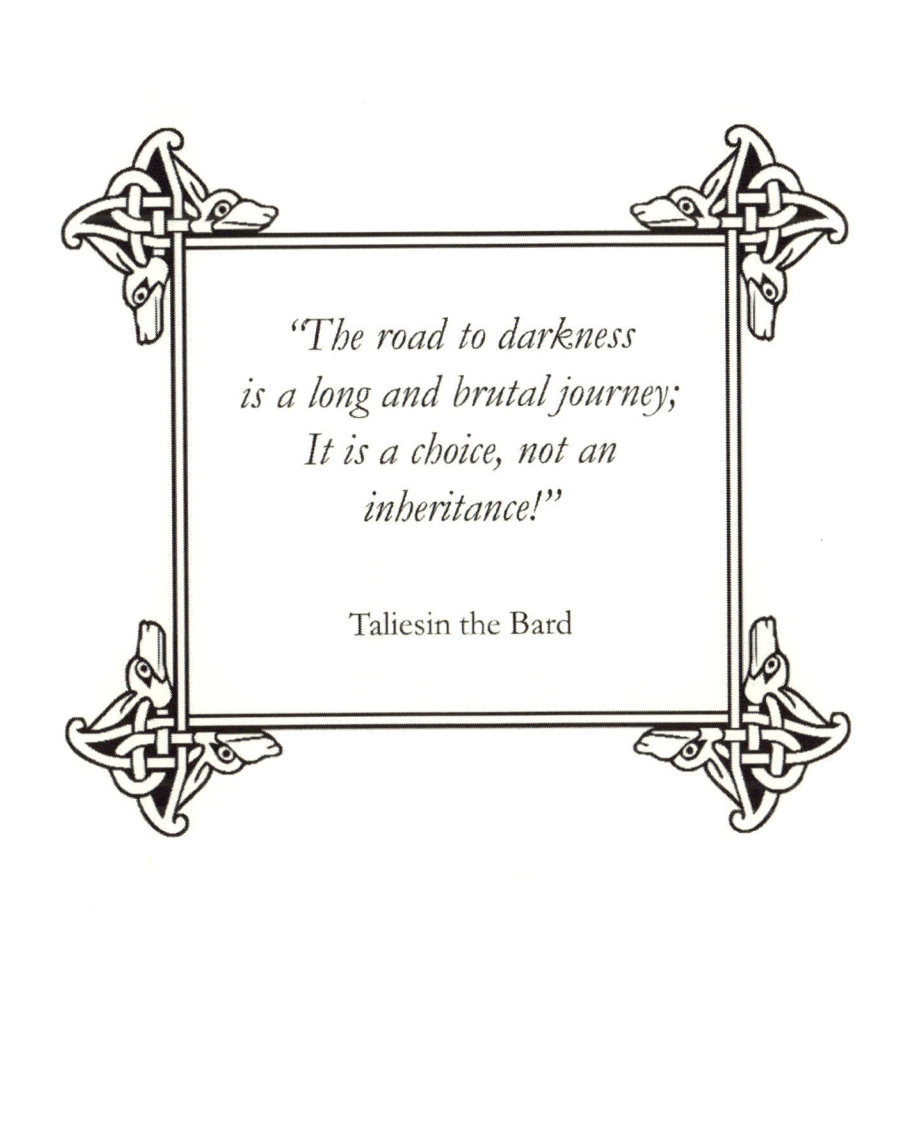

*"The road to darkness
is a long and brutal journey;
It is a choice, not an
inheritance!"*

Taliesin the Bard

CONTENTS

1	Through the Gateway	1
2	Secret Tunnels	14
3	My Enemy, My Friend	31
4	The Caves	46
5	The Mag Uidhirs	63
6	Taliesin Wakes	75
7	The Pirate Queen	89
8	A Fistfight	107
9	Trading Tales	115
10	Ambush	131
11	King Finnbheara	150
12	Glamour	171
13	The Castle at Inis Ceithleann	184
14	Let Us Leave	204
15	Cnoc Meadha	213
16	A City Under Ground	228
17	The Formoire Paths	241
18	Captured	258
19	The Gaol of Paiste	272
20	Freedom	285
21	Good-Bye	295
	Pronunciation Guide	307
	Author's Note	309

CHAPTER ONE

THROUGH THE GATEWAY

Thane took a deep breath and firmly held the reigns of Embarr as they burst through the rippling, liquid curtain of the waterfall into the blue-gray light of gloaming on the other side of the Færie Gateway. His mother's heavy gold medallion lay warm against the skin of his chest, a sign the Gate had worked as it was intended. They had left the Fæ lands of Tír inna n-Óc and were back in the mortal world.

Orphan's arms tightened painfully around his waist as they trotted across the pool of water at the base of the falls. Thane swallowed a laugh as he felt more than heard her muffled scream in the folds of the wool cloak covering his back. Orphan had a strange aversion to water, and he knew she had dreaded the fact that Thane's enchanted horse would need to walk across the surface of the pool to get through the Gate. As hard as she tried to appear fearless, Thane knew she had been afraid to cross the Færie Gateway.

The roar of the cascading falls drowned out all other sounds as Thane looked around him. He had no idea where they were. They could have emerged from a Færie Gateway anywhere in the world as far as he knew. This forest looked much the same as the ones he had traveled through with the Reivers or the one which they had been fleeing through when Taliesin was captured. A shallow stream led away from the falls and disappeared into the forest.

Embarr's hooves sent little sprays of water flying as he trotted across the top of the shallow stream, up the right side of the mossy bank, and into the forest. The horse didn't wait for direction from Thane as he galloped toward the north. Thane was confident Embarr knew where he was going and trusted his horse to get them there quickly and safely.

They were traveling so fast that Thane was only able to catch glimpses of their surroundings. Mist tangled through the leafless hawthorn trees as night began to settle around them. Thane could just see a full moon rising through the skeletal branches of the trees. From its position low in the sky, he could tell they were now heading northeast. He shivered as the chilly air hit him in the face, surprised at how cold it was for early autumn. He pulled his cloak tighter around him, wrapping his fingers in the soft, thick wool.

"Duck!" Thane yelled to Orphan as he flattened himself on Embarr's neck to avoid a low hanging branch. Orphan leaned over until she was nearly lying on top of him. Thane felt the warm weight of her pressing into his back. She may have been dressed like a boy, but at that moment he was reminded of how much of a girl she really was.

Uncomfortable thoughts plagued him as they wove their way through a dense forest of leafless trees. He was still trying to adjust to his discovery that Orphan, his best friend, was in reality, a girl. The boy he'd spent the last two years sharing laughs, chores and secrets with had been an illusion. Thane had worked through most of his anger at being deceived, but he was still coming to terms with the fact that his best friend was not whom he appeared to be.

After what felt like hours of riding through woods, across fields and over hills, Embarr finally slowed his frantic pace to a trot in the midst of a dense forest. Thane straightened up gingerly and stretched. Orphan loosened her arms from around his waist and lifted her forehead from his shoulder.

"How are you feeling?" he asked her. He was afraid their wild ride from the waterfall had reopen the poisoned wound the Roki had slashed into her side.

"Fine," she mumbled without lifting her head. "Stop fussing!"

"Well, then stop pretending nothing's wrong with you!" he retorted. He knew that she would never willingly admit to a weakness.

"Why is it so cold?" Orphan shivered and snuggled up closer to his back again seeking out some warmth.

"I don't know. Look at the trees. They have no leaves. It's strange. You'd almost think it is the middle of winter, not the end of summer," Thane whispered, staring at two lonely leaves clinging desperately to a branch on the naked tree they were passing.

Thane felt Orphan lift her face from between the folds of wool at the back of his cloak. "Time passes differently in Tír inna nÓc. Remember the tales of the mortals who stayed there. They believed they were only in the land of the Fæ for a couple years, but after returning to their homes, they found that hundreds of years had passed. I bet the same thing has happened to us. We were there only one evening, but obviously much more than an evening has passed here." She finished speaking then tucked her head back into his shoulder blades again.

"Hey! If it's winter, that makes me fourteen!" he cried in delight. He knew it would annoy her as her birthday was not until the spring. She was still twelve.

"Mum hum," was all he could make out of her reply.

The full moon was nearing its peak by the time Embarr stepped from the woods onto a wide riverbank. Across the river they could see a castle, its ramparts silhouetted against the torchlit walls of the keep. They stared in silence at the imposing figure of the immense stone castle...a stone castle he recognized. It was the home of his youth, but it wasn't the glorious home he remembered. Thane was disconcerted by the devastation stretched out before him. The gray stone edifice was crumbling apart; huge sections of the rampart were missing in the area where he had seen the most intense flames on the night of the attack. Many of the windows were missing or broken, and some of its walls had caved in.

Thane glanced anxiously at the flowing water as Embarr stepped effortlessly off the land and onto the surface of the river. They were across before Orphan had a chance to do more than squeeze the breath out of him and squeal into his back.

They stopped between his mother's garden and the edge of the woods. The once neat rows of carefully pruned yew hedges and flowerbeds were now in total disarray. His eyes searched the crumbling stone wall above the gardens for the window of his room. He remembered hiding in the bushes helplessly staring up at that window as Zavior confronted and murdered his mother.

Movement atop the castle wall broke him from his reverie; guards were up on the ramparts. It dawned on him that if he could see the guards this clearly, they could probably see him just as easily. He glanced down at Embarr's white coat glowing in the moonlight and was suddenly afraid they would be spotted.

Thane pulled on the reins and turned Embarr deeper into the shadows of the surrounding forest. Embarr stopped behind a dense copse of pine trees and prickly gorse bushes where Thane hoped they would be shielded from the view of the castle. Thane swung his leg over the front of his saddle and slid stiffly down to the ground. He pushed his fists into his lower back to stretch the kinks out of it and looked uncertainly up at Orphan. The last time he had offered to help her down off a horse, she had angrily slapped his hand away. He stood impatiently next to Embarr's head waiting for her to get down.

She cleared her throat.

When Thane didn't move she said, "Um, would you mind giving me a hand?"

Thane looked up at her and raised an eyebrow. "You're asking me to help you?"

Obviously, she also recalled the last time he tried to help her. She had the grace to look a bit sheepish for a moment then brushed aside her guilt and frowned down at him. "One glib remark and I'll kick you!"

"What? Me, say a word about you needing to be helped off a horse?" Thane teased as he took a step closer to Embarr. "Never."

He placed one hand on her hip and one on her back. "Lean forward and swing your leg over the back of the saddle. I'll help you."

He steadied her as she slid slowly off Embarr's back. Once on the ground, she turned, placed her small hands on his shoulders, and leaned on him. It was obvious to Thane that she was finding it difficult to stand without his support. When he looked down at her he noticed that she appeared to be even paler in the moonlight than she had been back in her room in Tír inna n-Óc.

"I'm sorry," she said miserably as she pulled slowly away from him.

"It's okay. Do you think you are bleeding again?" Thane asked hesitantly and was relieved when she didn't immediately bite his head off.

"No, I don't think so. I'm just tired," she admitted reluctantly. She reached around him and dragged her bow and quiver off the saddle before finally taking a few steps away from him. She walked slowly toward a thick stand of trees.

Thane followed Orphan, pulling Embarr behind him. He watched worriedly as she lowered herself to sit at the base of one of the largest trees. With luck, she would be hidden from view of the castle until he got back. Once she was settled, he took another look around the dark forest.

Through the thick trunks of the trees, he could just make out the castle. To the left, he could see the outline of the old church and graveyard. The royal crypt sat in the center of the graveyard. Thane turned his back on the crypt and purposefully pushed the memories of his flight from Zavior and the Roki out of his mind. He couldn't afford to be distracted by them now.

Thane surveyed the various leather bags hanging from Embarr's saddle. His bag was squeezed in between Orphan and Tally's bags and another one he didn't recognize that was bulging with food and supplies. He wondered again about the identity of the mortal they had met in the Fæ stables. He was so sure that he had met the man somewhere before, but try as he might, he couldn't remember where.

Thane eyed the sword peaking out from under Tally's lute and saddle bag. The stranger had thrust the sword into his hands as they were leaving the Fæ stables insisting that Thane would be needing it more than he would. Thane glanced back over his shoulder toward the castle and decided that the man was probably right. He was going to need a weapon to defend himself.

Shifting the lute out of the way, he slid the sword out from behind the saddle. Thane unwound the worn leather belt from the scabbard. The belt was too long for him but he tied it as securely around his waist as he could with the hope that it would stay put. Even though the weight of the strange weapon hung low on his hips, heavy and unfamiliar, it gave him a small sense of security. This time he would not be the defenseless child he had been when he had fled from the Roki during their attack on the castle.

"I think it would be best if you and Embarr stay here and wait for me," he whispered as he turned to face Orphan. "The castle is riddled with secret passageways. I can find the entrance to the bolt hole behind the crypt easily enough on my own. Once I'm in the catacombs, I'll look for the tunnel that'll lead me into the castle. From there, I should be able to make my way down to the dungeons where they're probably keeping Tally."

"I didn't come all this way to be left..." Orphan began to argue. She started to rise as he turned to leave.

"Look Orphan," Thane interrupted her. He took a step closer to her before she could do much more than lean forward. "You're too weak to be of any help, and you know it. You can hardly even stand up on your own," he said as he waved an arm down in her general direction. "If anything, you will slow me down and get us both killed."

Thane watched as she leaned against the tree and settled back down on the cold ground with a huff. She stared angrily up at him but didn't argue. There was nothing else she could say. He was right.

"If you think you are in danger of being seen by anyone," he continued, "get back on Embarr and find someplace to hide. I'll find you."

"Embarr, watch over Orphan." Thane said quietly as he rubbed a hand down his horse's nose. Embarr nodded solemnly. Without another word, he turned and walked away from the small, dense copse.

Thane moved from tree to tree, skirting the edge of the forest and working his way steadily toward the area where the trees abutted the rear of the cemetery. He took his time, careful to keep himself concealed in the trees and leafless underbrush. If he was spotted by anyone in the castle, it would be the end not only for him but also for Orphan and Tally.

Thane found the entrance to the bolt hole at the rear of the crypt exactly where he remembered it. He dropped to his knees and pulled out his small knife to cut the vines away from the opening and was surprised to find them already dangling loosely over the door frame. He jabbed the blade into the space between the door and the frame and pried it open. Thane cringed as its rusted hinges creaked and groaned loudly in the still night. He struggled with the door for a bit before he managed to make a space wide enough to squeeze himself through.

Thane looked nervously around the grounds half expecting to see men storming through the cemetery toward him. Except for the hooting of a lone owl, the cold graveyard remained silent. As he leaned toward the pitch black hole he'd exposed, a wave of foul, moist air rose out of the opening and settled around him in a thick malodorous cloud. He gagged on the smell; it was so strong he could taste it. He was dreading the prospect of crawling through the filth that he remembered had layered the floor and walls of the tunnel. He peered into the black hole and slapped the side of the door with the flat of his hand in frustration. The tunnel would be completely dark. He needed light.

Thane shut the door and stood up. He would have to return to the clearing to find something to use as a torch. He slowly retraced his steps back to where he had left Orphan and Embarr.

As he neared the copse, a huge branch swung up out of nowhere and hit him hard across the stomach. He was sent flying backwards through the air and landed with a hard flump on his back, as the breath whooshed out of his lungs. He lay there stunned, his sword sticking straight up in the air at his side and his arms and legs splayed out.

When he could breathe again, he opened his eyes fully expecting to be surrounded by a host of angry men. He was momentarily relieved to see Orphan's dark shadow silhouetted against the star studded sky. Relief spun instantly to annoyance as he realized that it was Orphan who had hit him. She must have used her Fæ powers because he had not seen it coming, and he was sure she did not have the strength to swing a branch of that size by herself.

"What are you doing?" she hissed, standing over him with her hands on her hips. Long trails of smoke streamed up from her shadowy head like two opaque ribbons as her warm furious breath rose in the cold night air.

"What do you mean, 'What am I doing?'" he groaned as he struggled to get air back in his lungs and sit up. "Why did you hit me?"

"How was I supposed to know it was you? You were creeping up on me. I thought you were one of the guards from the castle. You're lucky I didn't shoot an arrow into you instead!"

"I came back to see if I could find anything to use for light," Thane snapped back at her. "The tunnel is really dark and, considering the condition of the castle, I was afraid it would be dangerous without light. I'm also not sure the Fæ lights inside the crypt will still be lit," he grumbled as he got to his feet and followed her warily back to where Embarr was waiting patiently.

Thane watched her silhouette shrug its wool-covered shoulders. She wandered back toward the large tree and lowered herself gingerly to the ground. She picked up her bow, nocked an arrow, and leaned back against the rough bark with a sigh. Well, at least he was sure now that she could take care of herself. She may have been physically weak, but she had her bow, and her Fæ powers were obviously still as strong as ever.

"Shhh, boy. I won't be long," he crooned to Embarr. The horse appeared to be just as jittery as Orphan was. He pranced and whinnied as Thane fumbled with the ties on the large leather bag of supplies. Thane ran one hand soothingly along the horse's neck as he shoved his other hand down into the stuffed saddle bag and felt the sporran Natty had given him to keep his little treasures in.

He smiled to himself as he recalled the many times he had searched through saddlebags bulging with stolen goods during his years with the Kerrs. More often than not, he had given the small stolen treasures to Natty. He still had the pretty blue ribbon with the flowers that he had intended to give to her.

Again, Thane firmly shoved the memories to the back of his mind. It took him a minute of groping through packs of food, clothes, and water skins before his fingers finally wrapped around a thick waxy object. A candlestick!

Orphan opened her eyes, looked up at the candle he held in his hand, and laughed out loud. He didn't have to ask what she thought was so amusing. It was no secret between them that creating fire was not one of Thane's strengths; it was hers. He shoved the candle down into the side of his boot.

"Who is going to light that candle for you if you don't want me to come along?" she said in a halfhearted attempt to get him to take her.

Thane pulled a soft wool blanket out of one of the bags and turned back to Orphan, shaking it open. He knelt next to her and draped it over her shoulders, his movements hesitant and awkward.

"I'll manage just fine. You're staying here Orphan," Thane reiterated firmly. "I'm going to go back...just try not to kill me when I return...understand?"

Without giving her a chance to respond, Thane turned away from her and slipped into the surrounding trees.

Chapter Two

Secret Tunnels

Thane was careful to stay out of sight of the castle as he made his way back to the rear of the crypt. He knelt once more beside the rough wooden door of the bolt hole, took a deep breath, and crawled forward through the narrow opening. He squeezed into the tunnel on his hands and knees. It was a much tighter fit in the musty tunnel than he had remembered. Maneuvering awkwardly around the length of his sword, he reached behind him and pulled the door shut, then turned back toward the passageway.

Thane sat on the hard, damp floor of the tunnel in pitch black darkness. He had just enough room to sit up. His knees were bent at an uncomfortable angle, and his head was hunched forward between his shoulders, and his chin was pressed down into his chest. Robbed of his sense of sight, his sense of smell intensified tenfold. The stench was so much worse than he had remembered.

He pulled the candle out of his boot and held it out in front of his face. He tried to imagine it glowing with a bright flame.

Nothing happened.

He tried again.

Nothing happened.

Maybe Orphan was right he thought as his frustration mounted, but he'd come too far to give up for fear of the dark. Resolutely, he redoubled his efforts. After a few more moments of frowning into the dark at the spot where he imagined his hand was holding the long taper of wax, the wick began to glow, then smoke. He was relieved when it burst into a small, cheerful, golden flame.

He gazed at his surroundings and immediately wished he could have remained in the dark. The tunnel was so much worse than he imagined it would be. The walls of the narrow jagged tunnel were carved through rock, and a thick black slime covered almost every surface. Small bones and bits of rotting matter were littered across the floor. Taking short, shallow breaths, he tried to swallow the bile that was rising in his throat.

Holding the candle out awkwardly in front of him with one hand, he began to crawl forward on his elbows, wincing as his knees scraped across the rough surface of the sharply sloping floor. Thane felt as if the walls were pressing in on him, so he quickened his pace, desperate to get out of the vile tunnel.

It was a short tunnel, and before long he reached the other end. He was surprised to find that the exit to the bolt hole had been resealed. The last time he had been here a Roki had followed him through the tunnel, and he was sure the creature would not have covered the hole. Who had been in the crypt after he had disappeared, and why had they bothered to disguise the tunnel by covering the hole again?

Thane kicked at the barrel until it rolled away from the hole and thrust the candle through the small opening. He peered out into the dark catacombs. The two Fæ lights that had burned above the tomb belonging to his father's friend Monpier were extinguished. The only light in the room now came from the small candle in his hand.

Thane slithered completely out of the hole, got his feet under him, and gratefully stretched out. He took a couple deep breaths before he realized the air in the catacombs was almost as bad as the air in the tunnel. It smelled like the inside of a moldy old boot.

He straightened the sword at his side and brushed a hand vigorously across his knees in an attempt to dislodge some of the putrid debris from his clothes. He was afraid that even if the guards didn't hear him when he entered the castle, they were certainly going to know he was there by the stench his clothes had picked up in the tunnel.

When he got off as much of the muck as he could, he held the candle up in front of him and looked around. This room also seemed much smaller than he remembered it. A thick layer of dust and long strands of cobwebs covered every surface. The walls were cracked and had large chunks of stone missing from them. Pieces of stone and marble were strewn haphazardly across the floor and the tombs.

On the far side of the room, just visible at the dim edge of the light that spilled from his candle, was Monpier's massive broken marble tomb. Thane's heart began to pound in his chest as he walked slowly toward it, stumbling clumsily over the rubble and debris. He could clearly recall crouching behind the tomb shivering in fear. Zavior had just murdered his parents and he had been sure he would be the next to die.

A small piece of dingy yellow cloth on the ground in front of him caught his eye. He bent down and picked it up between two fingers. He remembered how one of Zavior's fearsome Roki had roared horrifically at him from this very spot as it held this little piece of Thane's blanket in its claw. He shook his head to clear the vision from his mind and dropped the cloth quickly as if it burned his fingers. Thane didn't realize how hard coming back to his family's castle was going to be. There were dark memories everywhere.

Thane turned to look more closely at Monpier's tomb. The marble was torn violently across the middle. The bottom half was tilted away from him and was facing the wall. The upper portion of the tomb that had the carved head and torso of the knight, was tipped toward him. As he approached the tomb, he held the candle closer to the carved face of a knight. He was looking into the cold, stone eyes of the mysterious man who had packed the supplies on Embarr and had helped them escape from Tír inna n-Óc. Shocked, Thane jumped back. What was Monpier doing in the land of the Fæ when everyone thought him dead?

Thane tore his eyes away from the marble face and shook his head. He was getting distracted and he needed to focus on finding Tally. That question would have to wait.

He knew there was another bolt hole in the catacombs that led directly into the castle, but wasn't sure he remembered exactly where to find it. Thane scrutinized the other tombs and ran his fingers along the walls but didn't find anything that felt like it might be a door or secret opening. Discouraged, he closed his eyes and tried to remember back to the days when he had played here with Damien. They had known all the secret passages into and out of the castle, but it had been so long ago.

Where was it? He took a deep breath and concentrated.

He remembered!

The access door that he was searching for was to the right of Monpier's tomb. His eyes flew open as he swung around and stumbled across the rubble to the far wall. He held the candle high to inspect the images of the dead carved onto the panels that lined the walls.

"There!" he cried softly when he recognized the life-sized relief that hid the entrance to the tunnel. He walked up to it and ran his hand along the outer edge of the panel, then traced his fingertips across the image itself. As he passed over the belt of the figure, his fingers caught the edge of a small hook. Looping the tip of his finger through it, he pulled on the curved stone until it clicked softly. A crack opened up along the length of the left side of the image. He tugged firmly on the belt and was amazed at how easily the stone door swung open.

Thane held the candle out so he could see into the tunnel and was relieved to find it was tall enough for him to walk upright and wide enough for two people to travel side by side. Wasting no time, he stepped through the portal and pulled the door shut behind him, grateful to be leaving the fetid crypt behind him.

This tunnel was very different from the dank, nasty hole he had just crawled though; it was dusty, dry, and stale. The air smelled almost pleasant; it reminded him of the toasted bread Tilda would make on cold winter mornings at the Inn. The ground beneath his feet was hard packed dirt, and the walls were haphazardly shored up with planks of crudely cut wooden posts. Spiderwebs were clustered in the corners between the beams and the ceiling.

The candle only illuminated a short distance in front of him. He walked forward slowly, waving his hand through the occasional web that stretched across the tunnel. He was sure it was only nerves and the eerie feel of the tunnel that had him imagining soft noises. Still, he stopped frequently to peer over his shoulder into the darkness behind him. There was never anything there. He was quite alone.

The tunnel ran underneath the whole length of the field between the crypt and the castle. It seemed like an eternity before the ground began to rise beneath his feet. It ended at a series of sturdy stone steps that Thane took two at a time. He stopped at the small landing to study the wooden door. If he remembered correctly, this was the passageway that opened into his father's library. If luck was with him, the room would be unoccupied. An iron latch near the top right corner of the door caught the light. He reached up and easily lifted it off its catch.

Thane blew the candle out and shoved it back into his boot before putting his ear to the door. He listened for a few moments, and when he was sure he didn't hear any noise coming from the other side of the door, he eased it open. He stuck his head slowly through the crack. The library was dark and empty.

Thane squeezed his body between the door and the deep frame and slid cautiously over the threshold. He took a step back to examine the unusually wide edge of the door. A tall bookcase had been mounted to this side of it. He turned, put his shoulder against the wood, and shoved it closed. The seam was so tight that it was impossible to feel even the smallest outline of the entrance. He hoped he could figure out how to open it again when he was ready to leave.

Thane turned and leaned back against the empty bookshelves to study the dark space around him. The library slowly revealed itself to him as his eyes adjusted to the bright moonlight streaming through the long windows across the room. His father's large wooden table was flipped onto its side, missing a leg. Chairs were tipped over and broken. Tattered books were strewn throughout the mess, their pages torn and scattered about like pale autumn leaves.

The shadows melded and shifted as images played across Thane's mind. His blood pounded loudly in his ears as pressure started to build in his chest. He fought to breathe as he remembered the night he inadvertently stumbled upon his father and Zavior arguing in this room.

The horrific scene played across the ransacked room as images of the beasts Zavior called his Roki superimposed themselves over the broken chairs, the big mahogany table, and rows of bookcases. He remembered the flashes of unnaturally red firelight that had filled the now cold and crumbling fireplace. He saw again the glint of his father's sword as he fought against Zavior's beasts. Thane stood frozen as the nightmare unfolded.

Thane squeezed his eyes closed and willed himself to stop shaking...to start breathing again. *The images aren't real! They aren't real!* He chanted frantically to himself over and over as he struggled to gain control of his emotions.

When he finally worked up the courage to open his eyes, the room was once again dark, silent, and empty. Thane had to get out of the library before he lost all control. With his eyes cast down, he stepped cautiously over the debris and, without looking left or right, he made his way toward the door that led to the hallway.

As he approached the closed door, he could hear gruff, angry voices. They were arguing, but he couldn't make out what they were saying. As they passed the door, he realized they were speaking a language he didn't understand. He threw his body flat against the wall next to the door and took some comfort in the soft hiss of his sword as he pulled it slowly from the scabbard.

Thane held his breath until he heard the footsteps fade away. He waited a few moments more to make sure they were gone before opening the door and stepping out into the cold, dimly lit hallway, shutting the door gently behind him. A few torches were mounted at odd intervals adding just enough light to see by but not so much light that he felt exposed. Thane was confident he still knew the way to the kitchens. He turned left and walked slowly down a corridor. He saw no one else. With a sigh of relief, he slipped through the open door at the end of the hallway. He stood silently just inside the large dimly lit room and looked around.

The main kitchen remained much as he remembered it, only now it was a great deal dirtier. The room smelled of cooked meat, but nothing Thane thought he would want to eat. The massive stone fireplace in the center of the room held the rancid carcass of an enormous, long dead animal that had been burned so badly it was almost black. Most of the meat had been torn off and presumably eaten, although a good amount had been scattered across the floor and left to rot.

Thane started to walk across the room. He stumbled over his feet when he realized there was a guard sitting at a long table on the far side of the room, adjacent to the short hallway that led to the dungeons and the outer garden door.

The man was immense. The bumpy mess that was his head was resting on his beefy, lesion-covered arms. Two ridges of boney protuberances ran in a line from just above his thick eyebrows, back over the top of his head, and looped down around his small misshapen ears. Long, brown, greasy hair splayed across the table he was resting on. If the awful noise coming out of his mouth was any indication, he was sound asleep. Whoever or whatever he was, he clearly wasn't completely human.

Thane retreated quietly through the kitchen door. He leaned back against the wall next to the doorframe and held his sword defensively in front of him, gripping the pummel tightly in his sweaty hands. He could feel his heart pounding in his chest as he tipped the flat of the blade against his forehead and briefly closed his eyes.

What should he do?

He could sneak up behind the warrior and stab him in the back.

No, he couldn't stab someone while they were asleep; that went against everything he was taught.

He could hit him over the head and hope that he was strong enough to knock him out.

But...what if it didn't work? That thing was huge!

He peeked around the frame of the door and inspected the kitchen again. All of the doors that led off of the room were closed. He knew that some of the doors led to storerooms and smaller kitchens. To the left of the nasty carcass was the bakery where he used to help Martha make pastries.

Thane took a deep breath. The only entrance to the dungeons was the one being guarded by the giant warrior. Thane was going to have to do something quickly. The longer he remained where he was, the more likely it was he would be caught. Glancing again at the sleeping guard, he took a deep breath and slowly and carefully crept across the filthy kitchen. The giant continued to snore contentedly as Thane tiptoed cautiously past him.

Relieved to have successfully made it past the guard unchallenged, Thane headed down the short hall toward the stairwell that led down into the dungeon. He wasn't sure what he was going to do if he found a room full of guards like the one in the kitchen. For the first time he began to doubt the viability of this hastily tossed together plan.

Thane gripped the sword in his left hand and trailed his right hand along the rough-hewn wall. He descended the curved stone staircase one step at a time, listening intently for the slightest noise from the dungeon below. It was eerily silent. Surely they would have Tally under heavy guard?

The stench of human waste and unwashed flesh hit his nose long before he saw the flickering yellow glow of torchlight. Hearing no noises, he continued to creep steadily down the stairs.

When he reached the last step, he held the sword up protectively in front of him again and peered around the corner of the stairs. There was no one guarding the dungeon. A rickety wooden table and stool sat between two rusty iron gates. The cells behind the gates were nothing more than low recesses that had been crudely cut into the rock wall. Even with the light spilling from the torch mounted on the wall, he couldn't see into either of the dark cells from where he was standing. He needed to get closer, and he needed more light.

Thane strode across the room and pulled the candle from his boot. He reached over the table and touched the wick to the torchlight; he was relieved that he would not have to waste precious time trying to conjure another flame.

With his newly lit candle, he bent over and examined the nearest cell. It was empty. Thane skirted around the table, held the candle out in front of him, and squinted into the other cell.

Thane's heart sped up as he realized that what appeared to be a lump of rags at the rear of the cell was a body huddled in a ball on the rough ground. It was too dark to know if it was Tally.

"Oi!" Thane whispered urgently to the lump of rags. It didn't move.

"Tally, is that you?" Thane called out again.

The rags moaned softly. Thane was relieved that whoever was under the smelly heap of clothing was still alive.

"Tally?" Thane hissed.

Thane realized that he would have to get the prisoner out because no matter who the man was, Thane couldn't leave him here. If he was Zavior's prisoner, Thane was sure he had done nothing to deserve his imprisonment.

Thane straightened up and searched around the chamber for a key to unlock the cell. There was nothing there. The key must be up in the kitchen with the sleeping giant. With a frustrated grunt, he blew out the candle and headed back up the stone stairs.

The guard was still right where he had left him, and thankfully still fast asleep. A ring of keys lay half hidden by his hair on the table next to his beefy left hand. Not wanting to get any closer than necessary, Thane stretched his hand out toward the guard and imagined the key ring lifting off the table and gliding toward him. The keys tinkled softly as they rose from the table and floated toward his outstretched hand. The man grunted loudly once, rolled his head around the table, but didn't open his eyes. Thane felt a large bead of sweat roll down his back as he snatched the keys out of the air with his other hand and returned to the dungeon.

The second key he tried slid easily into the lock, and the tumbler rocked open with a solid clang. Thane relit the candle, swung open the iron door, and crawled into the small cell. He laid his sword on the ground next to his knees and reached out a tentative hand to shake the mound of rags. Without warning, the prisoner rolled over, swinging his fists violently at Thane.

Caught unaware by the unexpected attack, Thane caught a solid punch to his jaw and fell back, knocking his head against the stone ceiling. Before his brain could fully register the fact that he was being hit, the pile of rags had its hands around Thane's throat and was trying to choke him. Thane tried to pull his knees up between their bodies to push the prisoner off, but his feet became tangled in the man's filthy robes. They tumbled out of the cell together, each one struggling to overpower the other.

Thane could tell that the prisoner was rapidly weakening, so with one last shove, he managed to roll them both over so that Thane was now sitting on top of him, his legs straddling either side of the man's filthy waist. As Thane sat up, the light from the torch on the wall behind him spilled across the face of the prisoner. Thane was looking down into the delirious brown eyes of the Bard.

"Tally!" he whispered.

"Thane?" Tally wheezed at him. He seemed to be having a hard time focusing on Thane's face. "What are you doing down here? Where did you come from?"

"We're rescuing you." Thane eased himself off the Bard and knelt at his side to take a better look at him. Tally's imprisonment had taken such a toll him that if Thane hadn't recognize his voice, he might not have know who he was. Tally's hair was so matted with filth that it was nearly black, not the familiar silver gray. Waxy, pale skin was stretched tightly over the Bard's cheeks and jaws. Bruises covered the right side of his face, and Tally smelled so awful that, in comparison, Thane thought the bolt hole in the catacombs had smelled like a garden.

"Rescuing me? Where did you get help?" Tally seemed to rally his strength a bit at the thought. "The Fæ? The Mag Uidhirs? Are they here? What is the plan?"

"Uh, well, it's just me…and…uh, Orphan too…but I left her behind in the forest with Embarr." Thane shrugged defensively. "She was still too weak to be of much help and…well…there really is not much of a plan. We're just figuring it out as we go along. So, yes…right now, it's just me."

"Are you crazy?" Tally suddenly railed at him in an angry whisper. "Are you telling me you just charged in here alone? No one watching your back? No plan? You are going to get yourself killed!"

Thane felt foolish and angry as he stared down at the outraged blustering Bard. Thane was risking his life to save Tally, and instead of the gratitude he was expecting, he was being scolded as if he were a misbehaving child.

"You know what? We don't have time for this. We need to get out of here," Thane shot back defensively.

"Can you stand?" Thane asked Tally curtly as he got to his feet and looked down at the old man.

"Yes, of course," Tally retorted.

Thane crawled back into the cell to grab his sword then turned back to find Tally still lying on the ground. His eyes were closed again.

"Tally?" he whispered urgently, his anger leaving as quickly as it had come.

The Bard's eyes fluttered open and he looked up at Thane in confusion for a moment then mumbled with a frown, "Actually...I do not think I will be able to stand after all."

Thane started to panic. It was beginning to dawn on him that getting into the dungeon had been the easy part. Somehow he was going to have to get out of this castle dragging a man who was so weak that he could barely stand, let alone walk.

Thane sheathed his sword then bent to help Tally get to his feet. He was shocked at how little Tally seemed to weigh. Thane wrapped his right arm around the man's waist and shoved his shoulder up under Tally's armpit. He swallowed a gag at the awful smell emanating from Tally's body.

Thane guided Tally across the small guardroom easily enough, but negotiating the stairs proved to be more difficult. The Bard was weakening, leaning more and more of his weight on Thane, until Thane was nearly carrying him up the stairs. Thane struggled to keep them both upright and silent, expecting the guard to wake up and discover them at any moment.

They had almost made it to the top of the stairs when Thane heard something that made his blood run cold. Angry yells and the metal on metal ringing of swords echoed beyond the kitchen. The noise was ear-splitting. This was more than just a fight between two swords; the castle was under attack. He needed to get them out of there before they were caught in the middle of someone else's fight.

Tally lifted his head off his chest and looked toward the sounds.

"They aren't friends are they?" he asked Thane breathlessly.

"No," Thane whispered back.

Tally's head fell forward again and he mumbled into his chest. The only words Thane could make out were "no sense" and "folly."

Frustrated and anxious, Thane stood in the stairwell, struggling under Tally's weight, and trying to decide in which direction they should go next. He knew that if they turned toward their right, away from the main kitchen, they would be at the door that led to the gardens and the graveyard beyond it. They might be able to sneak out the kitchen door but, with the castle under attack and Tally so weak, they would never make it across the open field and into the crypt without being seen.

A sudden fierce rallying cry rang out from deep within the castle. Sharp voices in the hall on the other side of the kitchen door barked out commands and the fighting momentarily escalated. Thane began to retreat down the stairs with Tally but paused as the sounds of the skirmish began to fade.

Thane forced himself to relax. He lowered Tally onto the step below him, returned to the landing. He stuck his head out of the doorway to take a quick look into the main kitchen. The sleeping guard was gone, his chair empty. Whoever had been fighting seemed to have moved away from the kitchens and taken the menacing guard with them.

Thane returned to Tally and shoved his shoulder firmly back under Tally's arm. This time he pulled his long sword out. They cautiously hobbled across the kitchen and out into the dim hall.

Chapter Three

My Enemy, My Friend

Their good fortune held as they made their way toward the library. It was taking all the strength Thane had to hold Tally upright and keep them moving forward one painful step at a time. He was desperate to get them to the tunnel where they would be safe at least for a little while. They could rest there for a bit before attempting to make the trek back to the clearing where he had left Orphan and Embarr.

Thane was surprised to find the door to the library slightly open. He was sure he had shut it behind him when he left. Maybe he had been so shaken by his memories that he was mistaken. He pushed through the door whispering encouragement to Tally as they stumbled awkwardly into the library.

Without warning, Thane's feet were swept out from underneath him. He lost his grip on Tally as he fell forward and skidded, face first, across the dirty rug and was lucky enough not to have been impaled on his sword. For the third time that night, he found himself knocked to the ground. He heard the door click closed behind him and scrambled to get to his feet. He brought his sword up and turned to confront his attacker.

"Who are you?" demanded the dark shadow from the doorway.

Thane could see the silhouetted length of a long sword pointing directly at his chest. He was afraid to take his eyes off the sword for even a moment to look for Tally.

"Who wants to know?" Thane stumbled over the retort feeling a bit stupid the minute the words were out of his mouth. What a ridiculous thing to say! Thane didn't wait for a reply; he attacked.

It didn't take Thane long to discover he was seriously outmatched. He hadn't been able to practice sparring since he had dislocated his shoulder during the fight with Zavior, and this borrowed sword was much longer and heavier than the ones he had used training. Also, his arms were already fatigued from the effort it had taken to get Tally up the stairs and into the library. The best Thane was going to be able to do was to block the blows the man was raining down on him and try to remain standing.

It was taking all of his skill to anticipate his opponent's blows. It wasn't long before his arms began to shake from the effort of fending off his attacker. In one last desperate effort, Thane swung his sword to the left and up. Thane's sword slipped. It slid up under the hilt of the other man's sword, and Thane somehow managed to slam his pommel into the stranger's jaw.

His attacker stumbled back shaking his head to clear it, growled in anger, then charged at Thane again. This time, he snaked the hilt of his sword around Thane's blade, and with one swift move, tore the weapon out of Thane's hand. It went flying across the room and landed with a clatter under a moonlit window.

"I asked you..." the man growled in his face as he pressed Thane back against the library door, the edge of his sword a breath away from cutting Thane's throat, "...who you are? Are you English? Or are you one of them? How did you know about the secret tunnels?"

Even up close, all Thane could see was the silver, square outlines of the windows mirrored in his attacker's dark pupils. The rest of the man's features were disguised by a mask that covered most of his face and head.

"I'm waiting," he sneered threateningly as he increased the pressure on the blade he had pressed into the soft skin of Thane's neck. "Give me a reason why I shouldn't kill you now before I go back to the forest and kill the accomplice you left there."

Thane felt every muscle in his body tense as panic flared inside of him. Orphan! What had he done to her? Was she safe? And, how did *he* know about the bolt holes?

"All right! All right! My name is Thane. We're only here to rescue..." He didn't get a chance to finish his explanation before he was grabbed roughly by the arm and twisted around so the moonlight spilling from the broken window illuminated his features.

"Thane?" the man repeated his name hoarsely. "Your name is Thane? Prince Nathaniel?"

Swearing under his breath, he dropped Thane's arm and backed swiftly away from him.

Thane watched as the stranger's gaze traveled up and down his tall, lanky frame. He imagined what the man was seeing as he looked him over. Thane's thick black hair and dark black eyes were strikingly at odds with his pale face. If Thane was lucky, his hair would still be covering his pointy ears. His richly tooled leather boots and the valuable jewel encrusted sword were incongruous with his shabby, coarse clothing.

"That's not possible. He's dead," he said in a matter of fact voice. "He died years ago!"

"No, I can assure you, I'm not dead!" Thane retorted as the other man searched the shadows.

"Who is that?" he demanded pointing to Tally who, Thane could now see, was sprawled out on the floor next to the door where they were first attacked. He was laying face down on the dirty rug unmoving.

Thane ignored the question. He brushed past the man and rushed to Tally's side. Although he didn't understand what was happening, he felt sure that the stranger didn't intend to hurt him now.

He rolled Tally gently onto his back. The old man was still alive, but his breathing was shallow, and he was unconscious. Thane had to get Tally out of here and get back to Orphan. Maybe her Fæ elixir could heal him.

Desperately, Thane turned back to squint into the silent shadows. "Look, I don't know who you are, but I'm beginning to think you're not a part of the evil living in these castle walls either. Will you help me get him out of here and back to...my friend in the forest?"

The man stared down at them so long that Thane was sure his answer was going to be 'no.' Abruptly the stranger stalked over to the window and snatched Thane's sword from the floor where it had landed during their fight. He walked briskly back to where Thane was trying unsuccessfully to rouse Tally and silently handed it back to him.

"We are running out of time. It is almost dawn and my men will be pulling away from the castle shortly. We need to leave now," he said as he watched Thane sheath his sword.

"He isn't going to make it on his own; I can't wake him." Thane looked up and said, "He'll need to be carried..."

The stranger walked around them and knelt on the other side of Tally. Together they hoisted him up between them. They half dragged, half carried him over to the bookcase. Thane watched as the stranger reached past him and confidently released a secret catch. The ornate wooden bookcase swung open. They awkwardly shouldered their burden through the narrow opening and paused on the small landing. Thane was surprised to see a torch burning in a bracket on the wall next to the door. The torch hadn't been there when he'd passed through just a short time ago.

Thane held Tally up against the wall as the other man disappeared back into the library. He returned a moment later. He pulled the door shut firmly behind him and the latch fell into place with a soft click.

"We should be safe in here," the man whispered to Thane as he grabbed the torch from the bracket. "I covered the tracks we left in the dust in the room behind us and the ones you carelessly left in the crypt. With luck, the guards won't find the entrances to the bolt holes."

The man took the lead as they maneuvered Tally's deadweight between them. They slowly made their way down the stairs and into the tunnel.

"We won't be able to escape through the rear bolt hole of the crypt. It's too small for us to carry him through. We'll have to go out the front door. Pray that no one is looking in our direction," Thane heard him grumble.

Thane didn't reply. There was nothing to say. It was taking all of his concentration not to stumble or bang Tally's head on the ceiling of the tunnel. He was anxious for Orphan's safety and desperate to get back to her. He didn't trust his new found ally. Who was this angry man, and what had he been doing in the castle?

Thane furtively studied the stranger's profile in the flickering torchlight. He was dressed for skulking about in the dark. Thane could now see that what he initially thought was a mask was really a dark woolen scarf and cowl of mail cleverly wrapped to conceal all but his intense amber eyes. Under his dark woolen cloak, Thane glimpsed a pair of black breeches, fitted tightly to his legs and coarse leather boots. They were almost the same height which was helpful since it enabled them to keep Tally's body fairly level while they made their way through the narrow tunnel.

The trip back through the bolt hole was difficult and painfully slow. Although Tally was a thin man, he was tall and unconscious. The tunnel was just barely wide enough for two people. They were forced to shuffle sideways carrying Tally's deadweight awkwardly between them.

After what seemed like hours of struggling with Tally's unwieldy body, they arrived at the entrance to the catacombs. They gently lowered the Bard to the ground near the door, and Thane collapsed onto the floor next to him. He was exhausted, and every muscle in his body was shaking.

Thane looked up in surprise as the man thrust the torch at him and whispered, "Stay in the tunnel with the Seanchaidh. You'll be safe here. I'll go get help and make sure we have a clear path out of here. Don't move, understand?"

Thane started to protest, but before he could push a word out past his clenched teeth, the stranger had slipped his body through the small exit and was gone.

Frustrated, Thane drove the torch into the dirt next to him. When he was sure it wasn't going to tip over and set his clothes on fire, he turned to examine Tally. The Bard had not regained consciousness once during the trip through the tunnel. Thane scooted closer to him and lifted the old man's upper body off the hard ground. He gently cradled Tally's head and shoulders in his lap.

In the yellow light of the flaming torch, he inspected the Bard's wounds. Thane was shocked and sickened by what he saw. Tally must have hit his head on something when he fell in the library because he was bleeding freely from a fresh gash on his temple. Dark rivets of blood ran into Tally's filthy hair. The left half of his gaunt face, and what Thane could see of his chest and arms, were covered with yellow, purple, and black bruises. It was an obvious mix of old and new injuries. What had they done to him? How long had he been held prisoner here? Just how long had they been in Tír inna n-Óc?

Thane mulled over the name the man in black had called Tally. He recalled 'Seanchaidh' meant storyteller in Gaelic. Obviously, the stranger recognized Tally. Did that mean he was a friend?

Thane leaned his head back against the hard wall and closed his eyes. There would be time enough to search for answers later. They had to get out of here alive first. Thane felt the fight slowly seep out of his body leaving him drained. As he sat there waiting for the stranger to return, his eyes began to droop and his mind began to drift. Even though he was half asleep, he was still aware of everything around him: the weight of Tally in his arms, the light of the torch flickering across his eyelids, and the sound of the burning flame.

††††

Soft noises coming from outside of the tunnel startled him out of his torpor. Thane reached for the pummel of his sword just as the stranger pulled the stone door open and looked inside. He held the door as a large, burley man squeezed his massive girth through the opening and slipped into the tunnel. A yellow, long-sleeved tunic covered most of his body, ending mid-thigh. He was barefoot. Thane looked up into a face that was pockmarked with scars from old blemishes and battle wounds. Heavy brows were drawn together over pale blue eyes that quickly assessed Thane and Tally.

He reached out his big hands and his thick fingers gently moved Thane's arms away from Tally. Without asking permission, he lifted Tally from Thane's lap. He ducked his large head and wrapped the Bard's unconscious body across his enormous shoulders as if Tally were no larger than a child. Thane stared in awe at the muscles of the man's powerful bare legs as they bunched and flexed under the strain of Tally's extra weight. The giant turned and maneuvered carefully through the doorway and into the crypt. Thane grabbed the torch and scrambled through the opening after him.

By the time he had closed the tunnel door behind him, the giant was gone. The man dressed in black stood in the center of the room holding his sword in one hand and a torch in the other. "You and your friends will be coming with us," he commanded. "It seems we have much to talk about."

"We don't have anything to talk about! My friends and I need to get as far away from..." Thane started to protest but was rudely cut off mid-sentence.

"We can't discuss this now. It's too dangerous to stay here. My men will come back and secure this room. You are coming with us," he ordered then walked out of the room leaving Thane standing alone next to Monpier's tomb feeling powerless and frustrated. This was not going the way he had anticipated.

Angry and feeling like he had lost all control of the rescue, Thane reluctantly followed the strangers through the catacombs, up the stairs, and onto the main level of the crypt. He passed the tombs of his forefathers without a glance; all of his energy was focused on getting them out of this situation.

"Who do you think you are? You have no authority over us, and you have no right to interfere!" Thane argued furiously. "We were doing just fine on our own. We're not going anywhere with you!"

The man rounded on him and replied, "You have no choice. The horse and the friend you so heedlessly left behind in the woods have already been taken into our care." He turned and continued to make his way to the front entrance of the crypt where the man carrying Tally had stopped to wait for them. He spoke briefly with Tally's bearer, then turned back to Thane.

"We won't harm you if that is what you fear." He looked appraisingly at Thane and in a voice full of contempt, he asked, "You don't have the slightest idea who I am, do you?"

When Thane continued to glare at him without replying, the man reached up and swiftly unwound his scarf. He pulled the cowl down to completely uncover his angry face.

The torchlight reflected off his dark, wavy hair as it escaped the confines of the wool. Thane caught a glimpse of a thin scar that ran along his left cheek and disappeared just under the edge of his jaw before a thick lock of hair fell forward and covered that side of his long, narrow face. Thane stared at the youth, for that was what he was…a young man. He was no more than a couple years older than Thane, although he had the eyes of a man many years older.

Thane took a step back in heart-wrenching disbelief as recognition finally slammed into his brain. He knew exactly who this man was for they had once been inseparable friends.

"Damien?" he whispered hoarsely. Joy at finding him alive after all these years flared in his heart. He took a step forward but his happiness was shattered by Damien's reply.

"You finally remembered me, huh?" he said, a bitter edge to his voice. "Didn't you ever once wonder where I was? Wonder if I was alive? Try to find me? What have you been doing for the last seven years while I…?" Damien stopped abruptly. He pulled his shoulders back and shook his head. "No, don't answer that. I don't have time to listen to tales of your grand adventures. Just follow us and try not to make any noise."

Damien snuffed out his torch then turned abruptly away from Thane. He slid out past the heavy front door of the crypt with the giant carrying Tally close behind him. Thane extinguished his torch and reluctantly followed after them. Cold air whipped across his body, pulling at his clothes as he skirted the front wall of the crypt, then turned to make his way toward the rear of the building.

For an agonizing few moments, they were painfully vulnerable as they ran across the open, moonlit field toward the rear of the cemetery. Thane expected to hear a cry of alarm from the castle walls and was relieved when they made the cover of the forest without incident.

Thane continued to seethe as they wended through the trees towards the small glade where he had left Orphan and Embarr. How dare Damien talk to him like that? He had no idea what Thane had been through over the last seven years…no inkling of the neglect and abuse he had suffered while in the hands of the Border Reivers. Damien had no right to infer that Thane had deserted the castle years ago because he had wanted to.

Thane looked up and glowered at the dark figure leading their small group…Damien. Thane had been sure Damien had been killed during the attack on the castle. Although he felt he should have been relieved to find Damien still alive, all he felt was a sense of betrayal. How had Damien escaped? For that matter, what had *he* been doing for the last seven years? Damien was strong and healthy. What about Martha? Was she alive too? Had they ever tried to find him? Damien was right; they did have a lot to talk about.

Thane tripped on a tree root and almost tumbled sideways into a thorny bush. He righted himself and took a deep breath. He tried to settle his riotous thoughts and concentrate on where he was going. He didn't want to find himself needing to be carried as well.

By the time they arrived back at the small glade, the sun had just begun to tint the sky gray. Thane shoved past Damien and bolted for the tree where he had left Orphan and Embarr. They were both gone. Everything was gone. He spun in a circle surveying the area. What had Damien done with them?

Without warning, men began dropping from the canopy of barren branches overhead and popping out from behind the surrounding trees and bushes. Thane had just enough time to draw his sword and thrust it out in front of him before he was encircled by a ring of axes, swords, knives and arrows. It looked like an army of saffron-cloaked, chain mailed giants. The big, burly men behind the weapons had the fierce scarred faces of battle-hardened warriors who, at this moment, all had their collective, enraged attention focused on him.

Damien pushed through the tight circle of men and stepped protectively in front of Thane, his arms spread wide. "Stop! He's under my protection and be assured," he smirked, "he is no threat."

For a heartbeat no one moved. Thane didn't breathe. Beyond the circle of men he could see Tally being gently lowered to the ground. The warrior stood guard over him as if afraid the frail old man might get up and run into the forest. Helpless fury washed over Thane. Damien was right, he really was no threat at the moment, and it galled him to have to stand here at their mercy.

Behind Damien, Thane sliced his sword aggressively through the air, more out of frustration than out of a need to defend himself. He glared at them to let them know he wasn't helpless or afraid of them before sheathing his sword. A couple of the men laughed out loud at his show of bravado before they all turned their backs on him and melded into the trees. They disappeared as quickly as they had appeared.

"Where have you taken them?" Thane grabbed Damien's arm and swung him forcefully around to face him. His stomach was a swirling knot of anger and anxiety. They should never have split up; he shouldn't have left her alone. Despite her insistence and the assurances he had made to himself that she was strong enough to protect herself, she had been in no condition to fight.

"Where's my horse?" Thane shouted to the trees.

Damien had repositioned the scarf and cowl around his head. Once again, all that was visible were his amber eyes, narrowed to hostile slits as he glanced down at Thane's hand on his arm.

"I told you not to make any noise! They are safe, a lot safer than we are standing out here yelling and arguing about them. We will be joining them soon enough, but it is a rough journey to our home and Taliesin's condition is grave. We will have to travel slowly. Derry will carry him as far as the horses. From there we will ride the rest of the way. Hope for the best."

Damien deliberately pulled his arm from Thane's grip, turned his back on him, and strode over to where Tally was lying on the ground. He spoke briefly to the man Thane assumed was Derry then strode into the forest. The immense warrior gently lifted Tally, hoisted him across his shoulders once more, and followed Damien.

Thane took a quick look around and realized he had been left to stay or follow as he chose. He closed his eyes and stood still for a moment listening to the barely discernible sounds of men moving away from the clearing. He blew a long breath, pulled his cloak tighter around his body, and trailed dejectedly after Damien.

Chapter Four

The Caves

Thane caught up to the group at the edge of the river close to the place where he and Orphan had crossed earlier with Embarr. The warriors were climbing silently into small currachs and swiftly rowing away. Thane turned to walk toward the boat Derry was lowering himself and Tally into when Damien grabbed Thane's arm and pulled him toward the last empty shell.

"Get in," Damien ordered. "You're going with me."

It had been many years since Thane had been in a currach, and he wasn't keen about climbing into one of them now. The small oval boats were all built in the same manner: animal skins stretched taunt over a shallow wooden frame and tarred to keep them watertight. Three narrow benches were fitted across the inside. He looked out at the retreating warriors. If those massive warriors didn't sink the currach, then he guessed the small boat would be able to hold his weight easily enough.

Thane snatched his arm from Damien's tight grip and climbed cautiously into the currach. It bobbed about in the water and tipped unevenly to one side as Thane stepped into it. He was still not used to maneuvering with Monpier's sword. As he swung the scabbard around his leg toward the front of his body, the tip caught between the wooden seat and the gunwale that rimmed the top edge of the boat. He lost his balance and landed hard onto the narrow bench behind him. The leather belt, also too big for him, rode painfully up his side only stopping when it hit his armpits.

Damien didn't offer to help. He just stood back and snickered at him. Thane felt like a bumbling fool as he struggled to pry the scabbard loose. He wiggled the belt back down to his waist and swung the sword forward so that it was now in front of his leg. He took another minute to straighten his clothes out then settled on the narrow bench. He glanced furtively around to see how many warriors had witnessed his humiliating display and was relieved to see that none of the men were looking at him.

Thane gripped the sides tightly as Damien hopped easily into the boat. He sat facing Thane, grabbed the oars, and thrust them into the water. Damien wasted no time pulling them across the current toward the opposite shore behind the little fleet.

Water sprayed up over the low gunwales as it hit the tar-covered animal skins on the side of their currach. Thane shivered as the ice cold drops hit his face and slid down his neck. He trailed his hands through the water to rinse off the grime he had picked up in the bolt holes. In the early morning light, he could see that his hands were not only covered in dirt but also Tally's blood as well. Even though the water was very cold, Thane felt oddly comforted by the silky feel of it as it trickled through his fingers.

Thane dried his hands on his cloak as Damien drove them up onto the shore next to three other boats. Damien jumped out and strode over to where the warriors had gathered near the edge of the forest. He appeared to be giving out orders. The men nodded at him and began to disperse. Thane found himself pointedly ignored by the warriors as he climbed awkwardly out of the currach.

Three of the men strode purposefully toward Thane. Feeling a bit unnerved by the strangers' approach, Thane reached under his cloak for the pummel of his sword, but the men brushed past him as if he weren't there. They pulled the boats effortlessly out of the water, flipped them over, and each lifted a shell onto his back. They carried them into the trees.

Thane searched the shore for Orphan and Tally. He didn't find Orphan among the strangers, but he did spot Derry's massive back and Embarr's white coat on the far side of the small clearing. Derry had draped Tally belly down over the neck of a sturdy, saddleless brown horse. Tally looked secure enough, with one arm and one leg straddling either side of the horse's body. A crude yellow cloth bandage had been wrapped securely around Tally's head to stop the bleeding, and a thick woolen cloth had been thrown over his body for warmth. Derry untied the horse and climbed up carefully behind the still unconscious man before turning and heading into the woods.

When Embarr saw Thane heading toward him, he began to neigh loudly and tug determinately on his reigns. Thane hurried over to him, relieved to find his horse unhurt and all their bags still hanging from the saddle. He ran his hands along Embarr's neck while Embarr sniffed anxiously at him.

"We're going to go find Orphan, then we'll take Tally from them, and be on our way. Don't worry," Thane said out loud. He wasn't sure if it was Embarr he was reassuring or himself.

Within minutes, the remaining men had mounted their horses. No one stopped Thane when he untied Embarr and climbed into the saddle. Damien rode up behind Thane and with a curt, "Try to keep up," he turned and rode into the woods, his men followed behind him.

Embarr had no trouble keeping up as Damien led them through the trees at a brisk pace. Damien ignored Thane for the most part, speaking only to the men around him. Occasionally, he glanced behind him to make sure Thane was still with them. Thane couldn't understand where Damien fit into this strange group. He certainly had the impression that Damien was in command of the small band of warriors, but he was much too young to be their leader, wasn't he?

Thane didn't have much time to mull over Damien's position within the group. He was too busy keeping his seat as they rode quickly over barely discernible paths through the trees and low growing shrubs. By the time they emerged from the forest, the sun had risen above the horizon and long rays of light cut through the thin clouds. The line of men wove through narrow, almost invisible trails that ran between a bog and the trees on their right toward a steep flat-topped mountain.

They turned back into the forest at the base of the mountain. Embarr picked his way through the thick undergrowth of shrubs and small plants that covered the ground. Without a word, half of the men broke away from the group and headed deeper into the trees on the right. Thane barely spared them a glance as he followed Damien and Derry up a rocky path, over uneven slopes between oak and ash trees. They were only halfway up the mountain when Damien and Derry stopped.

"We're here," Damien announced proudly.

Thane looked around in surprise. They were standing on the edge of a rocky ledge overlooking a dark opening at the base of the gully in the side of the mountain below them. Thane could just see a rapidly moving stream of running water. The surrounding trees were painted dull green and gray with moss. Patches of lichen covered the jagged rock wall that dropped down sharply to his left.

Thane hopped off of Embarr, spread his arms wide, and spun around in a circle. "Where's here?" he questioned angrily, raising his voice so he could be heard over the babble of the rapidly moving water. He was getting tired of being told what to do and being dragged blindly across rivers and through unfamiliar forests.

"Are we going to make camp half way up the side of a mountain, because I don't see anything here but big old trees and a rocky cliff."

Damien looked down at him. "I realize you don't trust me, and that's just fine; I don't trust you either, but the Seanchaidh needs to be cared for or he will die. So, until he either dies or is well enough to leave on his own two feet, we are stuck with each other. I'm sure you'll be able to get back to your grand adventures before too long."

Thane was bewildered by the continued hostility in Damien's voice. Grand adventures? Why would Damien think that Thane had been off having adventures? What wonderful things did he imagine Thane had been doing over the last seven years?

Thane opened his mouth, a sarcastic retort on the tip of his tongue, but Damien had already dismounted and walked away. He picked his way down a narrow path with his horse and disappeared into a narrow crevice.

Curious now, Thane gathered Embarr's reigns in his left hand and traced Damien's steps down the rocky slope. At the bottom, he found a small opening carved into the cliff wall and stepped carefully across the slippery threshold into a short stone tunnel.

It took a moment for his eyes to adjust to the intense darkness inside the cave. Even though torches were lit at short intervals over a path made of rough wood planks, Thane could see nothing beyond the short pools of light from the torches but utter blackness. Thane slowly made his way along the narrow path, Embarr trailing obediently behind him.

The tunnel opened up into a small dimly lit cave. Damien had tied his horse next to a brown mare on a narrow flat strip of rock near the shallows of a gently running river. The aroma of fresh horse droppings mixed with the sweet, musty smell of the wet cave made him want to sneeze. Thane held his breath in a desperate attempt to forestall the explosive noise. He didn't want to call unnecessary attention to himself.

By the time Thane reached the horses, Damien had already made his way down the crudely built stairs and was walking across a makeshift wooden dock that hung out over the river. Four shallow currachs were tied to an iron stake at the end of the dock. The boats were similar to the ones they had used to crossed the river. These were narrower and were made to be paddled not rowed. A flaming torch was mounted to each bow. The golden light flickered against the wet rock walls and the moving river creating dancing shadows and eerie patterns on the uneven surfaces.

Damien stepped into a currach, sat down in the back, and put a paddles into the water. Derry shouldered his way past Thane with Tally cradled securely in his massive arms. Thane tied Embarr off to a post near the other two horses, but by the time he worked his way down the path to the dock, Damien and Derry were already pulling away with Tally.

"Stay here," Damien yelled back to him. "We will be making several trips to our camps further down the caves. Your friend is already there. Someone will be along to care for your horse. I will return shortly." Damien disappeared around the bend in the river before Thane could reply.

Thane was left standing at the end of the dock with a handful of Damien's men. He surreptitiously studied the grim warriors sitting on the rocks around him. They wore similar loose, saffron colored, long-sleeved shirts under short leather tunics or chain mail shirts. Despite the cold, some of them were barelegged and barefooted, while others had on thick hose and coarsely made short leather boots. Many of them had thick beards and wore their hair short in the front and long in the back. Something in their rough manner reminded him of the Reivers he had lived with in Scotland. Not one of them acknowledged his presence.

Damien returned alone before long and loosely tied the currach to the dock. He gestured for Thane to join him.

Thane stepped carefully down into the front of the shallow half shell. This time he was careful to keep his sword under control. The whole currach swayed as he flopped clumsily down onto the bench and sat facing forward just as he had seen Derry do. Damien laughed out loud at Thane's awkwardness. The sound echoed through the cavernous tunnel. It sounded like there was a village of people laughing at him.

"Keep your eyes open for low hanging rocks," Damien lectured Thane. "If you manage to knock yourself into the water, you may want to just stand up. You will look like an even bigger fool if you flounder around trying to swim. The river is at the most waist high, so it is unlikely that even you would drown." Damien skillfully untied the mooring line and paddled the currach effortlessly away from the dock and deeper into the cave.

Thane ignored the jibe but took Damien's advice. He kept his eyes on the height of the ceiling, ready to duck his head if necessary. He kept his hands in the currach to avoid smashing them between the gunwales and the cave walls.

Between the torch on the bow and the torches that lit some of the larger passageways along the river, Thane was able to get a decent look at his surroundings. Tight tunnels led to open chambers then narrowed again as they glided through the rocky passes. Thane was shocked to see how many warriors had pitched tents in the larger caverns. They were paddling through an underground village.

The ceilings in most of the caverns were covered in hundreds of long icicles ranging in size from his pinky finger to ones that were longer than he was tall. As Thane got a closer look at them, he realized that they were made of stone not ice. It was both frightening and beautiful.

Damien paddled them through the river until it widened into a lake in an immense cavern. He guided the currach to the left side of the lake and drove the boat up onto the sandy shore. Thane hopped out. Damien clambered over the edge of the currach after him and together they pulled the boat out of the water.

Damien strode off to speak to a young boy who couldn't have been more than ten. The boy ran over to the currach and pushed it into the water. He hopped onto the back bench and paddled the boat toward the entrance of the cave.

A camp had been set up on the beach here as well. There were not only more mail-clad warriors here, there were also a dozen boys, some he guessed were as young as eight years old. They were all busy rushing around doing chores. Some were cleaning weapons, some were cooking, and one was sewing a large piece of yellow fabric. None of them looked up as he passed.

Thane had some difficulty spotting Orphan in the crowd as she wasn't the only one with red hair in the camp. He spotted Derry first, leaning up against the wall of the cave stoking an open fire near Tally. Derry was obviously standing guard. Orphan was kneeling over Tally's still unconscious body, gently stroking her fingers down his face.

"Orphan!" Thane yelled out.

Her head snapped up at the sound of his voice as it echoed through the cave. She jumped to her feet and rushed toward him. He met her half way and was startled when she wrapped her arms around him in a fierce hug. He stood still, awkwardly patting her back, as she babbled franticly into his chest.

"I'm so sorry! I was caught. I didn't even hear them," she leaned in even closer to him, "before I knew what was happening they had me surrounded. I didn't have a chance to even yell out before they'd thrown a blanket over my head and carted me off on a horse. They were rude, well, somewhat gentle but still rude! No one would tell me anything other than they were going after you. What's wrong with Tally? Is he going to die? What happened in the castle? Who are all these people? Where are we?

"I was so worried about you!" she whispered glancing around at the huge men sitting around the fires nearest to them.

Thane grabbed her arms, firmly pulled them from around his body, and set her away from him. She was certainly not acting like a boy! He glanced around to see if anyone was watching them, and while no one was looking in their immediate direction, he got the feeling that they were being closely observed.

"Calm down. I think we are safe enough for the moment. I know one of them. I think he may be their leader. Tally is in bad shape, and I'm not sure he is going to make it. I think Zavior or his minions must have tortured him for some time. From the condition of Tally's wounds, it looks like we have been gone months."

"I think so too. I couldn't wake him. What are we going to do?" Thane started to panic a little when he saw that her eyes were brimming with tears. He didn't know what he would do if she did something as un-Orphanish as cry.

"We'll give him some of your elixir!" Thane said desperately. "It worked well on your wound, didn't it?" He made a move toward Tally when Orphan grabbed his arm and pulled him back.

"NO!" she cried out then looked around anxiously as her voice eerily bellowed "no, no, no" back at her from the depths of the cave. Several of the giant men stopped to look over at them, ready to intervene if necessary. She took a deep breath and blinked. Thane was relieved to see that the tears were gone and she was in control of herself again.

She leaned closer to him and whispered anxiously into his ear, "I mean, I don't think we can use it on mortals. Back at your grandfather's castle, I heard the Fæ healer talking to someone about whether they should even be using it on me because I am not completely Fæ. I think it might do more harm to Tally than good. We can't risk it."

"Come." She dropped his arm and walked slowly back toward the unconscious Bard.

She was probably right, Thane thought as he followed her back to the fire. They really didn't know enough about the potion to give it to anyone but Orphan. They dropped to their knees next to Tally. Thane watched as Orphan lifted Tally's head and slid her legs underneath him. She pushed his hair gently away from the wounds on his face and whispered softly to him. Thane tried not to be disheartened when the Bard didn't respond.

"How are you feeling?" Thane asked her, suddenly afraid she was going to pass out as well. Even in the darkened cave, Thane could see that her face was just as pale as Tally's.

She looked up at him and said, "I'm all right."

At his skeptical look she said, "No really. I'm fine. Tired, but I feel better than I did at the castle."

A rumpled old man shuffled over to them and stood, looming over their heads. He had a ring of long white hair that wrapped around his head from one side to the other under a shining bald pate. Thane heard Orphan suck in a breath as the old man turned his head toward them. A scarred hole was all that remained of his left eye.

He squinted down at them with his one watery blue eye and thrust a wet cloth out to them. "Here. You take this," he grunted at them. "Do what ya can to clean his wounds. I'll be fetching a potion for him." When neither of them made a move to take it, he dropped it into Thane's lap then turned and blended back into the dark shadows of the cave.

Thane and Orphan exchanged a confused look.

Thane lifted the cloth off his lap, slightly annoyed at the damp spot it had left behind. He looked at the dirt and blood on Tally's face, unsure of where to start. He had only managed to drag the cold cloth awkwardly over Tally's chin a couple times before Orphan impatiently grabbed it out of his hands.

She went to work cleaning his wounds with firm but gentle hands. Orphan adjusted the wet cloth between her fingers frequently as she went so she aways had a clean spot to work with. It didn't take her long to wipe away the dirt and blood, allowing them to get a better look at Tally's face. One eye was swollen shut, multiple cuts and multicolored bruises decorated his skin. His lips were dry, cracked and bleeding. Still he didn't wake.

The old man was back, hovering over them again. "We must get 'im cleaned up and into fresh clothes. Whoa, he truly stinks!" he mumbled through his missing teeth.

Damien walked over and stood behind the old man. "I see you've met Guillius."

Guillius turned his good eye to Damien and said, "Rub that on any open wound you find. I'll find him some clean clothes." He thrust a small wooden cup filled with a yellow, gooey cream into Damien's hand and left again.

"Guillius was a healer in the Uí Néill clan, before he was wounded in a battle," Damien explained. "He has lived with us for the last few years. He is not as hale as he once was, but he is skilled. If you want your friend to get well, you will follow his directions without fail."

Damien knelt next to Orphan and set the cup down on the ground by his knee. He lifted the Bard's head off of her lap and told her to go lie down. "You look like you are going to fall flat on your face. We can see to this."

She looked hesitantly at Thane.

He nodded his agreement.

"We'll wake you if there is any change," Thane assured her. "Go lie down."

Thane smiled at her relieved sigh. He had seen her reaction when Guillius said they were going to undress Tally and knew she didn't want to be anywhere around them when they took Tally's cloths off. Despite her exhaustion, she got eagerly to her feet and moved to lie down on the other side of the fire.

Damien helped Thane remove Tally's outer clothing and together they wiped him down with the wet cloths. Thane tried to keep the Bard covered with the blanket as much as he could to keep him warm and protect his modesty. It made cleaning him awkward.

Guillius was back before long with an armful of clothes. He threw a long, brown shirt and thick, woolen hose in Thane's general direction. Thane caught them clumsily against his chest.

By the time they had finished treating Tally's wounds and dressing him, Thane was sure he wouldn't be able to stand, he was so exhausted. He looked over his shoulder at Orphan. She was fast asleep on the other side of the fire.

"She doesn't look like she is doing much better than your friend here," Damien said with an absent wave in Orphan's general direction.

Thane carefully schooled his face into what he hoped was a blank expression and said, "She?"

Damien's lip lifted in a derision, "Did you honestly expect me to believe she's a boy? Do I look dimwitted to you?"

Thane clenched his back teeth and rose angrily to his feet. Why hadn't Damien been fooled? Thane had believed she was a boy for years! Thane glanced at her, trying to see her as Damien did.

She was wrapped in her cloak and curled up on her uninjured side sound asleep. A few tendrils of red hair had escaped it's leather tie and fell softly around the curves of her smooth, high cheekbones and soft beardless chin. Fortunately, her hair still hid her small pointed ears. Finely drawn dark, red eyebrows arched over what he knew were bright, green eyes. The brown tunic and breeches she wore did more now to emphasize her attributes than they did to conceal them. She may have been dressed as a boy but Thane had to admit she did not look like one. Maybe she never really had.

Damien interrupted Thanes's musings.

"What's her name?"

"Orphan."

"Orphan?" Damien barked in disbelief. "You expect me to believe her name is Orphan? That's stupid! I'm not going to call her that!"

"Do as you like," Thane shrugged. He didn't know if he was more annoyed that Damien had seen through Orphan's disguise or that Damien's reaction to her name had been almost identical to the one he had had when she had first told him to call her Orphan.

Damien opened his mouth to make another comment but Thane interrupted him before he could get out more than, "She must..."

"Look! I'm not up to arguing with you now," Thane said belligerently. "I'm going to assume that since you brought us to your hideout or whatever you call this place, that I can trust you enough to lie down for a bit?"

"Suit yourself," Damien said indifferently to his back as Thane turned and walked away.

Thane stretched out on the hard ground on the other side of Orphan so that she was tucked safely between him, the fire, and Tally. He wrapped his cloak tightly around his body and lay flat on his back. As he stared up at the ceiling, he began to have second thoughts about sleeping in this cave. He could spot little black creatures hanging in the dark recesses of the cave, and the ceiling was covered with more of those sharp icicle shaped stones. If one of those spikes fell on him while he was asleep, he would surely be killed, but he was just too tired to care. He had only a few hours sleep since they'd left Muirghein's cottage on the beach more than twenty-four hours ago. He couldn't keep his eyes open any longer.

Chapter Five

The Mag Uidhirs

Something dripped on to Thane's nose.

Still half asleep, he raised a hand to wipe away the water and rolled over onto his side. He tried to snuggle into the bed, but something lumpy and hard dug into his shoulder and hip. The steady murmur of voices and a low moan were coming from somewhere to his right. The strangeness of it pulled him out of his sleep as another drop of water hit his cheek.

Thane's eyes fluttered open. He was expecting to see the gabled wall and pitched ceiling of the stable loft at the inn. Instead, he turned his head and was squinting through the flickering yellow light at a spike-covered ceiling. For a few frightening moments, Thane was completely disoriented. He had absolutely no idea where he was.

Thane bolted to a sitting position as it all came rushing back to him...rescuing Tally...Orphan...Damien...the cave...

Thane rubbed his knuckles into his eyes then squinted through the murky shadows. Orphan and the strange one-eyed old man, Guillius, were leaning anxiously over Tally. Thane wasn't sure he could muster the energy to stand because he was still so tired. He crawled over to them on his hands and knees and sat next to Orphan.

Tally's eyes were open but they were glassy and unfocused. He gazed right at Thane, but his eyes showed no sign of recognition. Bright purple, pink, and yellow bruises covered one side of his face. A long crusty wound marked the spot where he had hit his forehead when he fell in the library. He was still pale and weak, but at least he was conscious. Thane hoped that was a good sign.

Damien's healer looped one arm under Tally's head and shoulders. He pulled him up so that Tally's back was against his chest to help Tally drink from a shallow bowl. Orphan leaned towards them whispering words of encouragement to Tally.

It wasn't working. More of the thick, brown liquid was running down Tally's chin than they were able to get down his throat. Tally gagged and began to cough.

Guillius shrugged his shoulders in defeat and gave up. He laid the bowl next to his knee and gently wiped the mess off Tally's chin with a cloth. After he eased Tally back down onto the blankets, Orphan pulled a wool blanket up and tucked it around Tally's shoulders. She sat back on her heels as Tally's eyes drifted closed.

Orphan looked at Thane. "Guillius said he thinks Tally is going to recover...that he'll be fine. He just needs some food and a good long rest."

Thane glanced at the healer for confirmation. "Is that true?"

"Aye, he's burning with fever and he's many cuts and bruises, but, aye, he will most likely recover...if we can get his fever down. Seems that he was beaten many times for many months as his wounds are both old and new." Guillius speculated, rhythmically sucking air and spit in and out of the holes between what was left of his teeth.

"He must ha' done something mighty awful to have been treated so viciously by his captors." His bushy white brow rose high over his mutilated eye questioningly, obviously hoping to hear some good gossip.

"Tally didn't do anything wrong!" Thane growled defensively.

Guillius stared skeptically at Thane and shrugged, "If you say so, lad."

The healer waved his hand absentmindedly toward the shadows behind Thane. "Your saddle, bags, and weapons were brought down while you were asleep. They are over there on the wall when you have need for them."

Thane glanced over his shoulder in the direction Guillius indicated. All of their belongings were stacked neatly on top of a flat stone shelf that jutted out of the side of the cave wall behind them. He was relieved to see that they had brought Tally's bag and lute down too. Maybe once Tally washed properly, they could get him into some of his own clean clothes.

Wide awake now, Thane stood up and looked around for Damien. He wanted some answers. A handful of men were loitering around a fire near the water's edge but Damien wasn't among them. Thane turned back to Orphan and Guillius.

"Where's my horse?"

"Outside," Guillius replied.

"Outside the caves? Where?"

"Aye, out beyond the caves. The horses don't stay in the caves, they are taken out for fresh air and exercise near the training ground...it's no' far from here."

Guillius twisted his whole body around to look behind him at the men milling about near the water and yelled, "Tomás! Take the Prince to his horse."

Thane rolled his eyes. He hated being called a Prince! He was so far removed from that life now, and it only made him sad to think of all he had lost.

A big blond man detached himself from amongst his fellows without a word. He strode over to the shallow currachs, pushed one most of the way off the beach, and hopped down into it. He grabbed the paddle and stared expectantly at Thane.

Thane turned to look at Orphan. "I'm going to make sure Embarr is being taken care of. You want to come?"

Orphan shook her head. "No, you go ahead. I'll stay with Tally."

Thane grabbed Orphan's sleeve and pulled her to her feet. He guided her away from Guillius.

"How are you feeling? Have you had a chance to take more elixir? Did you sleep? Is your wound healing?" Thane whispered a rapid string of questions at her.

"I'm feeling fine...Yes, I had more elixir...Yes, I slept almost as long as you did...and Yes," she huffed, "my wound seems to be healing just fine! Don't worry about me. I'm fine."

Although she still looked pale, her green eyes were clear and steady. She looked around to make sure no one was listening and lowered her voice. "I was worried about our safety before you and Tally got here but not anymore. I don't think they mean us any harm." Orphan turned her gaze back to Thane.

Thane raised his eyebrow and tipped his head toward one of Damien's men. The warrior was sitting across the rocky floor, not too far away, sharpening a long two-handed ax and pretending he wasn't watching everything they did.

"Well, I don't think they feel the same way. Have you not noticed? We are never really left alone," Thane grumbled.

Orphan shrugged her shoulder at him, unconvinced. "I think you worry too much."

"And I think you don't worry enough!" Thane snapped back.

"As soon as Tally is feeling better we need to leave," Thane said, his eyes on the man with the ax. He wasn't convinced that these people were harmless. Why was Orphan being so naive? Damien had brought them here for a reason, and Thane wasn't sure it was because he wanted to help them.

"I don't trust them. Find the elixir. You're too pale, and we need you ready to fight." He turned without giving her a chance to argue with him again. He strode over to where the currach floated just off the sandy slope, Tomás sitting impatiently in the stern.

Thane climbed in and sat across from Tomás who barely waited for him to settle on the narrow bench before he dug the paddle into the water and pushed them out into the current. With long, efficient strokes, he paddled the currach through the narrow rock passages in silence. The gentle swishing of the water sliding along the outer lip of the boat reminded Thane how desperately he needed to find a bush and have a moment of privacy.

They pulled smoothly up to the wooden dock. Tomás loosely tied a rope to the iron stake to secure the currach to the dock, then pointed a long thick arm toward the exit. "Go out that way, turn left, then follow the cliff wall. You will find a path leading down the mountain; follow it until you come to a narrow stream. Follow the water north to a large clearing. There you'll find the horses."

Thane nodded, mumbled thanks, and clambered out of the currach. His foot was barely clear of the gunwale when, with a wave of his hand, Tomás paddled away. He looked up at the dim reflection of daylight shining through the tunnel and made his way toward it.

After the darkness of the cave, the sun reflecting off freshly fallen snow momentarily blinded him. Squinting his eyes against the glare, he looked up. From the position of the sun just visible between the bare tree branches, he guessed that it must be close to sunset. It looked like they'd slept the day away.

Despite the cold, it was a beautiful afternoon. There was no wind, and the forest was still and quiet. A thin coating of snow covered everything. It looked as if the trees and bushes were clothed in thin, wooly, white sweaters.

His warm breath created a halo of smoke around his head as he let out a frustrated sigh. He had wanted to be as far away from this place as possible before sunset, but between Tally's fever, Orphan's wound, and the impending dark, they were going to be spending at least one more night in the caves.

It took him a moment to get his bearings and still another moment to find a secluded place to relieve himself. He finished up quickly, cursing the fact that he had left his cloak in the caves. It was so much colder out here than it was in the caves. He wrapped his arms around his chest and rubbed his hands up and down his arms to warm himself.

He took his time picking through frozen underbrush along the rocky cliff until he found the path. It was right where Tomás said it would be. Thane quickened his pace and walked along the rough trail down the mountainside. Occasionally, through the frozen skeletal branches of the trees, he caught a glimpse of the immense peat bog that ran along the base of the mountain and a giant glittering lake far in the distance.

The long brisk walk through the woods warmed him a bit and took the biting edge off the cold. By the time he stepped out of the forest and into the large clearing, he was feeling more comfortable.

Bare trees lined the perimeter of the wide, snow-covered field. A stream flowed out of the side of the mountain behind Thane, ran along the outer edge of the line of trees to the left, and disappeared into the forest behind a stretch of land where at least a hundred horses were tied. On the right side, an extensive training field, crude quintain, and butts were set up.

Men were scattered here and there busy training with swords, axes or bows. Along the left side, others were caring for the horses or gathered around talking in groups of two or three.

Damien was nowhere to be seen, but Thane easily spotted Embarr's white coat amidst the browns and blacks of the other horses. Embarr blew his lips and whinnied as he watched Thane approach.

Thane spoke softly to him while he ran his hands along the horse's smooth white flanks. Someone had removed Embarr's saddle and brushed him. Embarr rubbed his nose into the crook of Thane's neck comfortingly.

"I'm glad you are being well tended," Thane whispered to his horse. Embarr blew his lips and nodded his head.

"I think Tally is going to be fine, but it looks like we are going to be here for at least another night. Stay here with the rest of the horses, I'll be back in the morning to check on you." With one last rub across the horse's soft nose, Thane turned away. He was relieved that Embarr was not upset and that the horse was safe.

As he started across the open field to return to the caves, a group of men on horses rode into the training field from the forest on the right. A richly dressed redheaded man swung down off his horse and looked around. He wore the same style of flowing yellow shirt that the rest of the men favored (Guillius had called it a léine) only his was much more elaborate. It was thickly pleated at his waist and had large billowing sleeves that draped from his shoulders to his wrists. The léine was tucked into his woolen trews and a sleeveless leather jerkin was fitted snug across his broad chest and narrow waist. His boots were not the common, poor man's leather foot wraps most of the men wore; his were neatly stitched, slightly round-toed boots. A long red woolen brat edged in tassels was pulled over his shoulders for warmth.

"Pádraig, the Mag Uidhir is here. Get Damien," one of the warriors yelled to the crowd of young boys who were milling about. A very small, pale-haired boy detached himself from a group and ran into the forest.

It was then that the Mag Uidhir noticed Thane. Confusion, then shock, flittered briefly across the man's face.

It was clear to Thane that this stranger recognized him. He had been told often enough that he had the looks of his father, and he knew that the contrast between his hair and his eyes and his face made him unique. After Damien's reaction in the castle he wasn't surprised, but he was beginning to feel conspicuous. He fought the urge to raise his hands to each side of his head to make sure his hair still covered his ears. Thane knew Damien was aware of his Fæ heritage, but he wasn't sure whether or not anyone else was. He didn't want to have to deal with the ridicule that might come to him if anyone saw his ears.

Damien must not have been too far away because he strode into the clearing almost immediately followed closely by Pádraig. The stranger turned his back on Thane and spoke urgently to Damien and to one of Damien's older warriors. From the snatches of conversation Thane could hear, he gathered a local village had been looted and burned to the ground. Most of the livestock had been stolen and dozens of families were now homeless. The Mag Uidhir was here to gather warriors to retaliate.

Damien scowled over the stranger's shoulder at Thane, and Thane was not surprised to hear his name mentioned. Damien led the Mag Uidhir away from the group and leaned closer speaking privately to him. Thane couldn't hear what Damien was saying, but, from the sneer on Damien's face, it couldn't have been anything flattering. What could they possibly have to say concerning him? The clan chief nodded his head. They walked back to his waiting men.

The Mag Uidhir mounted his horse, turned to Damien and said, "I have had word from Gráinne. She will be returning from Scotland within the next few days. She has more of your Mac Leòid kin. Send word to her if you are interested in hiring them."

Damien nodded and stepped away from him.

With one last searching look in Thane's direction, the Mag Uidhir turned his horse and led his retinue back into the forest.

Horns sounded over the field. Within minutes, men swarmed out of the forest in various stages of battle dress. Every one of them wore long shirts of chain mail over padded jackets and steel helmets reminiscent of the steel bonnets of the Scottish Border Reivers. Many of them were barelegged and barefoot.

Almost all of the warriors were armed with the sparrs, long handled crescent shaped axes, that they favored. Long-bladed scians were tucked into the leather sheaths that hung loosely from their belts. Thane was surprised at how many of them also carried claidheamh mórs, long two-handed swords. Quite a few warriors had quivers full of barbed arrows and bows slung across their backs. Dozens of young boys were darting between the men carrying even more weapons.

Where had they all come from? Thane would have sworn there hadn't been more than a dozen men and just a few boys in the caves. Either they had another camp close by, or the cave was far larger than he had thought. Maybe it was a little bit of both.

A hundred massive, mail-clad warriors and young boys surrounded Damien, ready for battle. Damien began to sort the men into smaller groups. To Thane's surprise, even though Damien must have been half the age of the eldest warrior, they all obeyed him. Before long, they had mounted horses and were riding off in a maelstrom of men and metal taking the host of young boys with them.

Thane left the empty field and walked back to the caves alone.

Orphan was sitting next to Tally who was still asleep. She didn't say anything as he dropped down beside her, stretched his legs out in front of him, and leaned back on an elbow. They shared a quick meal of breads and cheese.

She looked exhausted. Her eyes were now puffy and rimmed in red and she was still dangerously pale. Even though they had slept for a good part of the day, she was still recovering from her wound, and they had only slept for a couple of hours in Tír inna n-Óc the day before. It didn't take much encouragement to get Orphan to lie down.

Thane made sure Tally had enough blankets tucked around him to keep him warm, then wrapped his own cloak tightly around himself and eagerly followed Orphan's example. He was lulled to sleep by the soft lapping of the river against the shallow beach.

Chapter Six

Taliesin Wakes

The clanking and clamoring of weapons and the raised voices of the returning warriors jarred Thane from a fitful dream. Rubbing his eyes irritably, he rose slowly to his feet. His cloak fell from his shoulders, and he shivered as the cool air of the caves sucked the warmth from his body. He felt like he hadn't slept for very long. He was even more exhausted now than he had been before he'd fallen asleep.

Thane watched warily as warrior after warrior clambered out of the currachs and walked towards the far side of the cave where Thane could now see three torch lit openings in the rock wall. He glanced at Orphan as she came up behind him and pressed close against his side. She looked nervous. He didn't blame her, it was an intimidating sight.

As one group of currachs left another set quickly replaced them. The next group pulled their boats out of the water. They began unloading goods from the boats and laying them out on the beach for others to haul away. Thane had lived with the Reivers long enough to recognize the spoils of a raid. It looked like the fight had gone well for Damien and his men.

Out of the corner of his eye, he noticed Tally sitting up against the lumpy cave wall. Guillius was kneeling next to him, trying to get him to drink out of a wooden cup. This time, instead of trying to pour it into Tally's mouth, the healer held what looked like one of the long, narrow spikes from the ceiling of the cave to Tally's lips. Tally was slowly sucking the liquid up through the hollow spike.

Thane walked over to Tally and settled himself beside the Bard with his back against the wall. Orphan followed and sat down on Thane's other side. They watched in silence as the men and boys carried the goods away.

When Guillius was done fussing, he gathered his supplies. He mumbled something to Tally that Thane couldn't hear then pulled the Bard's woolen cloak closed across his chest. Guillius nodded to Thane and Orphan and left to join the commotion at the water's edge.

The returning men were in good spirits, laughing and discussing the fight amongst themselves. A few wounded were helped out of the currachs and waited patiently on the beach for Guillius to tend to them. It seemed that no one was hurt seriously enough to warrant much concern, and before long the healer disappeared into one of the tunnels that led deeper into the cave.

Thane turned his attention back to Tally. His skin was still a sickly ashen color under the bruises, but he was more alert. Tally caught Thane's eye and he lifted the corner of his lip in a self-deprecating smile.

"I'm fine, Thane," he said gruffly. "Truly."

Thane knew Tally was trying to reassure him, but it was hard to be comforted by the sight of a man who still looked like he was just breaths away from death.

"Do you know who they are?" Thane gestured to the warriors uneasily, "Or for that matter where we are?"

"Many of them are gallóglaigh...soldiers of fortune, mercenaries. Scotsman who came to the West fleeing persecution from the English or seeking their fortune." Tally spoke slowly and softly. "They pledge fealty to the clan who will pay them the most. Your father had many gallóglaigh. Do you not recall that Damien's father was one?"

"No," Thane shook his head and waited patiently for Tally to continue.

"Well, you were both very young when his father was killed. I recognize many of your father's men here as well. It appears they are all loyal to the new Mag Uidhir.

"The young boys you see milling about are their knaves. They are the equivalent of the English knight's pages or squires." Tally's breath was shallow and his voice shook a bit. He took a couple deep breaths, and after a few moments he began again. "I don't know how Damien found his way to this. It is not an easy life. Has he told you anything about how he came to be with this lot?"

"No," Thane said shortly. He didn't want to talk about Damien or voice his confusion about the animosity and thinly veiled accusations Damien had been throwing at him since they had met. Thane kept remembering the things they had done together when they were younger: fighting with sticks, snitching pastries from Martha, hiding in the secret tunnels in the castle and in the crypt. What had he done to make Damien so angry?

"The crypt!" Thane exclaimed suddenly sitting up away from the wall. He had forgotten all about seeing the stranger's effigy in the tomb until now.

"Tally! Monpier is not dead! Orphan and I saw him in Tír inna n-Óc!"

"What? Who?" Orphan said confused. She scooted around so that she was sitting facing them, her back to the commotion on the beach.

"The stranger, the man that helped us get away from the Fæ, was my father's advisor, Monpier. He's buried in a marble tomb in the crypt," Thane explained.

"What?" Orphan frowned at him. "He's dead and living in Tír inna nÓc?"

"Well, no...no! I don't know. Tally?" Thane turned to Tally to find the old man staring into the fire.

"He's still there then," Tally looked back at Thane as he spoke. "That is good to hear."

"You knew?" Thane asked.

"How could he be living there when he is supposed to be dead?" Orphan asked at the same time.

"He was gravely wounded in the Battle of Lough Erne. His wounds were so severe that he should have died within the first hour. Thane, your father was devastated. Monpier was not only his advisor but his oldest and dearest friend.

"Thane's mother persuaded your grandfather to take Monpier to Tír inna n-Óc with the understanding that if they used their powers to heal him, he would never be able to return to the mortal world. If he ever left the land of the Fæ, his wounds would return and the years he had been gone would fall upon him. He would die. Your father built the tomb to honor him, because in reality, Monpier was dead to them."

"From what we saw while we were there, Manannán mac Lir doesn't seem like the type to be altruistic." Orphan looked at Thane who nodded in agreement. "He refused to send someone to rescue you or to risk the Fæ getting embroiled in the fight against Zavior," she said with disgust.

"It does not surprise me that he would not want to be involved in my rescue. He would have done anything for his daughters and Alyse especially. The Battle of Lough Erne was a turning point for the Fæ," Tally explained slowly. "Your grandfather discovered that Zavior had planned the attack on the Mag Uidhirs, and that it had been Zavior himself who struck down Monpier."

Tally paused to catch his breath. "Soon after that battle the Gates were sealed against not only Zavior but also his offspring.

They cannot cross unless aided by the medallion you carry, by Embarr, or by any key to the Gateways that the Devine Ones may have."

"I'm sure that Embarr won't be offering to carry him or any of his descendants across the Gates!" Thane said fiercely. "So, we don't have to worry about that. I'll make sure none of them ever touch my medallion. I'll do anything in my power to keep them from crossing!"

Tally frowned and glanced at Orphan. He seemed uncomfortable with the direction the conversation had taken. Thane expected Tally to commend his fervent vows and felt a bit snubbed when Tally deliberately changed the subject.

Tally slid his body down the wall until he was comfortably lying flat on his back.

"Tell me about how all of you escaped from Zavior's ambush. The last thing I remember I was being pulled off my horse by a Roki."

"It all happened so fast," Orphan began. "One moment I was in the river fighting a Roki and the next, Thane was leaning over me shaking my shoulder and yelling at me. The Roki...you and Zavior...and the river were gone, and we were in a different forest. Thane helped me bandage my side before we mounted Emb..."

Tally reached out, grabbed Orphan's hand, and whispered, "You were hurt?"

"Just a little bit." She tried to make light of it. "I must have passed out again, because the next thing I remember I was laying in a soft bed in Muirghein's cottage."

Thane snorted and spoke over her, "The Roki had struck her with its claw. She had a large poisoned gash across her side. It wasn't until we got to Tír inna n-Óc where the Fæ healers could treat her that it began to mend. She won't admit it, but it is still bothering her."

"And you met Muirghein? You had better start at the beginning and tell me everything that happened after you were pulled from the fight with Zavior," Tally insisted. He let go of her hand, rubbed his fingers across her cheek, then settled weakly back on the ground between them.

"You should rest." Thane could see that Tally was getting tired. "We can talk again later."

"No. Continue. I want to know what happened after you shifted," the Bard insisted.

"When I saw the Roki strike Orphan," Thane picked up the tale, "I turned Embarr toward the river to help her. I panicked when I felt the familiar, deep burning pain inside of me. I knew I was about to be torn from the fight. I reached down and grabbed Orphan's arm, and both she and Embarr were taken with me. I don't understand why it happens or how they were able to go with me."

"It was the medallion. I have had much time to think over the last few months. Zavior was very...interested in finding out how you were able to disappear. I knew that the medallion was a Key to the Fæ Gateways and that it was a powerful heirloom given to Alyse by her mother. I believe your mother put an enchantment on the medallion to ensure your safety. Apparently, when your life is in peril, the medallion pulls you away."

"Why did I wind up with the Reivers? And at the Inn?" Thane asked.

Tally closed his eyes and was quiet for so long that Thane thought he had fallen back to sleep. He was just getting ready to stand up when Tally opened his eyes and spoke.

"Your mother often asked me about my travels...about my favorite people and places. She knew who I had trusted in the past. She knew who she could trust to take care of you. She must have found a way to get your dagger and the wooden practice sword to Asiag Kerr. The dagger and sword must have worked as a guiding beacon for the medallion."

"And the Inn?" Orphan asked.

Tally shrugged and said, "My only guess is that Thane was taken there because I was there. There are more forces at work here than just Thane's mother and the medallion. Continue your story. You were pulled from the fight..."

"As Orphan said, we woke in a strange forest. I had pulled my arm from my shoulder when I grabbed Orphan. It was hanging uselessly at my side. She was bleeding from the gaping wound in her side. With Embarr's help, I was able to lift her onto his back and he took us to Muirghein's cottage."

Leaving out the details of his discovery that Orphan was really a girl, Thane spoke at length about their stay with Muirghein and with his grandparents in Tír inna n-Óc. Orphan interrupted frequently to add a comment or opinion here and there.

"So, for us it has only been a few days since the fight with Zavior," Orphan finished, "even though you were in the dungeon for months."

"What did he do to you?" she asked softly.

"It is…" Tally stopped talking as one of the small currachs approached the beach. They looked around as a giant redheaded man yelled from the boat. "You there. Your Highness. You are wanted out in the training field."

Thane looked around the empty beach then back at the currach. "Me?" he shouted back.

"You see any other Princes down here? Yes, you!" he chuckled loudly to himself. "The Mag Uidhir wants you trained so bring your sword. You'll be aneedin' it." He sat in the boat impatiently tapping his fingers against the gunwale.

"Why does your Mag Uidhir want me trained? I don't belong to him," Thane shouted back at him.

"That, you'll have to ask him yourself. Come on now, I ain't gonna sit here all day!"

Thane looked at Tally who shrugged his shoulder.

"Go on. I doubt they mean you any harm," Tally said as he wearily shut his eyes. "Some of these men are familiar to me and I am sure many of them know who you are. You'll be safe enough with them for the time being. Keep your eyes and ears open. Ask questions."

"I'll stay with him," Orphan said to Thane when he looked like he was going to argue. "Go see what they want."

Thane unfolded his long legs and stood up slowly. He took a minute to rummage through their small pile of belongings and grabbed the long sword Monpier had given him. Glancing back to assure himself that Tally and Orphan were comfortable, he tucked the sword under his arm and walked toward the river. Thane eased himself down into the small boat in front of the giant redheaded man. The boat barely wiggled. Thane grinned, happy he hadn't made a fool of himself again.

"I'm Eoin Mag Uidhir. We'll be going on out to the training grounds. Seems you are lacking some vital skills," he said with a high pitched giggle that was so incongruous with his long sword and his massive frame that Thane was momentarily taken aback.

Eoin paddled through the rest of the narrow tunnel in silence. Thane was too annoyed for small talk, so he sat in the bow and fumed silently.

'Lacking in vital skills…' He'd bet anything that that comment had come from Damien.

When they reached the dock, Thane climbed carefully out of the currach and followed Eoin through the tunnel and into the early morning light. Although it was still very cold, the sunshine was rapidly melting the snow, leaving behind large puddles and shiny patches of mud.

Thane followed Eoin through the woods to the practice field he had visited the previous evening.

Embarr was exactly where he'd left him. The horse lifted his head when Thane approached. He gently nuzzled Thane's neck and nibbled at his hair with his big soft lips.

"Hey! That tickles!" Thane laughed out loud then pushed Embarr's muzzle gently away. Satisfied that Embarr was still doing well, Thane followed Eoin to the edge of the open field.

They found the men and boys gathered on the big field. Some of the warriors were training with scians and claidheamh mórs, others with spears, arrows, or long wooden poles. More were standing about giving instructions or just heckling the combatants.

Damien was instructing a group of young boys who were practicing with wooden swords when he noticed Eoin and Thane. He broke away from the group and headed purposefully in their direction.

"Done sleeping?" he mocked Thane. "Where is the girl?"

"Not here obviously." Thane retorted choosing to ignore the insinuation that he and Orphan were lazy. He had no intention of getting into a brawl with Damien, but he wasn't going to let himself be bullied by him either.

"The Mag Uidhir wants you both trained. You'll be joining that group," Damien commanded.

Damien pointed over his shoulder to the other side of the field where a small group of young boys stood around an immense gallóglach holding a sparr that was taller than he was. Each of the boys held a long wooden pole similar to a quarterstaff in their pudgy little hands.

Thane was surprised that they were teaching these young boys to fight with AXES and appalled that he was expected to join the youngest group. He didn't know what he thought was more appalling: training to use an axe to hack someone to pieces, training with little boys, or training to use an axe with little boys.

Thane, a biting retort on his lips, looked back at Damien, and found him smirking. He knew Damien was baiting him by placing him with the youngest boys. Thane clamped his teeth, together refusing to let Damien see how angry he was.

He remembered what Tally said about asking questions, so instead of telling Damien what he really thought about him, he blurted out, "Who is the Mag Uidhir now that my father is dead?"

Damien frowned at him and said scathingly, "You're joking?"

Thane glared at Damien a moment longer then turned abruptly away from him. He headed toward the group of boys. The gallóglach stopped in mid-swing to stare at him, then glanced over Thane's shoulder to where Damien stood smirking, then looked back at Thane. Thane could see comprehension dawning in the man's eyes. Thane's face heated with humiliation. Now everyone knew where Thane stood in the pecking order; he was on par with the eight and nine year olds!

The gallóglach shrugged and pointed toward a jumbled pile of sticks near the edge of the field.

"Go on and grab ya'self a pole," he grunted at Thane. "You'll be wanting one that's a wee bit longer than you are tall."

Thane dug through the pile until he found the longest pole. He put one end on the ground and sighed. It only came up to his shoulder. He threw it back onto the pile and was looking to see if there was another pile of longer sticks when the gallóglach barked at him.

"What are you waiting for? Pick up one and get over here. Ya waisting the day!"

Thane grabbed the nearest one, lifted his chin, and returned to the group.

Pádraig, the small boy he had seen following Damien around, was at the edge of the group. He had to be at least two years younger than most of the other boys around him. Yet, what he lacked in size, he made up for in eagerness. Pádraig grinned at Thane and moved over so Thane could join him.

The boys gripped their sticks near the middle, their hands close together. It was not the usual grip of a quarterstaff. Some were making striking and hacking motions with the stick as if they were cutting an enemy to pieces. Other boys were swinging their sticks over their heads or across the front of their bodies in complicated figure eight patterns. The most skilled boys were moving so fast that their sticks were a blur. The cuts and thrusts were to be executed with enough speed and force to drive through an enemy line allowing no opportunity for the enemy to get under their guard.

Out of the corner of his eye, he saw some of the boys shooting questioning glances at him. Thane heard bits and pieces of their whispered conversation as they tried to figure out if he was there because he was being punished or if he was just not very smart.

Thane planted his feet shoulder width apart with his right foot slightly in front of his left. Mirroring the grip of his trainer, Thane held the pole with both hands and began to swing it around. He imagined to himself that Damien was standing in front of him and that he was rapidly smacking Damien's arrogant smirking face. Thane tried not to think about how ridiculous he looked standing in the middle of all these little boys who were so much better at this than he was.

Chapter Seven

The Pirate Queen

Later that afternoon, Thane followed Pádraig back into the caves and together they scrambled into a small currach. Thane grabbed the paddle as Pádraig untied the line holding the boat to the dock. They bounced the boat off the walls a few times, but with some direction from Pádraig on how to hold the paddle and with a little practice, Thane managed to guide them through the tunnels. Pádraig chattered the whole way.

"Ya think it feels warm now? Ya won't for long. It stays the same temperature all year. Ya'll need your woolens even in the midst of summer down here." He looked up at Thane as he spoke.

"Did ya know ya eyes are black! Damien said there was once a Mag Uidhir with black eyes and hair just like ya have. He said the dead Mag Uidhir was your da! Did ya know?"

"How many caves are there?" Thane interrupted him, unwilling to talk about his father. He hoped that by changing the subject, he could get some useful information out of the boy since he seemed eager to talk.

"I dunno...lots and lots! Some of the cave rooms are as big as a castle...like the one we use as a great hall where you been sleepin'. That's the biggest cave room I ever seed. And some's only as big as me and ther's lots of sizes in between! The caves is all connected by the river and tunnels that run underneath the mountain."

Pádraig seemed eager to answer Thane's questions so he asked him another one, "Does everyone live down here?"

"Na, only a few of the gallóglaigh do, and Damien only lets em down here after they swears a secret oath not to tell anyone where it is, but nothin' is down here for good 'cause when it rains lots outside, the river gets real big and wild, and it floods the caves. Then we has to move out for a bit."

"What about all the rest of the warriors?"

"Them don't like to be underground. Says it makes em fidgety and some of the Mag Uidhirs says there's spirits in here too, and them won't even come close to the caves...them live in the forests around the training field. I like it down here."

Thane ducked as he rowed them under a low hanging formation of rock. He could understand why someone would hate it down here. "Orphan isn't too fond of being down here either. She hates being close to the water more than anything else," Thane chuckled, "Well, that and having to leave the caves to find privacy to relieve herself!"

Pádraig opened his mouth and laughed out loud, the sound echoed happily through the caves. "We don't go outside when we need to p...privacy. There's a small cave we use as a garderobe. I gets to go in with a few other boys and empty the large wooden buckets during the day." He said with a grin so wide Thane could see his missing front tooth. "Didn't Damien tell you about that cave?"

"No, he didn't," Thane said with a frown. He didn't think it was amusing. If he had known about that room earlier, it would have saved him many trips out into the cold.

"I live with Damien in a small room behind the main cave," Pádraig continued, "Damien thought you'd be more comfortable in a room you'd be able to keep warm, so he moved you, the Seanchaidh, and Orphan."

Thane had his own ideas about why Damien wanted them to remain in the caves...to ensure they would be easier to watch. He didn't share his thoughts with Pádraig. It was obvious the boy idolized Damien. Thane had felt the same way about him once.

They paddled into the main cavern and drove the currach up on the sandy shore. Thane left Pádraig to attend to the boat.

Thane followed the boy's directions. He walked through the middle of the three openings at the far side of the cavern. Just inside the tunnel, he turned left into a narrow opening and walked through a short, winding hall to his new room.

"You're finally back! Do you like it?" Orphan said. She sat in the center of the cave in front of a small fire.

Thane looked around. The babble of a small stream of water trickling down the rock wall at the rear of the cave masked much of the noise from the outer cavern. To his left, a translucent sheet of rock hung from the top of the cave to the floor in gentle waves like a huge stone drapery. It was so thin that the light of a small fire behind it made the entire curtain glow. A wool blanket had been hung across the opening to the space behind the stone curtain.

"What's this?" He pulled the blanket back to look inside. It was a small alcove.

"That's my room." Orphan had made a private space for herself just like she had done in the stable loft. Orphan had already made herself at home. Her bow and quiver were propped against the wall, and her belongings were unpacked and spread about into neat little piles.

"I thought you and Tally could share this side," she said to him as he dropped the blanket and stepped toward to her. She had arranged Thane's and Tally's belongings around the small cave for them.

"Where's Tally?" Thane asked as he dropped down next to her, surprised to find her alone.

"Guillius insisted Tally move about a little so he took Tally for a walk. Guillius said it would help him regain his strength. You just missed them. I doubt they will be gone very long. Tally did sleep for most of the time that you were gone, but he is still very weak."

At first glance, the fire in front of them looked like the other fires around the cavern, but when he looked closer Thane saw that the flames were not burning the wood.

"What did you do to the fire?" he asked Orphan in surprise.

"I didn't do anything special. I got tired of scrounging up fuel, so I made a fire that would burn without destroying the underlying wood or peat blocks." Thane just stared at her with his mouth open. She could do some of the strangest things with fire.

"Thane, I want you to see something."

"What?" Thane squeaked in surprise as she grabbed the hem of her tunic and started to raise it.

She laughed and said, "Oh, don't be silly! I want to show you my scar."

"Your scar?" Thane repeated stupidly.

She pulled her tunic up just far enough to show him her scar…or the place where her scar should have been.

"It's gone," she said needlessly.

Thane bent closer to get a better look. He reached his index finger out and trailed it over the smooth perfect skin of her lower ribs. There wasn't a mark on her. Thane recalled the last time he had seen her wound. It had only been two days ago and there had still been a jagged, blood covered tear in her flesh.

"That tickles!" she giggled. Slapping his hand away, she let her tunic fall back into place.

"Maybe we don't scar…" she rambled on, "…or maybe the elixir they gave me healed it. I'm not sure. All I know is I removed the bandage this morning and that's what I found. Then I realized I don't have any other scars."

"Thane, you don't have any either, do you?" she gestured to his body with a wave of her hand. "Think about it. After all the cuts and bruises you've received...just over the last couple days even...I've never seen one single scar on you." This time she took her finger and ran it across his smooth, slightly stubbly chin.

He looked down at his hands. His knuckles should have been a torn up mess, yet they were merely red and irritated looking. Thane recalled all the times he had been hurt over the years and realized that she was right, he didn't have any scars. He thought about all the marks and battle scars he had seen on the warriors here and the long, thin scar on Damien's left cheek. Was this the reason Damien thought he had had it easy the last few years? Because he had no scars?

"I guess I don't have any either."

"What about the scar on your thumb?" he asked her.

"I don't think it's a scar. I think it must be a birthmark or something. Remember how interested the healers were in it? Anyway, I think that is the only mark or scar I have."

"Why do you think we don't scar?" Thane asked.

"I don't know," she replied softly. "The elixir healed the poison in my wound. Do you think maybe we don't scar because we are part Fæ?"

Thane shrugged. He had no answers for her.

####

Thane began training the following morning with a group of older axe-wielding boys. They were closer to his own age and were using full-sized poles with blunt wooden blades. Thane grudgingly thought to himself that he was glad to have started with the younger boys the day before, so at least he had had a chance to learn some rudimentary skills.

Thane struggled with his attack drills. He found that wielding the long, wooden axe handle, even without a heavy steel blade, wasn't as easy as it looked. Moves that were supposed to be smooth and powerful were clumsy and awkward. He was grateful when he made it through the morning without accidentally breaking any of his body parts.

Unlike the younger boys who were chatty and happy to have him around, the older boys were much more reticent. They only spoke to him when they had to. When they did, it was with as few words as necessary. Thane tried a number of times to ask about the gallóglaigh and the Mag Uidhir Clan, but he didn't get far with his furtive questions. It was obvious to all that he was not one of them.

Orphan came out to the training field early in the afternoon. She was still a bit pale, but said she was bored in the caves by herself because Tally was till spending most of his time sleeping. She joined the sword fighting for a short time before moving to the butts, preferring to spend the rest of the afternoon with her bow and arrows.

Although Orphan was still dressing as a boy, Thane could tell there was no doubt in anyone's mind that she was a girl. The men treated her with deference. It's not that they were easy on her, they weren't. They expected her to keep up and to be as aggressive as they were. At the same time, they treated her with kindness and consideration for her feelings. When Orphan was knocked to the ground, hands would appear from everywhere to help her up with words of encouragement. When Thane was knocked down, he would scramble to his feet amidst the laughter and ridicule of all those around. He was trying not to feel resentful.

By the time Thane had moved on to sword fighting, he was exhausted. He had a hard time controlling Monpier's sword. It was heavier and longer than he was used to, and he had to struggle just to get it in and out of the scabbard. After just a few mock fights with a Mag Uidhir named Rian, the muscles in Thane's arms were burning, and his body was covered in bruises from the many times Rian had slipped under his guard and hit him.

Late that afternoon, a large group of warriors rode noisily onto the training field. Thane was grateful for the commotion that interrupted his sword training. Expecting to see the Mag Uidhir again, Thane was surprised when a redheaded woman dressed in trews, a shirt of mail, and a long woolen brat rode to the front of the group and dismounted. She stood with the confidence of one who was used to being in charge. Her short, red hair hung loosely at her shoulders, and her piercing green eyes took in everything around her. Thane was startled by how much she resembled Orphan in looks and stature; they could have been sisters. As little as Thane knew about Orphan, he wouldn't have been surprised to discover that she and this woman were indeed related.

The woman signaled to the large group of men on horseback behind her. They dismounted and within moments, they were mingling with the Mag Uidhir's and gallóglaigh warriors. Rian walked away and disappeared into the mass of men.

Thane assumed training was over, so he leaned his shoulder against a tree and listened to the conversations going on around him.

A young, very pregnant, woman was lifted off her horse by one of her large companions. As he lifted her, he mumbled something to her that made her smile then set her gently on the ground. She gathered the skirts of her ankle-length léine and waddled over to stand beside the redheaded woman.

"Gráinne! It is good to see you looking so well," Damien called out as he strode over to greet the redheaded woman.

"Damien, I see that things are going well here for you and your men. I've heard tales of your daring raids on the English last fall. Your successes have become legend." The redhead held both of her hands out to him.

"Congratulations on your marriage to Risdeárd Bourke!" Damien said as she took his hands and pulled him close for a brief hug. "May you be poor in misfortunes and rich in blessings."

She nodded her thanks and Damien continued, "Thank you for escorting the Scots to us."

"I'm happy to do it. I was coming this way to fetch Maighréad, my husband's cousin," she waved toward the woman next to her. "I am with child and will be in need of a wet nurse come spring. Maighréad has been recently widowed and is expecting soon so the arrangement will be of benefit to each of us."

"Then let me congratulate you both," Damien turned and indicated to Gráinne that she should accompany him across the field. Maighréad followed quietly behind them, the long brown braid of her hair swinging gently as she walked. "You are welcome to stay as long as you like."

"Thank you, Damien. We would be grateful for the hospitality of your fires for the evening."

"I understand Seanchaidh Taliesin is here? A good story or two would not go unappreciated," Thane heard Gráinne say as they walked by.

"Unfortunately, Taliesin has been injured and..."

As their voices faded away, Thane felt something hard hit him on the back of the head. He spun around to find Rian, his last sparring partner, standing behind him with a big grin on his face, wiggling his sword at him.

"What did you do that for?" Thane rubbed his head and glared at him.

"Never turn your back on your enemy, lad!" Rian snickered at his own jest as he raised his sword.

Thane had just enough time to swing his own sword up into a defensive position before Rian attacked. Gráinne and her warriors were pushed to the back of Thane's mind as he fought to stay on his feet and away from the bite of Rian's sword.

††††

Tally was not surprised to learn that Granuaile Ní Mháille had arrived at the training grounds with a new group of MacLeòid gallóglaigh.

"She asked for you by name," Thane said.

"I have known Gráinne since she was a very young child. She was always badgering her father to let her sail on the galleys with him. When he told her she couldn't go because her hair would get caught in the rigging, she took a knife and cut it off," Tally laughed fondly at the memory.

"She was headstrong and wild even as a child, a trait that has served her well in her life. She was married when she was about your age and has grown children of her own now."

"But I heard Damien congratulate her on a new marriage..." Thane said puzzled, "...to someone named Risdeárd Bourke."

Tally raised his eyebrows in surprise. "That is interesting. The Bourke Clan will be a powerful allegiance."

"Is it true that she is a pirate?" Orphan asked.

"A pirate?" Thane echoed in surprise.

"I wouldn't call her a pirate...at least not within her earshot...but she is a force to be reckoned with both on land and on sea. Gráinne has a way of earning the unwavering loyalty of all who serve under her command."

"I am sorry I will not get the chance to see her." Tally was still not feeling strong enough to leave the caves and Damien would not risk disclosing the caves location by bringing her down to him.

"You must go up to the festivities. Take my lute and play for them," Tally urged Orphan.

He scolded her when she resisted. "I did not spend all those years instructing you so you could play secretly for the birds."

Tally got slowly to his feet and grabbed the small lute from where it was propped next to his bag. Tally had been thrilled when he discovered that Thane and Orphan still had his lute. He had been sure everything he owned had been lost after the fight with Zavior. Since his bags had been strapped to Embarr's saddle, everything went with them when they shifted from the battle. The only thing Tally had lost was his sword, which Thane suspected was somewhere in his father's castle. Zavior would never have left such a useful and valuable weapon behind.

Tally played a few notes, adjusted the strings, then pressed the instrument into Orphan's hands.

"Go and enjoy yourselves," Tally insisted.

Thane and Orphan took their time walking to the training field. Neither one of them was eager to attend. Although it was going to be a celebration of sorts, they didn't really know anyone here. They agreed they would get something to eat then return to the caves and turn in early. It had been an exhausting day for both of them.

They were half way down the mountain path when Thane noticed an orange glow filtering through the trees and heard the roar of many voices. As they stepped out of the forest onto the crowded training field, they could see that the whole field was lit, as bright as day, by numerous large fires that the Mag Uidhirs had built.

Warmed by the long walk from the caves and the waves of heat radiating from the fires, Thane begun to swelter under the weight of his heavy wool cloak. When he felt a trickle of sweat run down his back, he pulled the cloak off his shoulders and lopped it carelessly over his arm. Thane glanced at Orphan. Her cheeks were shiny and pink, but she kept her cloak wrapped firmly across her chest. She was obviously trying to hide the lute. It just made her look lopsided and strange.

Large barrels of cold ale had been brought up from the caves and were tapped. Men were tending large kettles of stew and roasting animals on spits over the open fires. The smell of roasted deer, rabbits, and birds gathered from the surrounding forest made Thane's mouth water and his stomach grumble.

Many of the new Scottish warriors had kin in the camp. Loud voices, the sounds of backslapping, and great shouts of laughter filled the air as the men reacquainted themselves with their relatives, eager to hear news from home. Dozens of young boys were running among the men playing games.

Thane and Orphan ate and drank while wandering among the revelers. Orphan had a tough time juggling her meal and the lute, but when Thane offered to carry the lute for her, she glared at him.

They stopped here and there to listen to stories of battles, to listen to bagpipes, or to hear them tell tales about the families some of these men had left behind. The gallóglaigh were such fierce and intimidating warriors that Thane had never really stopped to think about them as sons, brothers, and husbands who must miss the families they had left behind in Scotland.

Granuaile and Maighréad sat near the largest fire with Damien, Guillius, Eoin and a few other Mag Uidhirs. As Thane and Orphan walked past their group, Granuaile called out to them.

"Come sit with us!" she commanded them. She scooted over and patted the ground next to her.

They hesitated for a moment, but there was no question in anyone's mind that that she had issued an order; it was not a request. Orphan made her way around the fire and dropped down between the warrior woman and Damien. Thane was left to squeeze between Eoin and Rian on the other side of the fire.

Once they were settled, Granuaile gestured to the lute sticking conspicuously out of the folds of Orphan's cloak and said, "Do you know how to play that lute or are you just carrying it around?"

"I can play," Orphan reluctantly replied.

"Please do so then," Granuaile commanded.

Orphan pulled the small lute out and settled it in her lap. She strummed her fingers over the strings much as Tally had done earlier in the caves and, when she was satisfied that it was in tune, she began. She played a sad, sweet melody, her fingers running skillfully over the strings.

Thane wasn't surprised to hear what she chose to sing next. The Ballad of the Warrior Goddess Scáthach was one of Orphan's favorite stories. Scáthach was a strong woman, a powerful seer, and fierce warrior with flaming red hair and a pleasing figure. Thane had often thought that Orphan liked this story because she saw much of herself and her dreams in Scáthach's life.

When she began to sing of Dùn Scàith, the home the Warrior Goddess shared on the Isle of Skye with the MacLeòid clan, the gallóglaigh cheered so loudly she had to pause and wait for the ruckus to settle down before she could continue. Scáthach was the mistress of a school for the greatest of warrior heroes including the legendary Ulster hero, Cú Chulainn. Scáthach taught Cú Chulainn his famous battle leap and war cry and gave him a lethal spear called Gáe-bulg. The spear, once inside an enemy's belly, would open up into thirty barbs and tear him to pieces…

Orphan had asked Tally to sing it so many times in the past that Thane was sure he could tell it himself. Bored, Thane let his mind wander as she sang.

Orphan cradled the lute nervously in her lap when she was done. The gathered crowd of men clapped and cheered. She looked uncertainly at Granuaile to gauge her reaction.

"Thank you. As you can imagine, Scáthach is a woman I also admire very much. You have many talents. I watched you practice at the butts earlier. You have exceptional skill with a bow. What are you doing hiding out here in the hills with these uncivilized brutes?" Granuaile asked with half a smile at Damien.

Orphan shrugged, her cheeks turned red with embarrassed pleasure.

Granuaile leaned closer to Orphan and said, "I could always use one with your skills on my galleys."

Orphan looked up at Granuaile in surprise. It was an incredible offer for the clan leader to make to an unknown warrior let alone a young girl. Thane held his breath as he waited for Orphan to reply.

"Thank you," Orphan finally said. "I appreciate your words but I am not very good on anything that floats. I am content here, though I will remember your kind offer."

"If you change your mind, a position in my clan is yours for the taking." Granuaile stood up gracefully and turned to help the ungainly Maighréad to her feet before any of the men had a chance to rise. Granuaile excused herself and with a brief nod to the others seated around the fire, she and Maighréad left.

Eoin and Rian began to regale Thane with their battle stories. They had been in many fights together and had an unending supply of amusing tales. In the middle of a long, bloody story, Thane glanced across the fire and noticed Orphan and Damien absorbed in a private conversation.

Orphan laughed out loud at something Damien said and Thane felt his anger rise. It seemed like they had found a lot to talk about. What was Orphan doing? Didn't she know Damien was not to be trusted?

Sensing they had lost Thane's attention, Eoin and Rian excused themselves and went in search of a more attentive audience. Thane was left sitting on the far side of the fire by himself.

He stared hard at the man who had once been his best friend talking to Orphan, the only friend he had now. What could the two of them possibly have in common?

Damien offered Orphan a mug of something. They were leaning close to each other, deep in conversation; their attention fixed on each other. Thane was forgotten.

Annoyed at being left out, Thane got up and walked around the fire. He stood behind them and waited to be noticed.

"I've always wondered what could have been so bad that my mother would choose to leave her home knowing she would die rather than stay there with me and live," Orphan confided to Damien, a slight quiver in her voice. She glanced over her shoulder at Thane.

"Thane!" she squeaked. She swung around like she'd been caught doing something wrong. Damien's only acknowledgement of Thane's presence was a slight stiffening of his back.

Thane leaned over and spoke softly in her ear, "I'm tired. I'm going to go see if Tally needs anything. You coming?"

Orphan didn't meet his eyes, "ah...no...well...I'd like to stay for a bit longer." She didn't wait for him to comment before turning away from him to face the fire again.

Thane hesitated a moment longer. He was eager to make his escape but was reluctant to leave her alone with Damien. When she didn't say anything else, he turned and walked quietly back toward the caves, alone.

Thane thought about Orphan's mother as he walked. He knew she had left Tír inna n-Óc on Embarr carrying a very young Orphan, but he didn't know why. She had placed her child in the arms of a stranger and chose to dismount. She must have been a mortal, and she must have been in the land of the Fæ for hundreds of years because the instant she touched the ground, her body had crumbled to dust. Thane had never thought about how much being abandoned by her mother must have hurt Orphan. She had never spoken to him about it, and he had never thought to ask. He was her best friend. Why would she tell Damien about her mother? Did she also tell him she was Fæ?

Thane curled up in his blankets to wait for Orphan to return. It was a long time before he finally fell asleep, lulled by the sound of Tally's snoring and the trickle of the water running down the wall of their room.

Chapter Eight

A Fistfight

Granuaile was gone by the time Thane and Orphan returned to the field the following morning. She left more than a score of MacLeòid gallóglaigh behind. Damien gathered the new men and introduced them to everyone. They were absorbed into the fold with little or no disruption and slid seamlessly into training with the group.

Thane and Orphan spent the rest of the day with the gallóglaigh. While Thane's training focused more on the sword, axe, and hand-to-hand, Orphan spent more time with her bow and sword. They were often at different parts of the field, so they didn't see much of each other during the day. Orphan usually went back to the caves long before Thane did.

After Thane was done training late in the afternoon, he walked over to the horse paddocks to care for Embarr. Damien was sitting alone on an ancient stone dolmen near the horses in a patch of weak sunlight. His elbows were on his thighs and he was staring down morosely at his folded hands between his knees. Damien didn't look up until Thane's long shadow fell over him. When he recognized Thane, he rose swiftly to his feet.

"Done already, Your Highness?" Damien mocked.

Thane had had enough of the insinuations and snide comments that Damien had been throwing his way. He'd done nothing to deserve the taunts and sarcastic comments he'd been getting from him, and now it looked like Damien was stealing the only friend Thane had left, Orphan.

Thane wasn't going to back down this time. He got in Damien's face and snarled, "What the hell is your problem?"

"You! You're my problem! You've been my problem from the very beginning when you showed up at the castle with no plan, no help, not even an idea of who or how many were guarding the dungeon…just you, a girl and a horse…and you can't even fight!" he scoffed at Thane, his lip lifted in derision as he ran his eyes up and down Thane's lanky body.

"Do you know how long we followed you that night? It was painfully obvious that you had no idea we were even there! We trailed you through the forest, through the tunnels, and into the castle. You never once guessed we were behind you, did you!"

Once Damien started, he couldn't stop. His anger came spilling out in a venomous diatribe. "If it hadn't been so obvious that you were breaking in, I might not have intervened. If I hadn't sent men to distract the castle guards, you would be rotting down in that dungeon in the cell next to the Seanchaidh!"

"What gave you the right to follow us? I didn't need your help! I didn't ask for your interference," Thane yelled back. Rage coursed through him, and before he could stop to think, he put his hands flat on Damien's chest and shoved hard.

"Do you have any idea how lucky you were to not get yourself...and us along with you, by the way...killed?" Damien put both his hands on Thane's chest and shoved him back.

"You nearly exposed the secret entrance into the castle. You're an idiot...Your Highness!"

After everything Thane had been through in the last few days, his nerves were raw, and he couldn't hold his rage in any longer. He pulled his clenched fist back and punched Damien in the jaw. He felt a tearing pain shoot up his arm, but he was too angry to care.

Damien staggered back a couple steps, stunned. He let out an angry growl, then threw himself at Thane. His first punch caught Thane square in the stomach. It doubled him over, driving the air out of his lungs. Before Thane had a chance to straighten up, Damien brought the same fist up and slammed it into Thane's jaw. Pain exploded across Thane's face.

Thane was dimly aware of the men who were gathering around to urge them on. He heard them yelling suggestions.

Thane dragged a ragged breath through his aching teeth and charged shoulder first into Damien. He brought both of his fists up and pummeled any part of Damien's body that he could reach.

Damien spun around Thane's bent body. He wrapped his left arm around Thane's neck, attempting to choke him. Thane pulled at

Damien's arm with both hands trying to get a breath, but Damien's arm was too tight; he couldn't loosen his grip. Desperate, Thane wrapped his leg behind Damien's and pushed hard with his knee. Damien's leg buckled and they both fell roughly to the ground in a tangle of arms and legs.

Before Thane knew it, they were rolling around in the cold mud pounding each other with their fists. One moment Thane was on top, and the next moment the world was spinning as he was forced onto his back. Thane struggled to breathe through the haze of pain.

Damien sat straddling him, his knees locked on either side of Thane's ribs. Damien pulled his fist back for another punch just as Thane lifted his hands and pushed hard against Damien's chest. With a flash of blinding white-blue light, Thane sent his once best friend flying through the air and across the clearing.

Damien landed hard, flat on his back, arms and legs thrown out at his side.

Shaken, Thane staggered to his feet. He stood doubled over in pain, gasping for breath.

Thane was stunned by the return of the strange blue light. It had not happened since he had been attacked by the group of children from the Reiver village. They had been just as suddenly and violently hurled away from him as Damien had been.

Damien lay still for a moment before he too rose unsteadily to his feet. He hunched over in pain, blinking rapidly as blood ran into his eye and down his cheek from a cut over his eyebrow. Thane watched in fascination as Damien's left eye began to swell. Damien shook his head to clear it and glared furiously at Thane.

Thane knew he couldn't look much better. His vision was blurry and there was a warm steady trickle working its way down his face from his nose and his lip. He wiped mud and blood out of his eyes. A sharp pain in his side made him glad he had relieved himself in the woods earlier, otherwise he was sure he would be standing in a puddle by now.

"You cheat!" Damien yelled furiously. "Can't you even fight like a man?"

Damien straightened up and thrust his fists out in front of him again ready to continue the fight.

Thane took an unsteady step back. He couldn't understand what was happening between them. Damien had been his best friend. The rage drained out of him, replaced by confusion and sadness.

"I don't want to fight you," Thane said wearily. He turned his back on the angry young man and walked away. He was embarrassed when he realized dozens of men were still standing around staring at them. Most were grinning, but some were now looking at him like he had just sprouted horns.

𝍶

Orphan and Tally were sitting around a small fire in the main cave when Thane paddled up to the beach. Orphan glanced over at

Thane as he gingerly climbed out of the small currach. When she saw what a mess his face was, she gasped and rushed to help him. Thane squinted at her through a half-closed swollen eye but didn't say anything.

"What happened to you? You're bleeding and covered in mud. Are we being attacked? I thought we were safe here." Orphan interrogated him, panic edging her voice.

"We're not under attack," Thane muttered angrily as he brushed past her. Every step he took sent an agonizing pain shooting up his side. He eased himself down close to the warmth of the fire next to Tally and wrapped his arms round his middle.

"I had a bit of a misunderstanding with Damien," he said as he wiped the dripping blood off of his chin with his sleeve.

"You had a fight? With Damien? Is he hurt?" she demanded of him as she threw herself down next to him. "What's going on with you two?"

"I don't know! He hates me!" Thane grumbled.

"He doesn't hate you..." she sputtered.

"Yes, he does!" Thane interrupted her.

"He doesn't hate you, Thane," she said, this time condescendingly. "He thought you were dead. Then you show up here...obviously alive, healthy, and strong...and now he feels like you abandoned him..."

"How do you know how he feels? And why are you suddenly taking his side?" Thane shouted at her. "No one bothered to come looking for me either you know!"

"I'm not taking anyone's side!" she shouted back at him. "You're just being unreasonable!" She stood up and stomped off toward their room.

Furious, and hurt by her defense of Damien, Thane turned his back on her retreating figure, wincing as pain shot up his side. He looked at Tally who was sitting propped against a couple of rolled up blankets, eyebrows raised, watching them argue. Thane was thankful that Tally didn't comment. He was relieved to see that the Bard was breathing a bit easier, and that he looked more alert than he had since they'd rescued him.

Thane felt a cold cloth being shoved in his hand. He turned his head and found himself looking directly into the concerned brown eyes of Pádraig. Surprisingly, the boy didn't have anything to say about the miserable condition of Thane's face, and he didn't stick around to be thanked for the cloth. He disappeared into one of the many stone passages that led off the main cave.

Tally looked Thane up and down, his eyes coming to rest on Thane's battered face. Thane knew that if he looked half as bad as he felt, he was probably an ugly mess. His cheek was throbbing painfully, and his lip and eye felt tight and swollen. He looked down at his hands; his knuckles were torn and bloody.

"Do you need to have Guillius look at you?" Tally asked quietly.

"Uh, no." Thane said as he rubbed his bloody knuckles self-consciously across his bruised cheek. "I feel fine."

Both Thane and Tally knew he was lying. He wasn't fine, neither physically nor emotionally.

"Did you know Damien? You know…before?" Thane asked, breaking the uncomfortable silence that had stretched between them.

"Did I know Damien?" Tally started to laugh, but it quickly turned into a groan. He pressed a hand flat against his chest and closed his eyes. When he could breathe easily again he opened his eyes and said, "Yes, I knew him well. How could I not? The two of you were inseparable. I take it by the condition you are in and from your argument with Orphan that Damien has not been happy to see you?

"No," Thane said shortly. "No, he hasn't."

They were interrupted by the arrival of another currach. Damien and Eoin pulled up onto the beach. Thane was delighted to see that Damien hadn't escaped their fight unscathed. His face looked just as bad as Thane's felt, and he was sure that Damien was trying hard to conceal a limp as he strode past them.

Chapter Nine

Trading Tales

Tally slowly began to regain his strength under Guillius' care. Before the end of their second week in the caves, he was walking unassisted and staying awake for increasingly longer periods of time. He was alert and his face had lost the scary pallor that had so worried Thane, and he had begun to gain back the weight he had lost during his imprisonment.

Thane was eating supper one evening with Tally and Orphan near a large fire in the main cave when Pádraig appeared beside them. He squeezed his little body between Tally and Orphan and sat down. Pádraig leaned in close to Tally and begged him to tell them all a story. He wanted a really good one, a story with Færies or dragons. Thane was not surprised when Tally readily agreed. He had been acting peevish and out of sorts lately, complaining about being treated like an invalid.

Orphan got up and disappeared briefly into their little cave. She returned a moment later to lay Tally's lute in his lap then dropped down on the ground next to Thane.

Word spread quickly that the Seanchaidh was going to tell a story. Before long, he was surrounded by giant Mag Uidhir and gallóglaigh warriors eagerly waiting for him to begin. Thane caught a glimpse of Damien through the thick gathering. He was sitting alone, with his back against the cave wall feigning disinterest.

The cave was so silent in anticipation of his tale that the sound of water could be heard dripping from the ceiling and lapping at the edge of the narrow beach. Tally fussed with the strings on the instrument for a bit before settling on a short sad melody. The soft notes echoed in the depths of the caves. Tally took a deep breath and began the tale of an unfortunate Formoire King...

Long ago, in a fortress on the cliffs of the Western shore, Balór, the young son of the Formoire King Buarainech, crept into a forbidden tower belonging to his father's druids. There he discovered a cauldron filled with a poisonous potion. As he leaned in to get a closer look, the brew exploded. Evil fumes engulfed his face and hot burning liquid splashed into his eyes.

The burns healed in time, but Balór was left with one giant eye in the center of his forehead that went through his skull to the back of his head. With this evil eye, Balór discovered he could not only see what was behind him at all times, but he could also kill a man with just one glance of it.

ORPHAN

Balór's gaze was so deadly, he had only to open his eye on the battlefield, and he could lay waste to all he looked upon. No army could triumph over him as long as his eye remained fixed upon them. To ensure the Formoire success in battle, a gold ring was woven through his eyelid and ropes were worked by four of his most trusted warriors to hold his eyelid open. Even if he tired, the battle could still be won.

Upon the death of Buarainech, Balór became King of the Formoire. And so it was, with Balór as their fearsome leader, the Formoire ruled for many years over the Tuatha de Danann.

In time, Balór learned of an ancient druidess prophecy that foretold of his defeat and death at the hands of his own grandson in a great battle. Full of fear for his life, Balór and his wife Ceithleann locked their daughter Eithne high in a crystal tower above the sea at Túr Rí, the Castle of the King. They posted guards and surrounded her with ladies in waiting. There they left her, confident she would be free from the attention of all men.

Cian, a Fæ warrior of the Tuatha de Danann had become furious with Balór for stealing his magical cow and sought revenge on the Formoire King. Cian conspired with the Druidess Biróg to gain access to Túr Rí and to the gaol of the beautiful Eithne.

Late one night, Biróg magically disguised Cian as an old woman, put the gaol guards to sleep, and snuck him into the crystal tower. Eithne became pregnant and gave birth to three baby boys.

In a fit of terror, her father gathered up her sons, put them in a wicker basket and ordered the basket to be flung into a whirlpool in the ocean so that the babies would be killed.

Biróg learned of Balór's plan but was only able to save one of the three babies. When the two lost boys drowned, their souls were transformed into the first selkies. Biróg brought the surviving infant, Lugh, to the sea god Manannán mac Lir, who fostered the boy and raised him as his own. Lugh Lámhfada grew to be a strong and skilled warrior. Manannán mac Lir bestowed many gifts upon Lugh such as an unbeatable sword Fragarach and a golden breast plate no weapon could pierce.

Many years later, the Second Battle of the Plains of Magh Tureidh took place between the Formoire and the Tuatha de Danann. It was a fearsome battle of sword and spear, blood and flesh, life and death. Lugh Lámhfada valiantly fought with the only people to whom he felt loyalty, the Tuatha de Danann.

On the field of battle, Balór met Lugh at the crest of a hill. There Lugh flung a stone at Balór and knocked the evil eye out the back of his head and killed him. The eye spun in circles on the ground killing the Formoire and sealing the victory for the Tuatha de Danann. The eye then burned a hole into the earth into which water settled to form Lough na Súil.

Lugh fulfilled the prophesy and slew his grandfather as the Druidess had foretold. The remaining Formoire Army were banished to dwell in cities under the sea. Balór thought to cheat his destiny by committing a heinous crime against his own flesh and blood in order to save himself. That act ensured his ultimate downfall and fulfilled the prophesy.

As Tally ended his tale, the crowd burst into applause.

"Another!" demanded one of the gallóglach from the other side of the fire.

"That is enough for tonight," said Tally as he placed the lute on the ground beside him and leaned back on one elbow. "I am weary; someone else tell a story," Tally suggested to the crowd.

No one spoke up.

"I'm curious," Tally's voice broke the silence. "How did the Mag Uidhirs find themselves up here, in these caves?" he asked no one in particular…and no one answered him. Many were casting furtive glances at Damien.

Thane sat up straighter, and he too looked towards Damien. At some point during Tally's story, Pádraig had moved to sit next to the young man. He was curled up, with his head tucked under Damien's arm, sound asleep. Pádraig's face was relaxed, and without his usual grin and precocious attitude he looked very much like what he was: a very small boy. For the first time, Thane began to really appreciate just how young Pádraig was. The boy couldn't have been much more than six years old.

Thane had seen Damien talking to each of the gallóglaigh at one time or another, but his conversations with them had been of an impersonal nature, the passing of information or instructions. He didn't share in the friendly banter the rest of the men engaged in. The only one Damien seemed to care about was little Pádraig. Whenever Damien was in the caves or up at the training grounds, Pádraig was usually not too far away. It was also obvious to Thane that the feeling was mutual; Pádraig worshiped Damien.

Damien disengaged himself from the sleeping child and stood up. Thane was not surprised when he bent down, gathered Pádraig up in his arms and carried him toward one of the tunnels that led toward the back caves. Thane turned and saw Orphan staring after them as well. He opened his mouth to comment, but she shook her head.

One by one, the gallóglaigh stood and followed Damien's lead. They too disappeared into the rear of the caves or left in the currachs until only a few of the Mag Uidhirs remained. The warriors moved closer to the fire and made themselves comfortable.

"It's good to hear your tales again, Taliesin. It's been a long time," the big redheaded Eoin said. He was grinning from ear to ear, proudly displaying the hole where he was missing one of his front teeth. "I remember sitting for hours in the great hall listening to you sing. Fond memories they are. Aye, very fond memories," he said nodding his head.

"I'm glad to oblige," Tally nodded his head in acknowledgement. "Would you return the favor?"

"Anything you need Seanchaidh, just tell us and we will do it," Jamie assured him.

"I need to know what happened the night the castle was attacked and young Nathaniel here disappeared. Will you tell me what you know? How did you come to be here?" Tally asked as he waved a hand at the cavern around him.

Jamie, Rian, and Eoin shared a brief knowing look that spoke volumes to each other without saying a word. Jamie nodded his agreement and Eoin began the tale.

"Well, as ya may already know, most of us were sent out to intercept the English up river. We traveled quite a ways along the river but didn't find any sign that the English had been anywhere near us, but we wanted to be sure, so we continued to search for them. We'd been almost home when we spotted the smoke coming from the direction of the castle. By the time we got back, the Uí Néills had stormed the walls and were inside the castle."

"The Uí Néills?" Thane asked in surprise. "You didn't see… any…"

"What? Monsters?" Eoin finished the sentence for him then put a massive hand across his mouth to smother his strange high pitched laugh. "Nowin' ya must have been talking to Damien." He giggled again. "No. We saw only the cursed Uí Néills. They'd already smashed through the castle's defenses and set parts of it afire."

"We were horribly out numbered," Jamie interjected. Although he was not as old as Eoin, he was equally as large. His long blond hair was tangled into the strands of his beard so it looked like he was wearing a long, yellow woolen cowl. "Those of us that were not fighting did what we could to rescue the folks from the castle.

"We discovered Damien crawling outa' some hole in the ground draggin' his half-conscious grandmother behind him. He was shouting about how some huge monsters had killed the Mag Uidhir and how the monsters were going to go after the Prince. He was frantic for us to stop them. I ain't seen any of them monsters myself either but by my way of thinking, if they were in the castle, we would have just been killed ourselves if we had gone back inside."

"Did anyone else say they saw the monsters?" Thane asked again. Why was it that Damien had been able to see them when no one else could? Thane knew Damien wasn't crazy because he had seen the creatures that night too. They were very real.

Eoin looked sideways at Thane before shaking his head and saying, "No. I don't know of anyone who saw anything like what Damien was screaming about."

"Regardless," Rian steered the subject back to their escape. "We did all we could do to hold Damien back. Took three of us, it did, to hold him down and keep him from going back into the castle after the young Prince here," he jerked his head in Thane's direction. "The boy was covered in blood from a long gash on the side of his face, and he had broken his left arm, but damned if he still didn't fight us for all he was worth, screaming his throat raw."

They sat in silence for a minute each lost in their own memories of the horror of that night. Thane looked at Tally who was staring intently into the fire. His face was pale and his hands were white where they were clenched together in front of him. Thane knew Tally was remembering his own frantic escape on Embarr and the guilt he carried for years believing Thane was dead and wishing he had done more to save him.

"Martha and Damien were both hurt quite badly…bleeding all over the place they were," Rian said. "It wasn't until Damien finally passed out from the pain and loss of blood that he stopped struggling and we were able to get them both away from the castle to safety. There were a few others beside Damien and Martha who had escaped the castle that night. None were as badly hurt as those two were. We escaped…fled into the cover of the woods. All of us had naught but the clothes on our backs."

"Where is she…Martha, Damien's grandmother?" Thane asked softly.

Jamie spoke up. "I think it was all just too much for Martha. Ya know, losing her son and his wife just a few years before and then to lose her home and so many others that night…" He stopped to shake the mop of yellow hair out of his eyes and swallowed carefully before continuing. "Martha never woke again. She passed quietly in her sleep a few nights later."

Thane felt as if a knife had been suddenly and viciously stabbed deep into his chest. He didn't realize until this moment how much faith he had placed in his belief that Martha was still alive and safe, living happily somewhere else. Thane felt a small warm hand take his and looked down. Orphan had wrapped her fingers around his hand and was squeezing tightly.

Thane watched in fascination as a drop of water landed on their hands and rolled down between their fingers. He looked up automatically for the source and found the ceiling above them was dry. The drop had come from him...he was crying. Not wanting to look weak, he pulled his hand from under Orphan's and surreptitiously wiped his cheek with his sleeve. He stared hard at the fire and tried not to let his emotions overwhelm him.

Eoin flicked a quick glance over his shoulder to make sure no one was listening and leaned forward, "I remember him as a mischievous, carefree, happy boy. But after the attack, Damien was quiet, intense, and angry. Once his arm healed, he spent every free waking hour in weapons training. It wasn't long before he could defeat all of his peers and a fair few of his elders. Many think for a time young Damien had a death wish...a wish to go with his parents and his grandmother."

"Pah!" Jamie broke in, "Me, I say the lad is out to make a name for his self like his father, who was as ya might recall, a fearsome gallóglach, one of ya father's most trusted."

"Whatever his reasons, Damien was fearless and daring," Eoin spoke over Jamie, "the gallóglaigh heard of his exploits and recruited him. They took him in, trained him, and eventually he joined them on their raids. Damien took the gallóglaigh Oath, to let death take him rather than to fail. It weren't long before they let him lead his own raids. Damien found a place with the gallóglaigh for those of us what wanted one. We swear fealty to the Mag Uidhir now for a price, but in the past we have worked for who ever would pay us the most."

"Damien may still be one very angry young man, but I meself would follow him anywhere." Rian said.

"Aye," both Jamie and Eoin agreed.

"Pádraig is too young to have lived with you in the castle isn't he? Who is he? Where did he come from?" Orphan leaned forward and held her hands out close to the warmth of the fire.

"Don't really know," Jamie answered.

"Damien just showed up one day carrying the lad in his arms," Rian said. "He'd found him in a village that had been razed by the English...his family dead. Pádraig was just a couple years old at the time, not much more than a babe. He was a quiet little boy, scared of everything and everyone but Damien. Not these days though, that urchin is more likely to be in trouble than out of it."

"Aye, and the only one Damien lets close to him is the boy," Jamie added.

Eoin thrust his elbow in Jamie's side and whispered, "Hush."

"Ouch! Well, anyways, it wasn't long before..." Jamie's eyes grew wide as he focused on something behind Thane. He stopped talking abruptly and stood up. "Uhh, goodnight, Seanchaidh."

Before Tally could reply, Rian had pulled Eoin roughly to his feet and the three men left. The reason for their sudden departure was apparent a moment later when someone cleared his throat. Thane, Orphan, and Tally turned in unison to find Damien standing not far behind them, his face in shadows.

"Get your sword, Your Highness. We're off to intercept an English patrol near Inis Ceithleann," was all Damien said before he followed Rian, Eoin and Jamie into the caves.

"Wonder how long he had been standing there?" Orphan stared off in the direction Damien had disappeared. She looked like she wanted to get up and follow him.

"Who cares? He shouldn't sneak around eavesdropping!" Thane shrugged as he unfolded his legs and stood up to retrieve his sword from their small cave.

Tally reached out and grabbed a hold of his hand to stop him. He looked warily into Thane's eyes. "Do you understand the implications of what those three just said?"

Thane shook his head. "What do you mean? They said many things."

"They can't see the Formoire, Thane. In their minds, Damien was imagining things. He has proven himself in battle, so they trust him with their lives, yet, in this, they have little faith," Tally frowned up at him.

"They should have believed him?" Orphan asked puzzled.

"The Formoire, like all Fæ are able to hide their true selves behind glamour, a false image they cast over themselves like a cloak. Mortals can't see past glamour to the real form beneath. My guess is that Damien may be able to see through glamour because his father was a MacLeòid."

"How does being a MacLeòid mean he can see through glamour?" Thane said puzzled.

ORPHAN

"Tatiana was a Færie Princess. She fell in love with the Chief of the Clan MacLeòid and they were married. She had a baby but wasn't able to stay in the mortal realm with him," Tally began to explain.

"She left her baby a silken blanket they now call the Færie Flag of Dunvegan. We heard about her at my Grandfather's," Thane said. "She wasn't allowed to stay. He said her baby was mortal, so she would have to leave him with his clan and return to Tír inna n-Óc."

"That's correct, but because of her, Fæ blood runs through that clan. It is not unheard of in the MacLeòid Clan for a child to be born with some Fæ traits even after all these generations. Damien must be one of her direct descendants. That is probably why he can see through their glamour when most others cannot. That may work in our favor as the Formoire will not expect it. They won't be able to fool him. I wonder if he has any other Fæ powers?"

"Will we be able to see past their glamour?" Orphan stood up and began to pace in front of the fire.

"Most likely. Glamour can only fool mortals," Tally reassured her. "Keep your eyes open. The Formoire are very different from the English. They will be large, their bodies deformed…abnormal."

"Like the one guarding you at the castle?" Thane asked him.

"That is correct," Tally nodded in agreement.

"What about Muirghein? She was an old lady when we first met her. How come we didn't see past her glamour?" Thane asked.

Tally smiled. "Muirghein was not using glamour. She is old and exceptionally powerful. She has the power to transform herself into whatever form she desires."

"I need to leave," Thane said.

"Wait!" Orphan demanded. She left abruptly, disappearing into their cave and returned seconds later with her bow and quiver full of white fletched arrows. "I'm coming with you."

Thane opened his mouth to argue but changed his mind when he saw the look on her face. Fighting with her would accomplish nothing. It would only make them late. He shrugged and turned to leave when Tally spoke again.

"You are your father's son, Thane. They will be watching you."

"Why?" he turned to look back at Tally.

"According to English law you are the heir and rightful Chief of the Mag Uidhir Clan and all its lands, but Brehon Law clearly allows the strongest of your uncles or cousins to claim Lordship. When your father, Cianán Mag Uidhir was killed and the castle overrun, the clan must have been in utter turmoil. From what I can gather, your cousin, Cúchonnacht Mag Uidhir stepped in and took over. He has taken more gallóglaigh into service to harass the castle hoping to drive out the intruders. He intends to seize the castle and take up residence there as The Mag Uidhir. He would be justified in believing that you would threaten his authority within the clan."

"What? He thinks I want to take over his clan?" he said appalled. "Is he mad? I want nothing to do with these people. I just want to get us out of here and get back to...to...I don't know... anywhere but here..." he trailed off futilely as he waved his hand to indicate the caves around them, his voice bounced tauntingly back at them.

"You may feel that way now, but there is no doubt they are concerned that you will change your mind. It is apparent to them by the way you speak that you have spent many years with the English. They will not so easily trust your loyalty to the clan."

They fell silent at the clatter of numerous feet. Gallóglaigh were streaming into the main cavern with Damien in the lead. Damien barely glanced at Thane as he strode past him and climbed into one of the many currachs lining the river's edge and left with the first group of men.

Thane ran back to their cave and grabbed his sword. He and Orphan joined Jamie and Eoin in a small, shallow-bottomed currach. The warriors were dressed for battle in bulky, quilted shirts that reached their knees, chain mail vests, and round steel helmets. Both men were silently checking and securing the multiple weapons they had attached to their bodies. Gone were the easy smiles and lighthearted banter of the past few hours as both men readied themselves for the impending battle.

Thane met Orphan's eyes in a sideways glance. He was sure they were both thinking the same thing: What had they gotten themselves into? Did they have enough weapons to defend themselves? Thane was feeling seriously underdressed and inadequately armed. No one spoke as they paddled their way toward the cave entrance.

Chapter Ten

Ambush

As soon as they came to a stop at the dock, Jamie and Eoin jumped out of their seats. They were replaced by a boy who would take the currach back into the caves to pick up more men. The boy sat impatiently waiting as Thane and Orphan climbed out and pulled away from the dock almost before their feet cleared the gunwale.

Thane and Orphan rushed out of the cave and through the forest. They emerged from the trees and onto the training field. It was crowded with dozens of armed gallóglaigh and Mag Uidhirs. They found Damien talking with the same richly dressed man they had seen just a couple weeks earlier. Damien looked to be receiving orders. When he noticed their arrival, he waved them over.

"This is Prince Nathaniel," Damien said to the stranger when Thane and Orphan came to a stop in front of them.

The man turned his pale blue eyes on Thane and nodded. "Nathaniel, I am Cúchonnacht Mag Uidhir."

Thane nodded in return and replied almost rudely, "I figured as much."

"Your father was a great man. I admired him immensely and was deeply sorrowed at his death. But you, young man," he said as he ran his eyes leisurely up and down Thane's long-limbed frame, "your worth is yet to be seen."

"What do you want from us?" Thane asked him boldly. He didn't feel like he had to prove anything to his cousin.

"For now, a show of loyalty to the clan will be sufficient. You will accompany Damien and his warriors tonight. There have been reports of English patrols pushing through the southeastern boundaries of our land. My men have become quite good at routing the outsiders, but they could always use another loyal warrior."

The Mag Uidhir swung himself up on his horse. He pulled on the reins to turn his horse and surveyed the armed men before him.

"Turn them back tonight," he reiterated to Damien. Then, amidst the clamor and clatter of his personal retinue, he rode away.

Thane looked at Damien for any indication of how he felt about having to take them along, but he may as well have been looking at a painting for all the emotion he could read in Damien's face.

Thane turned away from him. He and Orphan would go with them this time. He figured they owed the clan something for their care of Tally and for their hospitality, but he didn't intend to stay here and play mercenary for long. He had just taken a step toward Embarr, who was contentedly dozing next to two sturdy mares, when Damien called out to him.

"Prince! You can't take your horse. His white coat will be a beacon in the dark. Two horses have been brought to the field for the two of you to ride. Find Rian. He will fetch them for you."

Thane didn't turn around or reply. He grabbed Orphan's arm and led her in the direction of the other horses. Rian wasn't hard to spot as he was walking toward them, his big hands wrapped around the reins of two brown mares. They weren't saddled, only a pillow was tied to each horse's back.

"Where are their saddles?" Orphan asked.

"What'd ya need a saddle for? Don't ya know how to ride?" Rian asked puzzled.

The gallóglaigh and the Mag Uidhirs were already mounting their saddle-less horses and disappearing into the forest. Rian thrust one set of reigns into Thane's hand the other set into Orphan's. Thane gave his horse a cursory going over then hopped up on her pillowed back. He looked longingly over at Embarr then, squeezed his thighs tight against the mare's side, and turned to follow the line of warriors, Orphan close at his side.

They rode through the dense leafless forest in silence until they came to a river. Thane was surprised to see dozens of small currachs being pulled out of hiding places in the forest. He was even more surprised when the warriors began to dismount and tie up their horses. The younger boys were running around securing horses, adjusting weapons, and helping to launch the currachs.

Thane heard Orphan groan, "What is it with these men and their little boats?"

Eoin walked over and leaned his arm on the neck of Thane's horse. "You look a might puzzled."

"We're getting in boats?" Orphan asked, alarm pitching her voice a bit higher than normal.

"The fastest way to get where we are going is by currach," Eoin replied. "It's the easiest way to move so many men quickly and quietly as the forests are dense and difficult to move through. We'll be getting out a short ways up the river and we'll walk the rest of the way. We know the woods. Them English don't. We'll spread out and hit them before they even know we're there."

Thane couldn't see Orphan's expression in the dark, but he could almost feel her scowling at the river.

"Do we just pick one?" she muttered as she slid silently from her horse.

"Sure...whichever one ya like."

"What if I don't like any of them?" Orphan eyed the lineup of currachs with disdain.

Thane grabbed her by the hand and pulled her into the nearest currach with an empty bench before she could make a scene. The boat tilted wildly as the gallóglach with the oars pushed them away from the shore. Thane could feel Orphan sitting straight and tense beside him. Since the Mag Uidhir didn't request her, she could have insisted on staying behind when she realized they would be traveling by boat, but she didn't. He admired her for her ability to overcome her fear...well most of her fear.

The oars made little splashing sounds as the gallóglaigh rowed against the current. It sounded loud to his ears, each splash a metered betrayal of their position. He watched the other warriors in the currachs around him. They didn't seem concerned about the amount of noise they were making. As long they weren't showing signs of worry, he supposed it was not a problem.

Once he stopped worrying about the noises, his mind wandered to what lay ahead of them. His only raiding experience had been with the Reivers, and it had been a terrifying one. One moment he was gripping his sword, confident that he was skilled enough to fight with the Mag Uidhirs. The next moment he was gripping his sword in fear and doubt and sure he was going to get himself killed.

Eventually, they pulled onto a shallow bank. No one spoke as they climbed out of the currachs and dragged the boats out of the water. The huge gallóglaigh and Mag Uidhir warriors were swiftly and silently disappearing into the trees and the underbrush.

Eoin approached Thane and Orphan from behind and waved his hand as he passed them to indicate that they should follow him. Eoin whispered, "Stay with me. The rest of them are going to surround the camp on all sides. They'll need to get into position, so it'll take a little time. We'll be moving to the west, circling the camp until we see their horses. Our job will be to release the horses and drive them toward the north where others will meet them and take them to the Mag Uidhir. We get fresh horses and they lose their rides," he giggled softly next to them, then stopped abruptly as if he had just remembered something. He looked down at them with a scowl, "And don't ya be get'n in the middle of any fights. Damien says ya don't have the training for it."

Thane opened his mouth to argue when Orphan elbowed him in the arm and shook her head at him. Thane snapped his teeth together in frustration. It wasn't Eoin's decision, and this wasn't the time to discuss it. They followed Eoin.

There was no moon, the forest was almost completely dark, yet the warriors ahead of him moved through the trees and underbrush without making a sound. Thane and Orphan were not as quiet. No matter how carefully they tread, they couldn't seem to avoid stepping on the dry leaves, brittle branches, and frozen grasses of the forest floor.

Soon, the shimmering orange glow of dozens of fires appeared through the trees. Thane could see a contingent of at least two hundred English archers, pikemen, billmen, arquebusiers and other heavily armed soldiers lounging around well built fires. These were not untried villagers; they were battle tested soldiers of the English Crown at ease in the sure belief that they were superior in every way.

Thane heard an indistinct noise to his left and squinted through the dim light. He saw one of the gallóglaigh come up behind an English sentry. The ensuing struggle was silent and efficient. The guard's body was dragged out of sight. Thane was sure that the same thing was happening all around the perimeter of the camp.

The English remained oblivious to the threat surrounding them. Their confidence in the ability of their watchmen to protect them was obvious. Thane could see soldiers asleep in bedrolls, and sitting in small groups eating and talking. Dozens of tents had been set up in orderly lines in the middle of the camp and a large area had been cordoned off for the horses using posts and ropes to form a temporary fence.

Thane and Orphan followed Eoin as he crept around the west side of the campsite. They kept to the shadows, careful not to draw attention to themselves as they took cover behind a stand of pine trees to wait for the signal.

The woods suddenly exploded in sound. The gallóglaigh charged into camp from the cover of darkness. Several of the Mag Uidhirs dropped out of the trees on top of the sleeping men. Soldiers were tumbling out of their bedrolls and tents, momentarily confused and disoriented by the upheaval around them. Yells and the sudden ringing clash of steel upon steel filled the air. It didn't take long for the English to rally together and begin to fight back.

The loud crack of arquebuses reverberated through the air. Thane spotted a number of English soldiers loading the long heavy weapons. They were attempting to balance the guns on forked poles to fire them, but in the chaos of the battle, not many were succeeding. Despite that, it wasn't long before the disorganized skirmish became an intense battle.

Thane tore his eyes away from the fighting and ran after Orphan. Eoin had cut a bloody path through the men who had been guarding the horses and was trying to keep the others at bay so Thane and Orphan could get to the horses and set them free.

Thane didn't bother to try untying the knots, he raised his knife and began to chop through the ropes that were tied to the stakes. Orphan ran around to cut the ropes on the other side of the enclosure. At the rate Thane and Orphan were going, it would take forever to cut through enough of the fencing to free all of the horses.

Thane had an idea. He yelled at Orphan to get her attention, then held up his hands, wiggled his fingers at her, and raised his eyebrows conspiratorially. It took her a few seconds to catch on before a grin lit her face. Orphan nodded eagerly. She loved using magic.

They looked around to make sure no one was watching them and that Eoin, and the other gallóglaigh who had joined him, were still holding the English at bay.

"Ready?" Thane shouted over the noise. He saw her nod "yes," and together they went to work.

Thane put his right hand out in front of him, palm facing out toward the horses. He focused all his energy on the thick ropes, imagining the knots loosening, untying, and slipping free. The tethers slithered round the poles until, one by one, they began to pull free and fall to the ground. Thane grabbed the nearest ropes and pulled them from between the stakes so the horses wouldn't get caught in them.

Eoin's red hair came into view as he fought his way toward them. When he realized the horses were already free, he stood in the middle of the herd, axe held loosely in one hand, scratching his head with the other hand.

"What's wrong?" Orphan yelled over the noise of the surrounding battle.

"You're done already?" he yelled back surprised. He shook his head, then shouted, "We need to start driving them to the north. The two of you head to the other side of the field. Do your best to turn them toward me and get them moving. I'll take the first few and ride north; the rest will follow. When they're all moving in the right direction, find Damien and stick close to him. He said he'll take you back to the caves."

Thane and Orphan elbowed their way to the back of the herd, shouting and driving horses toward Eoin as they went. Just as Eoin had said, once Thane and Orphan got the first few horses moving, the rest were eager to follow. When the last of the animals was disappearing into the forest, they turned back to the battle to look for Damien.

Thane felt Orphan pulling frantically on his arm. He turned toward her and to see what had her so excited. Orphan pointed to the far side of the clearing. With all of the horses now out of the way, they could see two large wagons full of provisions.

"You think we should try to blow them up?" she shouted in his ear.

Thane nodded eagerly. "Yes! You do it! Let's get closer."

They worked their way around the edge of the camp, careful to stay out of the violent swings of swords and axes and flying arrows. When they were close enough to hit their target without accidentally burning anything or anyone else in their path, Thane yelled, "NOW!"

Without further encouragement, she opened her palms and sent twin balls of blue flame speeding toward the wagons. Thane held his breath as the fire hit each wagon dead center.

For a moment, nothing happened.

A sudden explosion rent the air and blew the two of them off their feet. Towering flames flooded the darkness of the night, turning it into the brilliant light of day. Flaming debris flew high in the air as the fires ignited smaller explosions. The clamor of battle stopped briefly as everyone turned in unison to stare at the fire engulfing what was left of the wooden wagons and their contents.

Thane lay on his back, the breath knocked out of him, momentarily stunned but grinning. She did it! His ears were ringing as he leaned unsteadily up on an elbow to look around for her. She was already on her knees not far from him, her eyes riveted on the dancing flames. He stood up and pulled Orphan swiftly to her feet. They had to get out of there and find Damien.

Thane searched the darkness. Everywhere he looked, men were fighting for their lives. Most of the arquebusiers had given up trying to load the guns and were fighting with knives and pikes. The steel sparrs of the gallóglaigh were flashing orange in the firelight as the warriors swung them in a complicated figure-eight that took out everyone that got in their way.

Damien was standing still, his sparr held out defensively in front of him. He was scanning the area near the burning wagons as if looking for someone. Thane pulled Orphan back into the cover of the dark forest. He had a feeling that Damien knew exactly who had blown the wagons up and exactly how they had accomplished it.

Some Mag Uidhirs were still hidden in the trees raining arrows down on the campsite. Others were fighting the remaining English in groups of twos and threes. Thane saw Jamie in the thick of the fight. He couldn't tell what was shining brighter in the firelight, his long blond hair or his sparr. Slowly, the fight was beginning to wane as the English who weren't wounded or dead began to retreat into the forest.

Thane looked back at Damien who was now at the edge of the camp battling an immense, horribly disfigured soldier. Thane and Orphan headed toward them. The tall, broad soldier fighting Damien looked very different from the other soldiers in the English contingent. It had the basic shape of a man, but it certainly wasn't human. The flickering orange light of the fires highlighted the many lesions covering the creature's skin. Like the guard Thane had seen in the castle dungeon, small boney protuberances formed a line from its eyebrows back along either side of its head and ended just behind its misshapen ears. It was a Formoire.

Thane saw Damien glance at them out of the corner of his eye as they approached. He was distracted a moment too long; his sparr was knocked out of his hands by his massive opponent. Thane ran toward him as Orphan shot first one arrow at the enemy, then another. The Formoire staggered back with a ferocious bellow, the white fletchings starkly vivid against the darkness. To their horror, the creature just pulled the offending arrows out of its side. The arrows had slowed him down but not stopped him.

Thane was close enough to them now to toss his sword, pummel first, at Damien. Damien snatched the sword from the air as his opponent charged at him again. In one smooth motion, with a mighty two-handed swing, he decapitated the creature.

The Formoire imploded, its body sucking in upon itself forming a large black hole before blowing out again in a shower of green mist. The acrid smell of burning flesh and hair stung Thane's eyes and burned his nose.

Damien looked through the grizzly mist at Thane and Orphan as they stared open-mouthed at the small pile of dust. It was all that was left of the monster's body. Thane and Damien locked eyes for a moment before Damien threw the hilt of Thane's sword back at him. He bent and scooped up his sparr from the ground. He turned away from them, then put his fingers to his lips. Damien blew two short piercing whistles as he ran back toward the edge of the clearing. Instantly, gallóglaigh and Mag Uidhirs began slipping away, disappearing into the shadows of the forest.

Orphan grabbed Thane by the arm and ran, tugging him after her. He stopped and stared at the devastation they were leaving behind. The small neat fires had been scattered, their flames spread haphazardly throughout the camp. Wounded men were lying on the ground crying out for help while other men were scattered, still and silent. Even more had fled when it became apparent the fight was not going their way.

"Come on! We need to go before they leave us here!" Orphan yelled as she ran for the cover of the trees. They were one of the few members of the raiding party left in the clearing; almost everyone else had disappeared.

Thane turned his back on the carnage and bolted after her. She was fast but his legs were longer. Soon he was in the lead, grabbing her hand, and pulling her after him.

At the river they threw themselves into the closest currach. This time they needed no encouragement to paddle. They wanted to get out of there as quickly as possible. They were traveling with the current now and Thane didn't give a moment's thought to how much noise they were making as he drove the oars aggressively into the water. Orphan was rowing hard. She didn't have time to remember her fear of being on the water. They made the return trip in half the time it had taken to get there.

They pushed their currachs up onto the shore. Dozens of Mag Uidhir boys rushed forward to help them pull the boats out of the water. Thane and Orphan found their horses right where they left them tied up near the edge of the river. They hopped up onto their horses, settled on the padding, and held on tightly as they raced through the dark. It was dawn by the time they reached the training grounds.

Damien called them together for a moment to commend them. The English were on the run, their weapons destroyed and the horses safely on their way to The Mag Uidhir. Tired and wounded men began to wander off.

"I'm going to get some rest," Orphan said as she waved a weary hand at Thane then disappeared up the trail that led to the caves.

Thane was too unsettled by the evening's events to sleep, both exhausted and wide awake at the same time. Thane left Damien to deal with his men and led the two horses back to the paddock. He handed off the reigns to one of the young boys and turned toward Embarr.

Pádraig was brushing the horse's white flanks as Thane walked over to them. The small boy looked up as Thane approached and quickly tucked the brush behind his back as if he'd been caught doing something wrong.

Thane gave Pádraig what he hoped was a reassuring smile. "Please don't stop. Embarr loves the attention."

Thane cupped his open palm gently on top of the horse's nose and rubbed his fingers over the soft hair as he looked down at the top of the boy's pale head. "I find I don't get a chance to do it as often as I would like lately. Thank you for looking out for him."

Pádraig peeked up at Thane through his eyelashes and began to run the brush along Embarr's long neck. "Ya welcome," he said shyly. "I like him. He's smart. Damien says when I grows up I can have a horse of me own too."

Footsteps crunched on the cold ground behind Thane. He turned and came face to face with Damien.

"Pádraig, Guillius needs your help with the wounded. He's in the main cavern," Damien said to Pádraig, his eyes never leaving Thane's face. "Go find him."

Pádraig stood uncertainly between them for a moment longer, then nodded. He shoved the brush into Thane's hand and murmured 'goodbye' to Embarr before running back along the path toward the caves.

"Did you blow up their wagons?" Damien demanded as soon as the boy left.

"No," Thane answered evasively. He knew Damien had seen them during the explosion, and that Damien would know he was lying.

"So, you're saying Orphan did it?" Damien persisted.

"I didn't say that," Thane countered. He didn't know if Orphan had told Damien she was Fæ so he continued to be evasive. He wasn't ready to relax his guard and cooperate with Damien yet.

Damien tried a different approach. "You saw what it was too didn't you?"

"What?" Thane pretended not to understand even though he knew Damien was talking about the Formoire he had fought.

Damien stared hard at him then, with a frustrated grunt, he turned on his heel to leave.

Embarr blew a disgusted breath between his lips and shoved his nose between Thane's shoulder blades pushing him toward Damien's retreating back.

"Yes, I saw him," Thane burst out reluctantly.

Damien stopped. He turned slowly around to face Thane.

"You saw him. That soldier wasn't normal, and he didn't die...he...he exploded. There's never anything left to prove...I'm not..."

"You're not crazy if that's what you think. He's a Formoire. I know you heard the same old tales I heard when we were young. Don't you remember? Tally spoke about their king last night." Thane took a step closer to him.

The sun was just peeking through the trees washing Damien's face in its cold morning light. His brows were drawn sharply down and his lips were drawn into a tight line as he stared back at Thane. The scar on his chin stood out pale in the morning light.

"They cover their true appearance in glamour. Mortals see what the Formoire want them to see, but glamour can't fool another Fæ." Thane tore his eyes from Damien's face and looked out over the quiet training field. "They can't fool me."

"I know you know what I am. I told you so myself when we were children. I trusted you once with my secrets and I won't lie to you now," Thane paused for a moment before looking back at Damien, "I don't have to like you to trust you."

Damien looked like he'd been slapped. Damien straightened his spine, and closed his eyes briefly. When he looked at Thane again, he had schooled his expression back to his normal indifferent visage, but the comment hung in the air between them.

"Why am I the only one who can see them? Well, besides you," he asked as he began to pace in front of Thane.

"And Orphan," Thane pointed his thumb over his shoulder in the direction of the caves. "If you're looking for those kinds of answers maybe you need to talk to Tally."

"Orphan? Is she Fæ or is she like me?"

Thane didn't reply immediately. He didn't know how much he should say.

Weighing his words carefully he said, "It's not my secret to tell. Like I said, you need to talk to Tally."

Damien didn't leave. After a couple seconds of uncomfortable silence, Thane said, "Anything else?"

"Can you change...the glamour thing...can you do it?" Damien asked him.

Thane shrugged. "Don't know. Never tried."

Damien opened his mouth to say something else then shut it abruptly as if he changed his mind. He turned and strode off toward the training end of the field.

Thane stood and stared after Damien as questions rolled around in his head. Could he do it? Change his appearance? He wished he had been able to do it long ago. It would have been a good skill to have when he was with the Reivers being teased for his misshapen ears.

Thane turned back toward Embarr. The horse was staring intently at him. He scowled back at him and said defensively, "What's wrong with you?"

Thane put his arm around Embarr's neck and leaned his face into the horse's warmth for a moment. He wished he could just climb on his back and ride away into the forest, but Tally was still not able to travel. "Since you have had someone sneaking you treats and fawning all over you already, I'm going to go get some rest."

Thane walked slowly back toward the caves along the path and watched the morning come to life around him. He startled a couple of rabbits who were foraging in the frozen fronds of ferns. They went still as he passed; their little eyes followed his progress. Once he passed them and they knew they weren't in any danger, they scurried off.

Thane found the stillness of the forest a relief after the noise and chaos of their skirmish with the English. He thought back to the battle. A sense of foreboding filled him. What would the Formoire be doing hiding out in an English camp? How many of them were running around this land masquerading as something else?

The voices of warriors coming up the path behind him broke into his thoughts. Thane quickened his pace; he wasn't in the mood to talk to anyone else.

By the time Thane got back into their little room, Orphan had already tucked herself into her little alcove. The thin woolen blanket was down over the entrance and there was no light and no sounds coming from behind it. Tally was not in their part of the room. After a quick meal, Thane settled down on his makeshift bed and tried to relax.

The medallion he always wore beneath his shirt caught under his armpit as he rolled over onto his side. He reached into his shirt and pulled it out. Even in the dim orange light of the fire, the light blue stone glowed with an iridescent, silvery light, the smoky substance inside swirling.

Thane wished he understood what it was and how it worked. Tally still avoided all discussion about it and would brush off Thane's questions with, 'you will know when it is time.' He tucked it back into his shirt and rolled over to watch the reflection of the flames from the fire flickering on the wet stone walls.

Chapter Eleven

King Finnbheara

Whenever Thane broached the subject of leaving with Tally, the Bard would glower and grumble that he was not quite well enough to venture a long journey. He seemed content to stay close to the cave and was in no hurry to leave. Thane found little support from Orphan in his attempt to persuade Tally. She appeared equally reluctant to leave for reasons she refused share with him. Thane resigned himself to spending the unusually cold and snowy winter with Mag Uidhirs.

When the weather permitted, they spent their days training with the Mag Uidhirs. If the weather was too bad to stay outside for long, they used the main cavern for training. Warriors gathered in shifts to practice with Claidheamh mór, sparr, and hand-to-hand fighting. None of the caves were long enough to use as a butts, so they were not able to practice with their bows.

Thane and Orphan occasionally accompanied the Mag Uidhirs on raids. The clan targeted mostly English patrols, but on occasion would lash out at rival clans. There did not seem to be any pattern to the clan's attacks and raids. They never went to the same location more than once. Sometimes they followed the river for miles before attacking an outpost, and other times they traveled the entire distance on horseback. The most unsettling aspect of the fights was the persistent presence of the Formoire.

One late February morning, just before dawn, they arrived back at the training grounds after a quick raid on an English camp. Pádraig was sitting on the stone dolmen next to the horses, a woolen blanket draped snuggly over his head and shoulders. If the layer of snow covering him was any indication, he'd been sitting in that position for quite a while. The moment he spotted them, he jumped off the rocks and ran toward them as he always did when they returned from a raid. The covering of snow blew off his back as he ran, creating a miniature blizzard behind him.

"Damien! Damien!" Pádraig cried out excitedly. "There was an old man at the entrance to the cave. He insisted he be taken to the Seanchaidh," Pádraig burst out almost before he was close enough to be heard.

"An old man?" Damien asked as he reached a hand down and swiftly pulled the boy up on the horse in front of him.

"Yeah! A really old man!" the little boy repeated excitedly bouncing up and down.

"How many others are with him?" Damien looped an arm around Pádraig's waist and pulled the boy tightly against his chest to settle him down and keep him from falling off, and Thane guessed, to warm up his little body. Damien nudged the horse in the direction of the cave entrance. Concerned, Orphan and Thane followed. What would an old man want with Tally? How did he know where to find them? How did he get away?

"He rode up alone on Embarr asking for Prince Nathaniel," Pádraig raised his voice to be heard over the drumming of the horses hooves. "Rollie was heading back into the tunnel when the old man stopped him. Before anyone could say anything, Rollie took him to a currach and they was disappearing into the caves. I thought we weren't supposed to bring strangers into the caves, Damien?" the little boy shouted.

No one answered him. They all knew he was right. The safety of the warriors who lived there depended on the location of the caves remaining a secret. How did he get to Embarr? Why would Embarr lead him here?

They arrived at the entrance to find Embarr standing outside the cave entrance swishing the snow off his back with his tail and blowing the snow with his nose. Small swirls of white snow danced on the ground in front of him.

"Embarr!" Thane called out. He slid off his horse and ran over to Embarr. "What are you doing?"

Embarr acknowledged him with a whinny and rubbed his soft, snow covered nose into his favorite spot on Thane's neck making Thane shiver. Once the horse had assured himself that Thane was well, he turned and trotted off down the path toward the training grounds.

Confused, they hurried into the dark cave. The four of them climbed into a currach, and Damien and Thane paddled quickly in the direction of the main cavern.

"Where's the old man, and who is that talking with Tally?" Thane whispered as they entered the main cave.

Tally was standing next to one of the fires arguing with a tall, young man.

Pádraig wrinkled his face at Thane like he'd just spoken to him in a foreign language. "That's the old man...there...talking to the Seanchaidh!" he insisted, pointing to the younger man.

Damien, Thane, and Orphan exchanged looks over Pádraig's head. Pádraig's 'old man' was a Fæ using glamour. Whether or not he was an enemy was yet to be seen. Thane was eager to hear what they were arguing about.

"I say he's not ready," Tally said furiously. Their voices echoed eerily throughout the stone room.

"Don't challenge me old man," the stranger insisted. "The prophe..."

The two men glanced over as the group clambered noisily out of the currach. A tense silence fell between them as they watched the group approach.

The Fæ was strikingly handsome. His long, pale face was surrounded by elbow length, reddish-brown hair, and his eyes were so pale they were almost white. Green robes rippled around his tall, lithe body and reminded Thane of fields of grass undulating in a gentle summer breeze. Thane couldn't tell how old he was, but no one could ever have mistaken him for an old man.

The Fæ fixed his piercing eyes on Thane as he approached. He looked him up and down as if assessing his worth.

Tally grabbed Thane's arm and pulled him forward to stand in front of him. Tally rested his hands possessively on Thane's shoulders and said, "Finnbheara, High King of Daoine Sidhe may I present Prince Nathaniel."

Thane stood and stared back at the Fæ. King of the what? Why was the Fæ here? Was he expected to bow?

Finnbheara stared into Thane's eyes. He felt like the King was looking into his soul; Thane's thoughts, hopes and fears were being laid out and examined.

Unnerved by the King's intense stare, Thane broke eye contact and shifted his weight from one foot to the other. He acknowledged the introduction with a simple nod then asked, "How did you get Embarr, and how did you persuade him to bring you here?"

"Thane!" Tally scolded him for his rudeness.

The King held up his hand, his eyes still boring into Thane's. "He is justified in voicing his concern for the horse, Taliesin. I will find no fault with him there at least.

"Embarr is intelligent and powerful in his own right, not an ignorant beast," Finnbheara said arrogantly. "Embarr and I are well acquainted. He will always present himself to me when I have need of him."

Looking past Thane to scrutinize Orphan, the King said, "You are Ceara?"

Orphan nodded but said nothing else. She too seemed to be unsure of what was expected of her. At the mention of her real name, Thane saw Damien turn his head to frown at Orphan. Apparently, even though Thane had seen them talking together a few times since Granule's visit, she hadn't shared that particular piece of personal information with Damien, and he didn't look happy about it.

"Word of your reappearance has reached the Daoine Sidhe," he said to her in a way that led Thane to believe the King might have preferred that she had remain missing.

Tally spoke up before the King could say anything else. "Perhaps we should move to our room. It is small but private."

Tally turned and led the way to their room. Once the King was seated, Tally motioned for Thane and Orphan to do the same. There was much jostling and bumping of arms and legs as they vied for a comfortable place near the fire. Damien sent Pádraig off to fetch some warm, spiced cider and food.

Once Pádraig returned, the food and drink was passed around. Damien and Pádraig remained standing next to the stone entry as the King explained the reason for his visit.

"You have managed to both surprise and anger your grandparents, Prince Nathaniel. They expected you to be grateful for the comfort and safety of Tír inna n-Óc. Yet within hours of arriving you managed to escape on a quest that you were specifically forbidden from undertaking." The King seemed to be scolding him, but Thane thought he saw a touch of glee in the Fæ's eyes.

"They had no authority over us. We didn't belong there and..." Thane began to bluster defensively but Finnbheara cut him off.

"No need to get angry with me, young Nathaniel. In this case, I applaud your reckless defiance of your betters for they were wrong." He raised his chin and looked down his nose at Thane.

"I am not in agreement with the verdict of the Fæ Council. The Tuatha de Danann would leave the fate of Inis Fáil in the hands of the mortals, but the mortals do not understand how vulnerable they are. They hold the belief that they are the masters of their destinies when in fact they are not. This land is about to be reclaimed by Zavior and his Formoire, and they will be unable to stop him. If that happens, they will have no say in their future. The mortals need protection."

"Is that what Zavior is planning? To take back Inis Fáil?" Thane felt a chill run through him at the thought. He dusted bread crumbs from his fingers then leaned in closer to the fire to warm his hands.

King Finnbheara nodded, staring pensively into the fire, "The Fæ Council is convinced that Zavior is determined to gather the Sacred Treasures together to that end, yes."

"What treasures?" Thane asked.

"Has the Seanchaidh neglected to tell you about the Sacred Treasures of the Tuatha de Danann? The Treasures we brought with us from our fair cities when we came to the West?" the King said sounding offended.

"No," Thane answered.

"Yes," Orphan said at the same time.

Damien snickered at their conflicting answers.

Thane looked around at the older boy and scowled. Damien was still standing behind them, arms crossed, leaning against the stone opening to the cave. He caught Thane's eye and wiggled his eyebrows mockingly at him.

He had forgotten that Damien didn't know much of what had happened to him since the castle was attacked so long ago. Thane had told Damien that he trusted him, but could he really? How much should he say in front of him? Thane finally decided that if Tally wasn't concerned, then he wasn't going to worry about it. Thane turned back to the King. Damien was the least of their problems now.

As if following Thane's train of thought, Tally looked back over his shoulder, waved to Damien, and said, "Please, join us. You are involved in this now, and you will need to know what is happening if you are to protect your people."

Tally moved closer to Thane to make room for Damien and, uninvited, Pádraig squeezed his little body next to Damien.

Once they were all settled, Tally cleared his throat and began.

When the world was new,
The God Dagda and the Goddess Brigid,

Fought to bring order to its chaos.

By the sacred waters of the Danu,

They formed the four great cities:

Falias, Gorias, Murias, and Finias.

The people of Danu,

The Tuatha de Danann,

Found contentment, success, and peace at the River's edge.

Dagda and Brigid blessed each of the cities,

Giving each of them a unique magical gift.

Falias was blessed with the Sacred Stone of Destiny.

It would sing in praise when touched by a righteous leader.

To Gorias went the Sword of Justice.

It was undefeatable and gave great strength to the bearer.

Finias was gifted with the Red Javelin.

Once cast it was destined to find its target.

Murias was honored with the Cauldron of Plenty.

It could feed a whole nation and heal all but the most fatal wounds.

Each gift was unique,

And each would bring glory to its owner.

Together they would wield a power,

So strong as to make the possessor invincible.

Tally paused for a moment.

Orphan prodded, "Where are the treasures now?"

"Have some patience!" Tally growled at her. "I was getting to that." He took a deep breath but before he could continue, King Finnbheara took up the tale.

"When our defeat came at the hands of the Milesians, it was swift and brutal. The Tuatha de Danann and many other magical beings: mer-people, unicorns, dragons, selkies and more, chose to leave Inis Fáil and retreat to Tír inna n-Óc. In the confusion of the withdrawal, two of the treasures were scattered, a third lost."

"You may already have surmised, your Grandfather, Manannán mac Lir has Undry, the Cauldron of Plenty," the King looked at Thane for confirmation.

"We didn't see any cauldrons," Thane shrugged his shoulders. He had no idea what Finnbheara was talking about.

"Well, I believe that is where the healing elixir you were given came from," Tally said to Orphan.

"It worked remarkably well, did it not?" the King declared with pride.

"Yes, it did," she agreed, sliding a glance at Thane. He met her eyes briefly, recalling how her poisoned wound didn't begin to mend until after she'd taken the potion. He hadn't given much thought to what had been in the sweet drink, or where it had come from; he'd only been grateful that it had worked.

"We are fortunate that the Cauldron is in Tír inna n-Óc as Zavior can no longer cross the Fæ Gates without either a Key or Embarr, and Embarr would never consent to let one so evil ride him," the King interjected before nodding to Tally to tell the rest. "Please, continue."

Tally looked a bit put out by all the interruptions but picked up the story from where the King left off.

"The English are now in possession of Lia Fáil, the Stone of Destiny. They acquired it from the Scots, who had taken it with them when they left Inis Fáil many, many years ago," Tally took a quick drink from his mug. "It will not be easy to retrieve as the stone is well guarded at Westminster Abbey, in London."

"Where are the other two artifacts?" Thane urged them to continue, feeling like he was finally getting some answers. He didn't want either the King or the Bard to stop.

"As for the rest, King Finnbheara will have to enlighten us as I am unaware of their location," Tally said.

"Lugh, Zavior's father, passed the Red Javelin on to Zavior not long after their retreat to Tír inna n-Óc," the King said. "I am confident that it is either with him or his son, Iagan."

"Fragarach, The Answerer, was the sword no armor can turn aside, the sword from whose bite no wound would heal, the sword to whom no lie could be uttered with it's blade pressed against an enemy's throat. The Fæ's most powerful sword was stolen by Paiste, the last remaining earthbound dragon, more than a thousand years ago."

"A dragon?" Damien scoffed. "Dragon's aren't real, they're myths."

Thane leaned around Tally to see him. He had been so involved in the tale that he had almost forgotten Damien and Pádraig were there.

"Dragons are as real as you or I," the King said angrily.

"Paiste was small as dragon's go, but he was one of the most cunning. He alone of his kind, chose to stay in Inis Fáil when the Fæ departed. A decision he would later come to regret. After many years of being hungry, bitter, and lonely, Paiste turned his anger on the humans. He terrorized them, plundered their farms of sheep and cattle for food. As I had pledged to protect the mortals, I agreed to aid them in their capture of him.

"It was during his binding that I discovered the dragon's theft. In a fit of rage, Paiste boasted to me of his possession of the sacred Fæ sword. A Formoire warrior named Gronsin had stolen the sword from Lugh with the intent of using its power to further his own nefarious desires, but events did not go as Gronsin had planned. The dragon felt the pull of the sword's power and was able to snatch it from the Formoire. It was not a crime that Gronsin was eager to share for not only had he stolen it from his leader's father, he had lost it within hours of acquiring it. It was a most grievous failure for him, and a loss that was devastating for the Fæ."

"I bet Paiste hid it in his den with his horde?" Pádraig exclaimed suddenly, bouncing up and down on his knees.

Damien shushed him and put a hand on his shoulder to calm him. Pádraig settled down, but his eyes remained wide with excitement.

"The boy is most likely correct, but I could not persuade Paiste to reveal the sword's hiding place to me. I do not believe Zavior has yet discovered what became of the sword. Paiste is still imprisoned in an enchanted iron cage in a cave beneath the waters of Lough Foyle. If Zavior knew, he would have found a way to release him by now.

"I have known Zavior since his birth. He was not always as he is now," the King frowned, and a sadness seemed to settle around him. "Zavior was an intelligent, charming and kindhearted young man, but he was also intense, impulsive, and had a very definite sense of what he perceived as right and wrong."

"He was what?" Thane scoffed, his face flush with anger. How could he say Zavior was charming and kindhearted? Zavior was a monster who had killed almost everyone Thane had ever loved. He had no desire to hear about Zavior's childhood, but Tally was frowning at him, so he clenched his teeth and swallowed the rest of his remarks. The King continued, ignoring Thane's outburst.

"Young Zavior fought desperately in the last battle against the Milesians, but it was to no avail. Our people were driven out of the Land of Promise, the land Zavior believed rightfully belonged to the Fæ. It was not long after that he lost his beloved mother. She was captured by an angry mob of mortals and convicted of witchcraft. After being bound in shackles of iron, the Fæ's most fatal weakness, she was tortured to death...well...it is enough to say...he has good reason to hate mortals.

"Lugh thought to bring Zavior onto the Fæ Council where he could keep an eye on his son's activities and guide him, but Zavior was too full of grief and rage. He was furious but much too young to have any influence on the ruling elders. Once he realized that he would have very little sway with the Council, he took the Javelin and left Tír inna n-Óc to make his own way. Zavior wants the freedom to roam the land that he feels should belong to Fæ."

"What you mean to say is he wants to use the mortals as his slaves, to be worshiped like his ancestors were, and believes it's his responsibility to rule over the land." Thane spat the words out, unable to keep his silence any longer. "Zavior has done horrible things in the name of reclaiming Inis Fáil."

Thane didn't want to believe they could share the same feelings of hurt and loss. He didn't want to think of Zavior losing the mother he had loved in such a brutal fashion when it had been Zavior who had taken Thane's mother from him.

"That is all true. Both he and his son have been banished from Tír inna n-Óc and cut off from his people for those very reasons," King Finnbheara said calmly.

"The medallion that I understand you carry upon your person," the King gazed at Thane's chest as if he could see through his shirt, "is many things, one of which is a Key to the Gateways of Tír inna n-Óc. Without a Key he will not be able to cross the Gates and retrieve the Cauldron," King Finnbheara said. "We must gather all the Treasures and take them to Tír inna n-Óc."

"Why haven't the Fæ retrieved the Stone of Destiny before now?" Orphan asked. "Surely they are skilled enough to take it?"

"You are already aware the Tuatha de Danann are not willing to become involved, and they are not willing to believe that Zavior is a threat. I am convinced that Zavior will not attempt to recover the Stone until he is armed with Fragarach and believes himself beyond defeat," the King answered without looking at her. "The Stone is quite safe for now; it is the sword that we must recover as soon as possible.

"Retrieving Fragarach will not be a matter of skill so much as…blood. The Fæ cannot get close enough to the dragon to question him for he is imprisoned in a cage of cold iron deep in the heart of Formoire territory.

"Even if Zavior discovers that Paiste was in possession of the sword, he will not be able to question him. His fear of iron is great, after what happened to his mother; Zavior will not be eager to approach that metal. However, it may make him all the more determined to find you."

Finnbheara stood up gracefully, glanced briefly at Tally, then turned to address Thane. "It must be you who finds the sword and returns it to Tír inna n-Óc. I will aid you in this task," King Finnbheara offered.

"Aid me?" Thane stuttered nonplussed. "You really expect me to do this? Why?" He rose angrily to his feet. He could feel the blood beginning to pound in his head.

"We must take action immediately. You are unique, Nathaniel, because of your mixed blood. You appear to have the best qualities of both the humans and the Fæ. Should he learn of Paiste's thievery, Zavior will be even more eager to make use of you."

Thane found it strange that the King was only referring to his mixed blood. He knew that Orphan shared the same qualities. Why was he not including her in his plans? Orphan must have been thinking along the same lines as she was frowning at the Fæ King.

"I can't be that unique," Thane argued. "There must be other children of Fæ and mortals. What about her?" Thane waved his hand at Orphan. Although he didn't want her singled out by Zavior either, he didn't understand why he alone was being targeted.

"Yes, why not me?" Orphan echoed.

"Zavior does not know about Ceara, and there are few children of mixed blood with your strengths…" the King paused and looked down at Tally while he carefully chose his words, "…you will be the one he wants."

"That's insane. How will Thane fare any better if he is also Fæ?" Damien added his doubts to Thane's with a frown as he too rose to his feet.

"Nathaniel has a resistance to the debilitating effects of iron because of his human half. He has been around iron and steel his whole life. I assume you have suffered no ill effects." The King looked down his nose at Thane.

"There are many other substances that can weaken us…potions of St John's wart, four leaf clovers, and spells…that we don't have time to go into now...that may yet prove harmful to him, but the fact is Nathaniel appears to be immune to iron whereas Zavior is not.

"The dragon is the only one who can tell us where the sword is hidden, and Thane is the only hope we have of persuading Paiste to divulge it's location," King Finnbheara said firmly. "He must find a way."

"But what if..."

Tally spoke up before Thane could say anything else. "You cannot force this decision on him. Nathaniel will be sent to Cnoc Meadha when he is ready. I will make sure of it, but you must promise me he will be protected."

"I cannot offer him any greater protection than he already possesses," he said as he glanced at Thane's chest where the medallion lay hidden.

With that parting comment and one last calculating glance at Orphan and Damien, King Finnbheara turned and left the cave.

"Where is he going?" Orphan whispered.

"He will most likely travel through the caves, and a myriad of tunnels to the Færie mounds at Cnoc Meadha. There he rules the Daoine Sidhe in a massive underground city."

"He doesn't live in Tír inna n-Óc?" Thane asked surprised.

"No. When the Tuatha de Danann left Inis Fáil, King Finnbheara made a pact with the Milesians to stay here. He swore his protection to the mortals in return for half of the land and he was granted his wish. The Daoine Sidhe were given half of Inis Fáil..."

Tally snickered, "...the bottom half...the underground half. Not exactly what he was expecting, but he made it work and still honors the pact he made many years ago. He will do all in his power to protect the mortals."

"What did you mean when you told him 'Nathaniel will be sent to Cnoc Meadha'? What about you and Orphan?" Thane asked as he lowered himself to the floor next to Tally. "You're coming with me aren't you, Tally?"

"I will take you to the Gateway but I cannot cross with you," Tally looked regretfully at him.

"What if I don't want to cross? What if I don't want to search for the missing sword? Will you force me?" Why did it seem that everyone felt they had the authority to make decisions for him? He felt like he was being swept along in a flood of others' expectations without being given an oar to steer with. Thane clenched his fists in frustration and looked over at Orphan for support. She looked as distressed as he felt, but for once she didn't offer an opinion.

"Thane, the choice to seek the sword is ultimately yours," Tally said softly. "You can choose to walk away, but understand this, you will never be safe if you do. There is no doubt Zavior will find you again, and then you will have few choices left."

Choices? It didn't seem like he had any choices. Now that he was being told he had to leave the caves, he didn't want to. He had begun to care about these people and had begun to feel like he was a part of the clan. Dread and resignation settled around Thane like a damp woolen cloak, its weight suffocating.

"I'm going with you." Orphan spoke up, looking purposefully between Thane and Tally. "You're not leaving me behind."

"I would expect nothing less," Tally looked at Orphan with a mix of pride and fear and nodded.

"It is not a decision that must be made today, but know that if you stay here too long, you will risk the safety and wellbeing of everyone here. Zavior has already proven he will stop at nothing to get to you. He will kill them just as surely as he killed your parents, the Reivers, and Markus."

"Markus deserved what he got for telling Zavior we were at the Inn," Thane retorted disdainfully.

Tally squinted at him, his eyes peered quizzically into Thane's. "Thane, do you really believe anyone deserves to die as he did? Strangled in the woods by a brutal villain?"

Thane took a deep breath and shook his head, "No."

In his heart, Thane knew that what Tally said was true. Although Markus was a mean drunk and an all around unpleasant man, his brother, Marsden, was not. Marsden had gone out of his way to protect them. Thane knew that, although Marsden was sorry Markus brought Zavior's malevolence to their door, he would grieve for the loss of his brother.

Thane looked across the fire at Damien's expressionless face and wondered what he thought about all of this. He hadn't offered an opinion, and he didn't offer to go with them.

"I must go speak to Rollie. He should never have led the King down here." Damien turned away and nudged Pádraig to his feet.

"Damien!" Tally called after him.

Damien paused at the stone archway, Pádraig's hand gripped tightly in his. He didn't turn around.

"You must not be angry with Rollie. He could no more disobey Finnbheara than he could have changed the course of a river," Tally said to Damien's back. Damien nodded stiffly then strode out of the cave, dragging Pádraig along behind him. The boy glanced back over his shoulder longingly as they left.

Tally, Thane, and Orphan remained seated around the fire, each lost in their own thoughts.

"You do still wear the medallion around your neck, do you not?" Tally asked.

"Yes," Thane tugged on the leather cord around his neck until the gold medallion pulled free from his tunic. He cradled the warm medallion in his hand and tilted it toward the light so that Tally could see it. Tally reached out a long finger and ran it along the golden forms of the animals surrounding the stone.

"I do not understand it all myself, but this medallion is worth killing for, so keep it secret and keep it hidden. It must never leave your possession, do you hear me? Zavior must never have control of it." Tally brought his other hand up and gently closed Thane's fingers around the piece.

Tally watched Thane carefully tuck the medallion back into his shirt then stood slowly. "Thane, do not fear the future. You will do what is right when the time comes." He placed a gentle hand on Thane's shoulder before turning to leave the alcove.

Chapter Twelve

Glamour

Thane found himself flat on his back again. The gallóglach he was sparring was taking great delight in continually knocking him to the ground. His knuckles were a bloody mess from being smashed numerous times by his many opponents' various weapons and he was sure he had more than one cracked rib. It was getting harder and harder to force himself to get back up on his feet after he was knocked down.

He leaned on his ax practice pole and pulled himself to his feet. He turned to face his last sparring partner of the afternoon...Damien. The older boy looked as if he had been training all day as well. Despite the cold, sweat dripped down Damien's face and blood was smeared across his cheek from a small cut over his eye. He had a self-confident look on his face that made Thane grit his teeth. This was not going to be an easy match. Thane took a deep breath, gripped the middle of the pole in his hands, and brought it up in front of him in the guard position.

They started off tentatively testing each other's limits, each swinging their sticks at the other. It wasn't long before Thane found himself being driven back, always on the defensive. He was working too hard at fending off Damien's attacks to get a strike in against him. Thane's frustration mounted as he realized that even after weeks of training, he was still considerably out-matched. Damien had a strength and ferocity that went far beyond anything Thane had attained.

Thane was driven back until he was against the outer edge of the practice field. In desperation, he raised his ax handle high to drive Damien back.

Damien took advantage of Thane's change in position and slid his long pole up around Thane's and slammed the top of the stick into the side of Thane's head, then spun it around the top of his hand. Thane was swept off his feet in a move that he was sure would have cut him off at the knees had there been a blade attached to the end of it. As it was, Damien sent him flying backwards. He landed hard on the ground, the wind knocked out of him.

Thane lay there, flat on his back, as he fought to catch his breath. Pain radiated up his calf and spread through every part of his body. His arms felt so heavy it was as if someone had filled them with iron. He gazed up at the beauty of the setting sun through the naked trees over Damien's shoulder and wished he could remain on the ground watching the clouds drift by.

"Up on your feet!" Damien demanded, his chest rising and falling rapidly as he too fought to catch his breath.

Still, Thane didn't move.

"I said get up, Your Highness!" Damien took his staff and prodded Thane none too gently in the hip. "You're weak! You'll never be a warrior at this rate! GET UP!"

Thane felt anger surge through him. He wasn't weak; he just hadn't spent the last few years training with giant gallóglaigh warriors. He rolled gracelessly to his feet, reaching for his pole as he rose. Anger gave him the unexpected burst of energy he needed; he attacked.

Damien took a quick step back in surprise, but he was a second too late to avoid a hard strike to his side. He rallied quickly and came at Thane with renewed vigor. They circled around each other swinging furiously. The sound of wood hitting wood and the grunts and groans of both of them filled the slowly darkening clearing. Shouts of the gallóglaigh egged them on.

Finally, after several minutes of fighting, they stood exhausted staring at each other. Sweat and blood from their many small cuts and bruises ran in streaks of red down both of their faces. Damien lifted one corner of his bloody lip into a smile and nodded to Thane. He was gone before Thane could say anything.

Thane limped his way slowly back to the cave, exhausted but proud that he hadn't quit.

††††††

Late one afternoon, in the last week of March, Thane overheard a conversation between Damien and a small group of Mag Uidhir clansman. They were planning to go back to the castle at Inis Ceithleann where Tally had been held captive. The Mag Uidhir needed to determine how many soldiers were billeted there and what type and quantity of weapons they had. He wanted to regain control of the castle, and to succeed he would need to know what they were up against.

Thane waited until the small group finished talking and dispersed before approaching Damien. "We're going with you," he informed him.

Damien raised an eyebrow at his boldness. "What makes you think we want to take you? Last time you were there you almost got yourself captured!"

Thane had been thinking about going back for sometime now. He was convinced Zavior would not have left Tally's sword behind after the fight. He ignored Damien's retort and continued, "We think Tally's sword may be there. We need to retrieve it before we leave. We're either going with you or we'll go alone. Your choice."

"Let me talk to the Mag Uidhir," Damien hedged.

"Talk to him if you want; we are going either with or without you," Thane shrugged and walked away. Damien growled in frustration behind him and Thane couldn't stop himself from smiling. He got a perverse sense of pleasure from annoying Damien.

ORPHAN

It was almost a certainty that he would be permitted to go with them, because there was no way the Mag Uidhir would let him go alone.

As Thane hurried back to the caves, he couldn't help but notice the signs of spring in the forest surrounding the training camp. Early blooming flowers were open, and he could see the tiny buds of new leaves on the trees. The weather had been getting warmer until last night, but now it felt like a winter storm was approaching.

Thane ducked into the cave entrance, and waited a moment for his eyes to adjust to the darkness. He hopped effortlessly into a waiting currach and paddled toward the main cavern. He had fully acclimated to life in the caves, and it had been a while since he had thought about leaving. The threat of Zavior discovering his location and his search for the sword Fragarach had been pushed to the back of his mind until now.

He thought about how much he had changed over the last few months. He had grown taller over the winter, his shoulders were broader, his limbs were stronger, and he was more agile. The training sessions still left him exhausted but there was an underlying exhilaration to the tiredness and a feeling of accomplishment. He was now skilled enough to go head to head with some of the biggest and fiercest warriors and often could hold his own against them...for a short while at least.

Orphan too had changed during their winter stay in the caves. She was almost thirteen, and although she had not grown much taller, her arms and legs had filled out and were now firm and strong. Her ability to handle and manipulate fire was almost frightening, and her skill with a bow rivaled all but the most skilled archers in the camp.

By the time Thane finally dropped down next to Orphan in their cave, he realized he was starving. He helped himself to some of Orphan's bread and cheese and sipped some cider out of her cup.

He expected her to scold him for not asking her first, but she just continued to chew her bread thoughtfully, the fire reflecting eerily in her eyes. Thane could swear he could see the mischief bubbling up in her as she half-listened to him recount his conversation with Damien. He had assumed she would be as excited about returning to explore the castle as he was, but she obviously had something else on her mind.

"Are you listening to me?" he asked frustrated.

"I've been thinking about this glamour thing Tally told us about," she said to his surprise.

"What? Glamour?" Thane repeated, puzzled at her sudden interest in something they hadn't discussed for weeks.

"I think we can do it. How hard can it be?" she grinned at him.

Thane rolled his eyes at her. Tally had given them some guidance initially on how to use their powers, but since he wasn't Fæ he hadn't been able to teach them very much. Mostly, Tally taught them how to focus. Orphan was the one who was always experimenting with their powers and pushing them to try new ideas.

If it weren't for her, they would never have attempted to make fire. She excelled at it, while he still struggled to make the simplest of flames. His strengths lay in the more physical powers; he was really good at moving things. He could lift much heavier objects and transport them for much longer distances than she could.

Thane didn't protest. It wouldn't have done him any good anyway. He reached for the last of her drink and food before she could take it away. Orphan wasted no time in clearing everything from the middle of the cave. She sank back down on her knees in front of the fire and looked across the flames expectantly at him.

With a sigh of resignation, he dropped the cheese back on the oilcloth and waited for her to say something. They stared at each other for a few moments, neither knew precisely where to start.

"Tally said glamour is a false image the Fæ can cast over themselves like a cloak. It must be like an image you cast over yourself to disguise your real features. So, I should be able to change the color of my hair." She wiped her palms on her knees nervously, closed her eyes, and scrunched up her face in concentration.

Thane stared expectantly at her. The light from the fire reflected off her red hair giving the impression that her head was covered with flames.

"You look like your hair is on fire. Is that what you're trying to do?" he said with a snort.

She frowned at him, "No! I'm trying to make it look black, like yours."

"Well, it didn't work!" Thane laughed at her frustration.

"You try something then!" she huffed at him.

Thane held his hands out in front of him, closed his eyes, and imagined that the back of his hands were covered in fur. He opened his left eye just enough to peek through his dark lashes. His fingers looked no different than they had a moment before. Nothing changed. He opened both eyes and glanced at her. She looked thoughtful.

"My turn. I'll try becoming a cat." This time she didn't close her eyes, she squinted into the dancing flames between them as if she could force the image to life from the fire. Still nothing happened.

While she was concentrating on changing her image, Thane thought about the bats he had seen skimming the surface of the river that ran through the caves. He spread his arms out and imagined what it must feel like to be free to fly across the water.

Thane was so absorbed in his vision that he didn't hear the footsteps approaching the alcove until it was too late. Before he could say anything, Pádraig burst into the small room.

"AHHHHHHHH...DAAAMIEEEEN."

Orphan and Thane jumped to their feet in fright. "What's the matter Pádraig? What's wrong?"

Orphan started toward him but stopped when he backed away from them both, his eyes wide and terrified. The most awful noise was coming out of his wide-open mouth.

Eoin came bursting through the opening right behind Pádraig, closely followed by Tally and Damien. Eoin stopped short, his sparr clutched tightly in his fist, prepared to strike. He too looked ready to scream. Damien pushed Pádraig protectively behind him, and held his sword defensively in front of him.

Thane and Orphan retreated to the other side of the fire as far away from Eoin's sparr as they could get, their backs flush against the wall

"Wait," Damien ordered as he grasped Eoin's arm to prevent him from attacking them.

Thane could hear the anxious murmuring of the clansmen gathering in the outer cave. Tally turned and disappeared behind the thin curtain of rock.

"It's nothing. Pádraig was just started by a couple animals. Nothing to see here," Thane could hear Tally's soothing voice getting further away as he hustled the men away from the cave.

Damien released Eoin when he was sure the man was not going to attack. He then turned to lock his hand on Pádraig's shoulder to keep the small boy from running. He slowly sheathed his sword looking confused.

"What are you two playing at?" Tally demanded angrily as he stormed back into the little room.

Thane and Orphan looked at each other in bewilderment.

"What do you mean?" Thane asked. Pádraig looked like he was going to scream again and Eoin lost what little color he had left in his face.

"You hear that, Damien! They can talk!" Pádraig stammered, his voice squeaking in panic.

"Of coarse they can talk! It's Thane and Orphan using glamour!" Tally barked pushing between Damien and Eoin to stand in the middle of the room. "Cease this nonsense immediately."

Thane and Orphan looked at each other again. They couldn't see anything different in their appearance.

"It worked?" Thane asked incredulously.

Tally looked from one to the other and closed his eyes. He looked like he wanted to take them both by their pointy ears and shake them.

"Of course!" Orphan grinned. "We can't see the changes in each other because we're Fæ! Right, Tally?"

Thane felt a shiver like a trickle of water run down his back as he released the image of the bat from his mind. It must have worked because he saw both Eoin and Pádraig take another step back toward the entrance of the alcove. Pádraig's mouth dropped open in the shape of a perfect 'O' but thankfully no more sound came out.

"You are both lucky it was poor Pádraig and Eoin that walked in on you and not one of the gallóglaigh or you would both be dead. They would not have stopped to ask why a giant black cat and a giant bat were warming themselves by your fire; they would have sliced you both to pieces," Tally said angrily. "Have I taught you nothing about discretion?"

"We thought we…" Orphan began before Tally interrupted her.

"You two will be the death of me yet!" he lamented before he turned on his heels and stormed out. Thane saw Orphan's smile crumble. He knew she was thinking about how close he'd come to dying defending them and how true that statement could easily have been.

"I was just coming to find you," Damien said quietly. He stepped further into the room dragging a reluctant Pádraig with him. Eoin stood uncertainly by the door, his sparr hanging loosely at his side.

"Stay or go as you please but say nothing about what you saw here. You were startled by an animal. Understand?" Damien commanded. Eoin nodded and chose to leave, backing quickly out of the room. The look on his pale face said more than words; he didn't want to hear anymore about what had just happened.

Damien turned back to face Thane and Orphan who had returned to their places at either side of the small Fæ fire. As Damien moved closer to the fire, Thane could see how tired he was; dark circles rimmed his eyes and lines of fatigue were etched around his lips. His hand was still resting lightly on the pummel of his sword as he watched Thane gather the spilled bread, cheese, and oil cloth.

Pádraig stared wide-eyed at Orphan and Thane as they settled back down in their respective spots. Orphan gave him a quick reassuring smile and he gazed back at her, more curious now than scared.

"You can come with us to the Inis Ceithleann…on one condition," Damien announced.

"What condition?" Thane asked without looking up from the food he was carefully wrapping up.

"You can come along if you help identify and count those you call Formoire."

Thane turned and looked over his shoulder at Damien. "That's the Mag Uidhir's idea?"

Damien shifted his weight from one foot to the other. "That's the condition. Agree to it or remain behind," he said stubbornly.

Thane turned back to the fire. It didn't matter to him one way or another. He could count Formoire for Damien if it got him safely inside the castle. He met Orphan's eyes above the fire and she gave him a quick nod.

"We'll help you," Thane agreed.

"Meet us at the dolmen in one hour. This may be an information gathering mission, but you need to be prepared to fight." Damien left, Pádraig trailing along behind him.

Orphan began to braid her hair. She'd taken to wearing it in one large plait down her back when they went out claiming it kept it out of her face. He watched as she worked the thick red cords of hair swiftly through her fingers. She tied the ends together with a length of brown leather and carefully tucked the points of her ears under the thick strands of hair on the side of her head.

She bent to gather her weapons and said, "Should we tell Tally where we are going?"

"No," Thane said flatly. He didn't want to worry him and he was afraid that if they told Tally what they were up to, he would insist they remain behind.

Thane turned to his small pile of belongings. The sporran Natty had given him when he lived with the Reivers was lying on the ground next to his pile of clothes. He had taken it out earlier in the day and was showing it to Pádraig. Pádraig was captivated by Thane's little collection of treasures. The boy especially loved the shiny silver horse head emblem and smooth piece of green glass. Thane picked up the sporran and tucked it back under his pile of clothing. Maybe he should give it to Pádraig one day.

"What are you doing over there…let's go!" Orphan prodded him.

Thane grabbed his weapons. He strapped his small knife to the inside of his boot and cinched the thick leather sword belt tightly at his waist. He turned to Orphan and nodded for her to lead the way.

Chapter Thirteen

The Castle at Inis Ceithleann

A dozen or so horses were being strapped with the strange pillows they used in lieu of saddles by young knaves when they arrived at the dolmen. It looked like only a small group would be going tonight. Thane and Orphan took over the preparation of their own horses. By the time they were done, Damien had arrived with a handful of Mag Uidhir clansmen, all of whom were dressed in unusually dark clothing. There would be no gallóglaigh on this trip.

"We need to get a good accounting of how many..." he paused briefly, "...men they have protecting the castle. Nathaniel, Orphan, and I are going to enter the castle by the bolt hole in the stables across the river. We'll count how many we find inside."

"Eoin, Jaxs, Paddy and Rian," he pointed to the men as he spoke, "you take the North side of the castle. Murray, Finn, Brecc, and Niall, go around to the South side of the island. Stay out of sight. Just count soldiers. You must not be seen. We'll meet back here at dawn."

The eight clansmen acknowledged his orders with grunts, nods, and waves. The men swung up on their horses and disappeared into the darkness of the surrounding trees. When they were alone, Damien turned to Thane and Orphan.

"You agreed to help." He looked each one of them in the eye and said, "I think those things I'm seeing with the English are coming from the castle at Inis Ceithleann. The first time I saw one was when they attacked the castle when…you left," he stumbled awkwardly over his explanation. "As you know, I have been seeing them in our lands ever since, and there are almost always some at the castle."

Thane turned and walked a few steps away from Orphan and Damien. He didn't want to admit it to himself, but he was scared. He needed a moment to think.

For years, he had blocked out the memories of his young life at the castle and that horrific night but he remembered it all clearly now: the horror of watching his parents fight for their lives, of standing next to the church watching strange soldiers, of Roki scaling the walls, and warriors battering down the doors. He recalled the two huge, misshapen soldiers that were guarding the front door of the crypt that he now realized were Formoire. Both his grandfather, Manannán mac Lir, and King Finnbheara had said Zavior had willingly joined forces with the Formoire. Yes, he had to agree with

Damien. The monsters were probably coming from the castle. They were under Zavior's command.

Thane turned back to Damien and said, "I remember seeing them that night too. How do you explain their presence on the English patrols?"

Damien shrugged his shoulders. "I can't."

"What do you need us to do tonight?" Orphan interrupted them to bring them back to their present situation. "You said you would give us time to search for Tally's sword."

"I want you to help me verify that they are still in the castle and how many of them there are."

"That's all you want?" Thane said. He didn't bother to remind Damien that he had just said he'd seen them there.

"Isn't that enough? Getting in and out of the castle unseen will not be an easy task," Damien retorted.

Thane shrugged and mounted his horse; Orphan followed his lead and pulled her horse around to stand next to Thane.

Damien looked up at them for a moment before he too mounted his horse. No one spoke as they made their way quickly through the trees. The stars were hidden behind a thick blanket of clouds and the night smelled of snow.

Thane couldn't keep the cold, wet air from freezing the fine hairs in his nose and sneaking its fingers through his cloak. He pulled the ends of his cloak tighter around his shoulders wishing he had something to pull around his face. By the time they stopped to tie the horses in a stand of trees at the edge of the forest, he was frozen solid. Just when he thought it couldn't get any worse, it began to snow.

Damien led them toward a small cluster of bushes near the river's edge. Thane looked around as they crouched behind the frozen foliage. On their side of the river, at the top of the small hill to their left, he could just see a long, low building through the trees. That must be where the bolt hole was that Damien had mentioned earlier.

Across the river, Thane could see the flickering light of torches along the walls of the castle. There was movement on the battlements, but he was too far away to clearly tell if the warriors were mortal men or Formoire.

Damien saw the question in Thane's eyes and pointed toward the hill. "Do you remember the bolt hole in the stables and the tunnel that goes under the river and into the castle?" he whispered to Thane.

"Vaguely. One of the entrances to it was in my parents' bedchamber. I don't remember ever being allowed in those tunnels. Although, I don't recall that that ever stopped us, am I right?" Thane whispered back with a small smile.

Damien nodded and grinned at him. For a moment, Thane caught a glimpse in Damien's face of the young boy who had once been his best friend.

"From your parents' bedchamber, if you recall, the tunnel splits into a series of hidden passageways that wind throughout the thicker walls of the castle. One passage leads to an escape tunnel that exits into the rear stall of the stables. I've used it a couple times to get in and out of the castle over the last few years."

Even though it was a cloudy, moonless night, Thane felt sure they were going to be spotted as they made their way through the bare trees to the top of the hill. They were no more than half way up the hill when they heard a loud rhythmic sound coming from the river. Damien pulled them down onto the snowy grass and whispered to them to lie still. A boat slowly passed on the river between them and the castle, oars splashing noisily through the surface of the water.

Thane let out the breath he was holding when the boat finally moved upriver out of sight. Afraid they might be spotted through the barren trees if they stood up, they crawled slowly on their hands and knees up the hill. Damien hid himself behind the trunk of a large tree. After he checked to make sure there was no one around, he signaled to them, and they ran across the short field toward the rear of the stables.

As they got closer, Thane could see that the long, low building was built out of large river stones. He could hear the muffled voices of several men coming from the front of the stable.

The few windows that were on the side of the building were shuttered to keep the cold out, but small slivers of light still managed to seep through the cracks between the shutters and the window frames. The snow had begun to fall faster and was swirling around the building like small white ghosts, giving the stables an eerie feeling.

Thane glanced behind him to see if they were leaving a trail in the snow. He was relieved to see that their prints were not the only ones on the ground and at the rate the snow was falling, they would be covered in no time.

Damien led them to the back of the building. He crouched low, slid his knife into a crack between the ground and the wall, and pried two large stones loose. The ease with which he removed the blocks proved that he had done this many times over the last few years.

"It's filthy down here so watch yourself," he whispered. He listened briefly at the opening before sliding through it. Orphan pushed her bow and quiver through first before she too disappeared. Thane glanced around the dark one last time before he followed them.

They found themselves crammed into a small stall at the back of the stables. The smell was horrendous. Thane had spent many years sleeping in the rear or lofts of stables and was generally fond of the smell of horses, but this stench was something entirely different. Mixed with the smell of horse, manure, and sweat was something else...something that smelled dead! Orphan had pulled her tunic up over her nose, but by the look in her eyes, it wasn't helping.

Damien reached around Thane, through the opening and maneuvered the stones back into place in the wall. In the dim light, Thane could see that there were little ridges broken into the sides of the stones that Damien had used to grab them. Once the stones were securely in place, you would have to know exactly where the cracks were to be able to find them.

Damien turned back to them and pointed across the aisle to a long wall covered with a tangled collection of leather harnesses, saddles and bits. Thane looked back at him confused. He wasn't sure what he was supposed to do. Damien rolled his eyes and pushed past him. He peeked around the end of the stall to make sure they wouldn't be seen by the men at the front of the stables before darting across the aisle.

Damien ran his fingers behind a shelf in the middle of the wall and, when he found what he was looking for, he pulled hard. The bottom half of the shelf split silently apart, from top to bottom, to form two short doors that opened into a dark space beyond. He waved Thane and Orphan across one by one and guided them through the narrow opening before following them, shutting the doors carefully behind him.

They crouched in the dark while Damien fumbled with a flint and small torch. Orphan elbowed Thane sharply in the side as she maneuvered around him. The narrow room burst with light as she held out a soft blue flame in the palm of her hand. Damien jerked violently away from her, banging his head on the door behind him making an alarming clatter.

Thane swiftly threw his hand over Damien's mouth to stifle the noise he was sure was going to come bellowing out of it at any moment. Damien's eyes were huge, staring over Thane's hand in shock. Orphan closed her hand abruptly and they were plunged back into darkness. No one breathed as they all strained their ears to listen for signs that they had been discovered.

Footsteps stomped through the stables on the other side of the wall as the men rushed back to look for what caused the noise. They argued and fought over various explanations until they finally gave up and settled on blaming the horses. After a few moments, they wandered noisily toward the front of the stables, the murmur of their voices could just be heard over the snorts and snuffles of the horses.

Minutes passed in tense silence as Damien, Thane, and Orphan waited to be sure they were safe.

"Don't do that!" Damien hissed when he finally found the wherewithal to push Thane's hand from his mouth.

"Sorry," Orphan whispered back defensively. "I thought you needed a little light?"

"A *little* light?" he squeaked. "You can make fire with no wood? Never mind, of course you can." He breathed forcefully through his mouth a couple more times before he said, "Can you do it again…only smaller? We just need to see where we are going, not set the tunnel on fire."

She lit a fingertip's worth and held her hand out toward him.

Still looking a bit horrified, Damien took another deep breath and, with a wave of his hand, gestured for her to lead the way. Damien went next leaving Thane to pull up the rear in near darkness.

This tunnel was similar to the one that led from the castle's library. It had a hard-packed earth floor, a rough stone wall on one side, and packed dirt on the other. Thane found it hard to see much past Damien's bulk so he kept his hand on the stone wall as he walked for guidance. The tunnel floor suddenly tipped sharply down; he just stopped himself from stumbling headfirst into Damien. As it was, he knocked Damien forward a few steps.

"Sorry," Thane mumbled into Damien's back as they started forward again.

It was warmer in the tunnel than it had been outside. Thane was grateful for the chance to thaw his frozen fingers. Without the biting wind, he was warm enough to loosen his cloak.

Thane knew they were going to have a long way to walk because the stables were quite a bit farther away from the castle than the crypt was. They traveled through the tunnel in silence except for Orphan's occasional complaints and grumbles about the absurdity of a tunnel being dug under so much water.

"What if the tunnel collapses?" she asked Damien at one point.

"It's been here for longer than I've been alive. You have nothing to worry about; I'm sure it's safe." Damien patted her shoulder gently, and he calmed her fears without making her feel stupid. Thane was surprised at both Damien's thoughtfulness and the fact that Orphan didn't bite Damien's head off.

It felt like forever before Thane felt the ground begin to rise. They were finally walking in the part of the tunnel that was under the castle itself. When they came to a split in the tunnel, Damien pointed them down the narrow passageway that led to the right. They climbed a short set of stone steps, followed another narrow hall, then made their way up a series of long wooden staircases. Thane was glad for Damien's guidance because he wasn't confidant that he would have been able to find the way himself. There were more turns and passageways than he remembered.

"Put out your light," Damien whispered to Orphan. "There are small cracks in the walls here that will not only let light in, it will also let light out. We should be able to see before long. Use your hands to follow the wall until your eyes adjust. We must be very careful now not to be seen or heard."

Thane put his left hand out to touch the back of Damien's cloak and trailed the other along the rough wall next to him. Before long he was able to make out the shadowy outlines of the other two and the dark walls of the passageway. Damien paused frequently to peek through cracks that showed the dimly lit rooms beyond. Thane caught glimpses of rooms he recognized from his life as a child here. Most of them were destroyed and filthy. The treasures that had once graced each room were either plundered or destroyed.

To Thane's shock, the only occupants they had seen so far had been Formoire. Although they could hear voices filtering through the thin walls of the rooms, they couldn't understand what was being said.

Damien pulled Orphan and Thane to a sudden stop next to a bedchamber. Thane could just glimpse the large ornate bed that sat against the opposite side of the room and instantly recognized the dark wooden posts, carved headboard and red velvet curtains. They were looking into his parent's bedchamber.

They paused and listened intently for any noise or movement from inside before Damien slid back a hidden latch. He slowly swung open a full length wooden panel and scanned the room beyond before holding the panel open for them to climb through. The room was dim, the only light coming from the small fire in the fireplace.

Thane looked around the room. In some ways it was much the same as he remembered, yet it was also very different. It was much smaller and dirtier now. A large pile of weapons was carelessly heaped in the corner between the bed and the nearest window and the rugs that had once covered the floor were gone.

Thane remained standing just outside the secret door. Even though he could hear Damien's and Orphan's whispered conversation, he was lost in the past. His unfocused eyes saw the room he remembered as a place he had once felt safe and loved. He would crawl into that very bed in the middle of the night to lie warm and comforted between his parents. He'd spent many mornings sitting in the middle of that bed talking to his father as he dressed for the day.

Now, the red curtains that hung from his parent's bed were tattered and threadbare, and the room was scattered with their murder's belongings. The once warm and happy place had turned dark and foreboding. Thane felt rage build inside of him. Zavior had taken all this from him and moved in as if he had the right to possess it.

Damien sifted through some parchments that were strewn across a small table near the fireplace. "Hey, look at this," Damien whispered. "I think they're maps."

"To where? What do they say?" Orphan asked as she walked across the room and peered over his shoulder.

He looked back at her and shrugged. "I don't know. I can't read," he said a bit defensively. He shifted slightly to make room for her as she leaned closer to the table.

"They're maps of English troop movements, lists of weapons, stocks and look…" she pulled out a very old piece of parchment from the bottom of the pile and read out loud, "…the Four Sacred Treasures of the Tuatha de Danann."

"Then it's true. He's looking for the treasures." Damien looked back at Thane and nudged Orphan. She walked back to Thane and put her hand on his arm. "Thane, are you doing all right? You look pale."

It took him a moment push the rage down. He was no longer that little boy, and his parents no longer lived here. He would find a way to defeat Zavior and make him pay for what he had done.

He straightened his shoulders and said, "I'm fine. Sorry. What did you find?"

He forced himself to join Damien at the small table as Orphan wandered away from them. It looked like Zavior was planning a major military campaign.

"Do you recognize any of these places?" Thane asked him softly as he leaned closer to Damien to leaf through a large pile of parchments himself. He didn't recognize any of it, but then again, he hadn't really expected to. He knew very little about these lands.

"Some of them look like the rivers right around this area, and these here I recognize as maps I've seen of the coast," Damien whispered back pointing to some of the other maps. "These here I'm not familiar with at all."

A great clanging and crashing of metal made Thane and Damien jump. They spun around to find Orphan standing on the other side of the room amidst a scattered pile of weapons. A huge smile spread across her face as she brandished a very long sword triumphantly in her hand.

"You found it!" Thane cried. "I knew it would be here still!"

"We need to go, now! Someone may have heard her. Hurry!" Damien urged, suddenly panicked. He quickly began to shuffle the papers back into some semblance of order. Thane rushed over to help Orphan as she tried to shove the weapons back into a pile without slicing her hands open on the many sharp edges. They only succeeded in knocking more over and making more noise.

None of them were surprised when they heard the sound of booted feet running toward the room. Someone was coming. The three of them scrambled over each other as they rushed to stuff themselves back into the secret passageway. They just pulled the panel closed as the bedroom door burst open. They were pressed tightly together in the narrow passage behind the hidden door afraid to breathe for fear of making even the slightest sound.

Over Orphan's shoulder Thane could see Zavior storming around the room through the small cracks in the wood. The Fæ looked exactly as he had the few times Thane had seen him. A tall and thin Færie, he had long fair hair that hung loose down his back. His double-braided beard swung across his chest as he pivoted about the room trying to find the intruders.

Zavior's pale eyes flared red just as the embers in the fireplace burst violently to life, illuminating the room in a fiery red glow. He searched under the bed, behind the window drapes, and under the desk. He waved his arms and the doors to the massive wardrobe flew open. The few robes hanging in the wardrobe waved wildly about as if an invisible hand was riffling forcefully through them. He stalked over to it and pushed the clothes aside to feel the back of the panel and into the far corners. Thane felt Orphan flinch against his side when Zavior sliced his hand through the air in a rage, and scattered the pile of weapons across the floor.

Finally convinced that the intruders were no longer in the room, he spat out what was obviously a vicious curse in another language. He strode over to the desk and carelessly leafed through the maps and lists sending pages sailing off the table in his haste. Sliding what he wanted from the middle of the pile, he turned to leave, then hesitated. His pale eyes scanned the room one last time as if he could feel their presence. The malevolence in Zavior's eyes sent a shiver of terror through Thane. The tension in their little hideout was so palpable he was surprised Zavior couldn't smell their fear.

Zavior turned abruptly and left, slamming the door behind him. They waited a few more moments to make sure he wasn't coming back before they moved. Thane sagged with relief against the rough wall. He could feel Orphan shaking beside him.

"Let's get out of here!" Damien whispered.

"No!" Thane hissed into the dark. "We need to find out what he is going to do with the parchment he took. Maybe we can find out what he's planning to do next."

"Fine, we'll make for the Great Hall. Chances are that he is headed there, but we are not going to stay long, understand? Tuck that sword away," Damien ordered Orphan.

"They'll be looking for us now, so we can't chance a light," he continued. "Stay close and be quiet. There is no room for mistakes. Let me go first since I know the way."

Damien slid past her and began to move cautiously down the dimly lit tunnel. They made several quick turns before they came to a stop. Thane could just hear the whisper of Damien's fingertips as he dragged them along the rough wall looking for the catch. With a soft click, he'd opened a short door.

Damien took Orphan's arm and guided her through the narrow opening, then reached back and did the same for Thane before he followed them, easing the door shut behind them. It took Thane a moment to recognize the space. They were stuffed into a tiny alcove cut high into the wall overlooking the Great Hall. The lower half was enclosed by a wall of stone and the alcove was hidden from view by a thin, deteriorating tapestry. The alcove could not be seen from the floor of the Great Hall.

This was yet another secret place he'd played in with Damien. They would hide for hours up here spying on the warriors and Thane's parents below. There used to be a lot more room to maneuver up here when they were little boys. Now with the three of them crammed in the alcove it was all elbows, knees, and weapons.

Tiny holes and tears in the old tapestry allowed them to see most of the large room below. Zavior was standing on the right with his back to them in front of a large, stone fireplace. There was a fire burning in the hearth, but instead of giving the room light and warmth, it filled the unkempt room with undulating shadows that made the room appear ominous and foreboding.

The doors to the hall burst open with a bang. A tall man strode purposefully across the room and came to a stop an arm's length away from Zavior. All Thane could see of him was a shock of dark red hair that skimmed the tops of the very stiff shoulders under his long black cloak. Whoever he was, it was clear that he wasn't happy to be standing there. He tipped his head respectfully to Zavior but said nothing.

"Someone has infiltrated the castle...AGAIN! This time they were in my chamber! MY CHAMBER!" Zavior burst out furiously. "They were pawing through the maps and the Fæ weapons! They have taken the Bard's sword!"

"That is impossible. I have numerous guards patrolling the grounds and stationed on the battlements," the stranger argued. "No one can enter or leave the castle or the grounds without my knowledge."

"So, if they didn't gain entry past your vigilant guards, how did they get in?" Zavior sneered.

The other man stood silent as Zavior's anger rolled over him.

"It must be the Prince!" Zavior's robes billowed out behind him as he paced angrily in front of the man. "He must know another way into the castle. I know it was the Prince who freed the Bard from the dungeon. It is the only possible explanation for the prisoner's disappearance, that and your abysmally inept guards. Have you discovered the location of the boys yet?"

"I have Formoire placed with nearly every English patrol here. They are not hiding amongst any of them," the stranger reported to him. "They do not appear to be in this area."

"What you really mean is you cannot find them." Zavior snarled. "The prince will be with that red haired boy. The boy must have been very important to him or he would not have been able to shift with him when we fought at the river. Find the storyteller and the redhead and you will find the Prince," he commanded. "You are not looking hard enough."

Orphan elbowed her arms up to put her hands over her hair in a futile attempt to hide its vivid color. She looked horrified. Thane smiled to himself. There were so many redheads amongst the clan, if they were seen, the least of their problems would be the color of her hair.

"He may be with his father's people, here in the Mag Uidhir lands. They must be hiding here or somewhere nearby. I want them found! Be discreet with your inquiries. We don't want him to get word we are looking for him and run away again."

Damien glanced back at his companions, his dark brow furrowed. Thane was sure they were all thinking the same thing. It would not be long before they were found.

Zavior held up the map that they had just watched him remove from his room. "Take this." He thrust the rolled up parchment at the other man and waited for him to unroll it before he continued. "Study it!"

"Send in Baihnen. Maybe he has seen what you have not," Zavior said with a dismissive wave of his hand.

Thane shifted forward slightly to get a better look through the hole nearest his left eye. The stranger carefully rolled the parchment back up before turning to leave. As he crossed the hall below them, they got their first clear look at him. A long thin nose was set between clear, pale blue eyes. His high cheekbones were flushed with anger and humiliation, but surprisingly, no fear. He may not have been pleased with the reprimand he'd just received, but he wasn't afraid of Zavior.

There was something very familiar about this man. Thane was sure he'd seen him somewhere before, but he couldn't place him. Could he have been one of the Fæ at his grandfather's castle? No, not likely. If he had been, he'd have known Orphan was not a boy. Who was he?

"Iagan," Zavior called out below them.

"Yes, Father." The man paused as he reached his hand out to push through the large wooden doors but didn't turn around.

"Don't underestimate him. He has the medallion and apparently the ability to use it."

The redhead below nodded curtly before walking out and closing the door firmly behind him.

Damien tugged urgently at their sleeves. He pulled Thane and Orphan carefully through the door at the back of the alcove into the narrow tunnel. "We need to get out of here...now!" he whispered.

They finished their search with a cursory check of the remaining rooms as they made their way silently back through the narrow passageways to the tunnel.

It was only after they were in the relative safety of the tunnel and headed back toward the stables that Damien whispered a request for light. With minimal fuss, Orphan obliged him. After running a good distance away from the castle, Damien slowed down and looked back and forth between the other two.

"I've seen that one with the red hair before...Zavior's son. He rides with the English patrols sometimes," Damien whispered to them. "He never participates in the battles and he is nearly always gone when the fighting is over."

Orphan looked at Thane. Then she said, "We need to get back to the cave and tell Tally."

Chapter Fourteen

Let Us Leave

It was well after dawn by the time they reached the training ground. Pádraig was waiting for them at his usual perch on the dolmen. As soon as he spotted Damien, he jumped off the rocks and ran toward them.

"Damien!" Pádraig waved, his pale face flush with excitement.

Damien threw a leg over his horse and in one smooth motion was on the ground and walking toward the little boy. Damien barked directions at a couple of the boys who were standing around and Thane and Orphan were immediately relieved of their horses.

Pádraig grabbed Damien's hand and started to tug him toward the caves. "We was gettin' worried. The others returned hours ago! I was scared so'mat was wrong. Tally is really, really mad." Orphan and Thane followed close on their heels, sliding a nervous glance at each other. Thane had hoped that they would be back long before Tally found out they were gone.

They hurried through the forest and into the caves. The four of them clambered into a large currach and Damien paddled them stiffly in the direction of the main cavern. For once, Orphan didn't complain about their mode of transportation. She was too focused on all they had learned and was just as anxious as Thane. They needed to get back to Tally as soon as possible.

Pádraig wiggled impatiently on the narrow bench as he chattered animatedly to Damien. Damien's occasional grunts and nods kept the boy happy until they pulled up on the sand in the main cavern. Pádraig scrambled eagerly from the boat, a step ahead of Damien.

Damien put a gentle hand on the boy's head, and turned him toward the tunnels. "Go find Tally. Tell him we have returned and we have news," he commanded him then shooed him along with a gentle push on his back. "Run quickly."

Thane felt a painful tug of regret in the middle of his chest as he watched Damien and Pádraig together. Thane had a sudden vivid memory of being just about Pádraig's age. Damien was a couple years older than Thane and, even though Thane was a Prince and heir to the Mag Uidhir clan, Damien had always treated him like a younger brother. Damien had always been there looking out for him, getting him into trouble and out of trouble. Now, it was Pádraig he treated like a younger brother, Pádraig he looked after.

When Damien turned back to Thane, his usual aloof expression was back. "We will meet you in your chamber once we locate the Seanchaidh. I will see that food and drink are brought in for us and ensure that we are not disturbed." He turned and headed toward the rear of the cavern.

Orphan preceded Thane into their room. She swung the cape from around her shoulders and laid it gently on the floor and placed the sword on the ground next to it. She waved her hand over the neat pile of wood in the center of the small cave and a bright blue fire burst to life. Before long, they felt toasty and warm.

Orphan stood close to the fire warming her hands over the flames. Thane had to smile. Considering her affinity for fire, he wasn't surprised to hear her mutter, "I hate being cold!"

Thane had just taken off his boots and stretched his stocking toes toward the fire when Guillius arrived with a large tray full of food and warm mead. He placed them on the ground next to Orphan and after a couple disapproving glares in their direction, he left.

Thane had finished a whole loaf of bread and was working his way through the bowl of spiced apples by the time Tally stormed into the alcove. Damien and Pádraig followed right behind him. Tally was furious.

"What were the two of you thinking? How could you go back there?" Tally's face was flushed with anger. "After all that we have done to keep you safe, you go willingly to the stronghold of a monster! What if you all had been caught? Did you not see how he treats his prisoners?" He took a shaky breath and continued to rail at them. "Orphan, why didn't you talk him out of such a foolhardy stunt. Instead you join him...without so much as telling me of your intentions?"

Thane stood slowly. He had not seen Tally this upset since the day Tally had first laid eyes on him at the Whyte Wyndmyl Inn. Shamefaced, Thane felt his head involuntarily sink down between his shoulders as his guilty conscious weighed on him. He'd known Tally would be mad that they had gone to the castle, but he didn't stop to think about how frightened Tally would be for their safety. Tally knew exactly what they were walking into. When they didn't return with the rest of the clansmen, he must have imagined that they were either being tortured or were dead. He must have spent the last few hours in a state of panic.

"Tally, we're sorry. We didn't tell you because we didn't want to worry you. Look, we got your sword back!" Orphan said as if she was going to make everything suddenly better by presenting him with his sword.

She scrambled to her feet and retrieved the sword from the ground next to her discarded cape. She shoved it into his right hand then threw herself at him, wrapping her arms tightly around his waist, and hiding her face in his chest. Tally stood stiff in her embrace for a moment before he finally relented. He hugged her fiercely then patted her back soothingly with his left hand. He pulled abruptly out of her embrace. The sword clattered loudly on the stone ground as he let it go to grip her upper arms tightly in his hands.

Tally's voice shook as he stared into her eyes and whispered brokenly, "What were you thinking, Orphan? You could have been captured or killed!"

"We were safe. Damien made sure no one saw us!" Orphan reassured him.

The Bard cleared his throat a couple times before letting her go and turning his gaze on Thane. Thane shivered and took an involuntary step back at the look of stark fear he saw in the Bard's eyes. He didn't want to think about what had put that awful look onTally's face...about what he must have gone through as Zavior's prisoner.

"I'm sorry, Tally," Thane said with genuine remorse.

"We have so much to tell you." Orphan touched Tally's arm in an attempt to change the subject and break the awkward silence that was stretching between them.

She scooped the sword from the ground, grabbed hold of Tally's hand, and pulled him forward until he was standing next to the fire. Kneeling down, she tugged on him until he folded his long legs appearing to crumple down as he sat next to her. She placed the sword gently on the ground between them.

Damien and Pádraig stood near the entrance looking unsure of their welcome. Thane sat down on the other side of the fire and let Orphan take the lead. She had been with Tally the longest, so he assumed she would know what to say to reassure and calm him.

Not giving Tally a chance to resume his tirade, she launched into a detailed description of what they had discovered: the

Formoire, the piles of papers, the maps, and the weapons they found in Zavior's room. She even managed to repeat every detail of the conversation Zavior had with his son, Iagan.

Tally was enthralled. Anger and fear momentarily forgotten, he looked at Orphan with his eyebrows raised in surprise. "Iagan was there...with him? Zavior's son? Now that we know Iagan is involved it is even more imperative the Tuatha de Danann recover the sword. If Zavior finds out about Paiste, he may try to use Iagan to break through the iron prison. Iagan's mother was a mortal."

"He was married to a mortal?" Orphan gasped in surprise.

Thane sat silent as they spoke around him. His thoughts drifted to the dragon and what King Finnbheara had said during his brief visit weeks ago. As the King had said before, handling iron had never been a problem for him, so he would have no problem approaching the iron prison. Thane could not wait around for Zavior to find him or to discover what they'd learned about the Fæ sword. Waiting would only endanger them all and everyone around them.

"I'm going to find Fragarach," Thane said suddenly.

A tense silence fell.

"What?" Thane said defensively. "Isn't that what you are saying Tally? We can't wait for Zavior to figure out that the dragon had it before he was captured, and we already know that the Fæ refuse to be involved. Did you all forget that they were willing to let Tally rot in that dungeon! We all know Finnbheara was right. I must try."

"You expect to find your way to an underwater gaol and convince an angry dragon to give you a missing magic sword? Doesn't that sound just a bit unwise to anyone else?" Damien looked at the faces of those around him.

"If Zavior finds the sword first he will be one step closer to being invincible." Thane leaned forward and looked Damien in the eye. "Right now, the only thing preventing him from getting the sword is that he doesn't know where it is, and it is only a matter of time before he figures it out. I know who has it, and approaching the iron bars will pose no danger to me. You would do the same if you were in my position, and you know it."

Tally sighed in resignation. "King Finnbheara will guarantee you safe passage through Cnoc Meadha to the Gates of the Formoire's territory. Once there you will have to find the entrance to the dragon's underwater prison through the underground Formoire Paths. The rest will be up to you."

Thane stood up and said, "We need to leave now then if Zavior is looking for us. He has a suspicion that we are with the Mag Uidhirs."

"Now, calm yourself Thane," Tally soothed. "It sounds like we are safe enough for the next couple of days at least. There are not many people who are aware of the existence of these caves and remember, they are still looking for two boys not a boy and a girl. Although," he paused frowning, "it is concerning that word is out that Prince Nathaniel Mag Uidhir has returned."

"We can take care of ourselves," Damien said defensively, "and there is no one here who will betray your trust."

"We are not questioning your loyalty, young Damien," Tally reassured him, "only the wisdom of staying too long in one place, and we have been here a long time. Nevertheless, we should have been thinking about moving on."

Damien turned away. Thane caught a glimpse of his face as he turned on his booted heel and left. He was furious, but beneath the anger, Thane saw something else...fear. Could it be Damien was upset by their talk of leaving?

Pádraig rushed out after him.

"You have had a long night and I am weary," Tally got slowly to his feet. "We will make plans after you have rested," he said in a tone that brokered no arguments. He retrieved his sword from the ground and moved to where his blankets were arranged. With a sigh of contentment, he laid down and faced the wall.

𒑫

Later that afternoon Damien sought out Tally and Thane on the training grounds. Thane was brushing down Embarr while Tally sat nearby. Damien stepped up behind them and cleared his throat. He avoided making eye contact with Thane and spoke directly to Tally.

"I have just returned from speaking with the Mag Uidhir. He confirmed our fears. A red haired man matching the description of

Zavior's son has been moving among the clan furtively asking questions about the location of two boys, one with red hair and one with black. He is making no secret that the boy he is looking for is Prince Nathaniel Mag Uidhir. So far, they've told him nothing, but it won't be long before he finds someone who will be willing to talk for a price. Too many people know you are here."

Damien finally looked at Thane. "Your time has run out. You should leave here, tonight if possible."

"It is possible. We will make for Finnbheara's Castle," Tally said.

Chapter Fifteen

Cnoc Meadha

Thane was surprised at how rapidly their departure was accomplished once the decision to leave the Mag Uidhirs was made. It had been easy enough to gather their few belongings as they didn't own much. Guillius made sure they had one last warm meal of stew, hard bread, and cheese. Thane took one last look at Guillius as he handed Tally a package of food that he had prepared for them. Thane had become so used to seeing him around that he realized he no longer saw the scars and the missing eye; he was just Guillius. Thane was going to miss the old man.

Many of the Mag Uidhirs and the MacLeòid gallóglaigh gathered at the cave entrance to see them off. Jamie unexpectedly wrapped his arms around Thane, picked him up and swung him around in a circle. Others just slapped him on the back and wished him well.

Pádraig was unashamedly miserable. He had grown very attached to Thane and especially Orphan, and they felt the same way about him. Just before they had left their room for the last time, Thane gave Pádraig his sporran and all the treasures in it. Pádraig was clutching it between his hands now, his pale face pinched up, trying not to cry.

Damien was much more reticent, although he hugged Orphan longer than Thane thought was necessary. He gave Thane the briefest of nods as he clasped forearms with him and wished him safe passage and a successful...hunt.

Rian came out of the forest leading a properly saddled Embarr and one of the Mag Uidhir's sturdy brown horses. As he stopped in front of them, a brilliant flash of blue flew around Rian's head and landed on his shoulder. It was a dragonfly. Its long iridescent body glimmered like a jewel in the late afternoon sun as it sat for a moment fluttering its wings before it flew off into the forest.

Eoin giggled and said, "I heard that dragonflies will lead you to the Færies if you're not careful! We don't want to lose you to those creatures."

Eoin thought of the dragonfly's appearance as a bad omen, but Thane saw its appearance as a good sign. No one but Damien and Pádraig knew that that was exactly where they were headed...to the Fæ underground city at Cnoc Meadha. Thane hoped Tally knew where he was going otherwise they just might need to follow the dragonfly.

Tally would ride the Mag Uidhir horse and Thane and Orphan would ride together on Embarr. Tally planned to return to the caves once Thane and Orphan had safely crossed the Færie Gateway. If all went well, Thane and Orphan would eventually meet him back here when their task was complete.

They mounted the horses and with a final wave turned toward the forest. Thane looked back one last time and found himself feeling disheartened at the flatness in Damien's eyes as he stood, his hand on Pádraig's shoulder, watching them leave.

†††††

After two hard days of travel, they stopped on the crest of the hill at Cnoc Meadha near nightfall. Thane had spent much of the trip worrying about his ability to find the sword. Doubt and fear ate away at his confidence. Embarr danced restlessly under Thane and Orphan as if sensing Thane's reluctance to go any further.

The day had been full of the promise of spring, the air unseasonably warm and moist. Tendrils of fog wove through the trees like loose threads on a loom. Thane couldn't see much between the deepening shadows and the thickening fog. There was nothing that resembled what he imagined a Fæ Gateway should look like. The saddle creaked softly under his weight as he turned to look back at Tally. The old man had stopped a few feet behind Embarr. There was a strange look on his face as he stared off into the trees.

"This is as far as I can go." Tally slid carefully to the ground and walked over to Thane. He stood near Embarr's head, rubbing his hand down the horse's long nose.

"I'm not sure I'm ready for this," Thane confided anxiously to Tally.

Tally nodded. "I would think you a fool if you believed this to be an easy task. You must look inside yourself and make sure you are doing this for the right reasons. If not, then tell me now and we will leave."

Thane felt Orphan squeeze his waist as she whispered in his ear, "I'll follow you wherever you decide to go, but if you want my opinion, we can't let Zavior get his way in this."

Thane was heartened by the knowledge that this was truly his decision, and Tally and Orphan would support him in whichever path he chose. An image of Zavior storming around his parents' castle came to mind, and he felt a rage-filled determination build in him. The King was right, he had to find a way to do this.

Thane reached down, grabbed the arm Orphan still had around his waist and gave it a quick squeeze. "How do we find the King?" he asked Tally.

"The Gateway is just beyond those hawthorn trees. You will know it when you get there." Tally looked up into Thane's eyes, "Be vigilant Nathaniel; watch your back. Zavior has shown more than once that he will stop at nothing to reclaim this land, and King Finnbheara will have his own reasons for lending his aid to you. Those reasons may not be as noble as he would have you believe. Remember, the Fæ are not to be trusted. They have their own interests at heart...always."

Thane stared down at the Bard in surprise. Tally never called him by his given name. Before Thane could swallow the lump in his throat and muster a reply, the old man had turned his attention to Orphan. Tally didn't say anything to her, just patted her gently on the knee and turned away. He mounted his horse and they watched silently as he disappeared back the way they'd come.

The silence Tally left behind was oppressive. Thane could feel the slight tremors that shook Orphan's body as she struggled not to cry. Thane didn't dare meet Orphan's eye or attempt to comfort her. He was afraid she was regretting her decision to come with him and, selfishly, he didn't want to give her a chance to change her mind. He also didn't want to admit, even to himself, that he was scared and he was grateful for her support.

He nudged Embarr toward the stand of ancient trees Tally had indicated. The entrance to Finnbheara's Fæ city was unremarkable. There was nothing to give away its presence except for an uneasy feeling of power that seemed to permeate the air around them. Thane looked around the woods and felt the hairs on the back of his neck stand up. The medallion around his neck felt unusually warm against his chest, as if it too was sensing the enchantments surrounding the Fæ Gateway.

Thane and Orphan rode slowly into the stand of hawthorn trees. The further into the trees they went, the warmer the medallion felt and the harder it became to see as the fog thickened around them. Thane looked back at Orphan as her arms tightened painfully around his waist. Her eyes were round with apprehension yet she held her chin up in determination.

The fog closed in and began to swirl around them, gently at first, then faster and faster, until it became so dense and white it blinded them. Intense heat traveled across Thane's flesh, but instead of burning him, it felt warm and soothing. Thane had no more than blinked when he opened his eyes and found that they had crossed the Gateway. They were now in an enormous circular chamber with a high arched ceiling. Nine wide passageways spread out at even intervals from the room like the spokes of a wheel. The color of the polished stone floor was similar to the warm colors of the Mag Uidhir caves. Light came from hundreds of fist-sized emeralds embedded randomly throughout the walls. Their gently pulsing light cast a subtle green hue over everything.

Orphan slid off Embarr's back, Thane following along right behind her. She walked over to one of the walls and ran her open hand along its uneven surface. Thane came up behind her and splayed his hand next to hers on the wall.

Up close, he could see that the walls were formed from hundreds of thin intertwined ropes that ran from the peak of the ceiling and down the walls, before digging their delicate tendrils into the floor. He could feel energy flowing through the twisted, intricate patterns under his palm. Were the walls alive? How was that possible? It suddenly dawned on him that they must be underground...below the hawthorn trees.

ORPHAN

"I think that these must be the roots," Thane whispered, "of the hawthorn trees in the forest above us."

They jerked their hands quickly away from the wall and glanced uneasily at each other.

"Where do you suppose everyone is?" Orphan turned toward the center of the room.

"I don't know. I assumed we would appear...I don't know...right in front of the King..." Thane spun around and looked at the different passageways. How do they pick one?

"Do you think they know we're here? Should we look for the King?" Orphan prodded him.

"Do you know which way to go?" Thane said sarcastically. "Because no one bothered to give me directions, and we can't just wander..."

Embarr swished his tail and whinnied at them. He raised his head high, turned purposefully away and headed down one of the passageways.

"Looks like he knows the way," Orphan grinned.

Thane shook his head, "It's more likely he knows where to find food!" He gave her cloak a quick tug and turned to follow Embarr into the passageway. "Let's go."

The ceiling and walls of the tunnel were covered in mosaics depicting gods, goddesses, trees, and animals. The images were made from millions of sea shells in a variety of shapes, sizes and colors. While Thane recognized the cockles, oysters, whelks, and mussels, there were others he had never seen before.

The incredible tunnel twisted, turned and angled beneath their feet as the hall sloped downward. Occasionally, they walked through a space that had a circular, domed ceiling where the shells swirled upwards toward a small hole at the apex. Thane wondered if the holes led to the world above them and if the holes would allow sunlight to shine down into the tunnel.

Eventually, Embarr stopped in a simple chamber, much smaller than the one in which they first arrived. There were no doors or passageways other than the one they had just come through.

A miniature tree, no taller than they were, rose from the ground in the center of the room. Leaves of gold shimmered on the glowing amber trunk and branches as if caressed by a gentle breeze, though Thane couldn't feel one. The yellow light from the tree reflected off the smooth surfaces of the leaves, and sent shards of color flickering on the stone walls like miniature bolts of lightening.

Orphan sat down on one of the low stone benches that were set at intervals along the curved wall as Thane walked the perimeter of the room. He didn't find anything to indicate that there was an exit here. They had reached the end. They would have to go back the way they'd come and try to find a different path.

"I was so sure Embarr knew where he was going," Thane grunted in frustration. He flung himself down next to Orphan, tipped his head back against the wall, and closed his eyes.

A section of the curved wall suddenly slid open. Thane and Orphan jumped to their feet and stepped closer to Embarr. It opened so quickly that they didn't even have time to draw their weapons.

King Finnbheara stood in the open doorway.

"Welcome, Nathaniel...and...Ceara. I am pleased to know that Taliesin is a man of his word. Come, we will settle your belongings in your rooms before we discuss more serious matters."

Beckoning them forward, the King turned and disappeared through the open stone doorway. Orphan glanced at Thane and, with a shrug of her shoulder, she followed. Thane guided Embarr through the narrow opening, then spun around to watch as it firmly slid shut of its own accord. The space sealed up behind them with not even a crack to show where it had been in the stone wall. He heard Orphan gasp and turned forward to see what had startled her.

They had stepped through the doorway onto a wide ledge that overlooked a city with a small mountain at its center. If they were underground, as Thane was led to believe they would be, they had to be very far underground. There was no discernible ceiling as one might expect down here. The sky, for lack of a better word, was the color of twilight.

Thane could see the streets of the city, lit with thousands of twinkling green lights, fanning out from the mountain in the same spoke-like pattern as the room they had first arrived in. If his guess was correct, there would be nine of them. A labyrinth of smaller streets and alleyways wound between each of the main roads.

"It is a long way to the castle. It is best we ride," King Finnbheara said as he mounted a horse that had been waiting on the ledge. Thane and Orphan did the same with Embarr. Once they were ready, the King turned and descended toward the center of the city at a gallop. Orphan threw her arms around Thane's waist and held him tightly as they raced after the King.

They rode past heavy, dark stone buildings that lined the sides of the wide cobblestone street. The structures towered four or five stories above the road. They had ornately carved wooden doors and window shutters, and they were inlayed with finely wrought gold, silver and copper trimmings.

There were many Daoine Sidhe, the Fæ of the city, on the streets walking or riding horses, but Thane thought it was strange that there were no children among them. They were all so perfect and beautiful that after a while, Thane began to wonder if he would be able to distinguish one from another. The Fæ barely had time to acknowledge their King with a bow as they raced by. The presence of the Fæ was the only thing he found similar to his Grandfather's castle. Everything else here was very different. Whereas Tír inna n-Óc was airy, bright, and full of a variety of flowers, trees, and plants, this city was oppressive, dim, and, other than its Fæ dwellers, bereft of life.

The light began to fade as if night were falling over the Fæ underground city. There had been no sun to gauge the time by, but Thane felt that it had taken them at least an hour to reach the base of the mountain. They slowed their pace as they continued to follow the narrow road that led up and around the side of the mountain.

They were a quarter of the way up the mountain and had reached the far side by the time they finally stopped. A crescent-shaped polished stone courtyard spread out before an immense stone castle built directly into the face of the mountain. Nine torch-lit, tiered levels rose to the peak of the mountain. Each level was narrower and set further back into the rock than the one below it. Arched windows were spaced evenly across the front, and at the top, golden spires tipped the points of three square towers.

Two Fæ sentries stepped out from the castle and bowed to the King. They were dressed in tunics of green so dark they appeared almost black, and they were belted at the waist with a length of wide gold braid. Long capes of the same dark green, held in place at the shoulder with large gold leaves, fell down their backs to their knees.

"Gather your belongings," the King ordered Thane and Orphan as they dismounted. "Brecc will show you to your rooms. Please, take all the time you need to avail yourselves of an ablution. Fresh food and clothing will be brought for you. You will be escorted to the throne room when you are presentable." The King left them in the care of the sentries and disappeared into the castle.

Thane leaned over and whispered questioningly, "Ablution?"

"He wants us to bathe!" Orphan snickered back at him. "In other words, he doesn't like the way we smell."

Thane and Orphan gathered their bags, weapons, and supplies from Embarr's saddle. One of the sentries came forward to take Embarr's reigns, but Thane hesitated. He was unwilling to relinquish Embarr to a stranger.

"He will not be able to follow you into the castle. Have no fear. He will be well cared for, and he will find you once you have completed the task King Finnbheara has set for you. He is not unfamiliar with the Daoine Sidhe and will be quite at home here," the Fæ guard assured Thane.

Embarr rubbed his white nose on Thane's shoulder. Thane rubbed his open palms along the hard edges of the horse's jaw and leaned his forehead against Embarr's forehead. Thane whispered, "We'll find you when we are done. Take care of yourself."

Embarr nuzzled his nose into Thane's neck one last time, then gently tugged his reigns from Thane's hands, and followed the Fæ. Thane had learned the hard way to trust Embarr's assessment of those around them as he had never led them into danger. He was no longer worried about Embarr's welfare, but he was going to miss him.

Thane and Orphan followed Brecc through the front doors of the castle. The walls were carved out of stone and the moldings had the same intertwining scrolling patterns he had seen at his Grandfather's castle. Long, glassless windows, arched and pointed at the top, lined one side of the hallway and looked out onto courtyards of blooming trees. As he passed he could see stone benches, tucked into the standing halves of scallop shell-shaped stones that were as tall as he was, scattered randomly beneath the trees.

Brecc led them through a bewildering series of hallways before stopping in front of a door that had the same pointed arch as the windows. He opened it and waved Thane and Orphan into a small sitting room with a brightly lit stone fireplace. A low table sat between two chairs and was set with an array of fruit, meats, pastries, and two chalices filled with a dark liquid.

Doors, open at either side of the sitting room, led to identical bedrooms. Thane picked a room and stepped through the doorway to explore it.

A large tree root came down through the ceiling of Thane's room, widened as it touched the floor then curved over the rug like a giant wooden leaf forming the bed. Thick green blankets were piled in the center of the strangely shaped bed. Thane threw his bag and weapons on the blankets and took a moment to look longingly at it. It had been awhile since he had had the opportunity to sink into the softness of a real bed, and he was desperately hoping he would get that chance before much longer.

Reluctantly, he turned his back on the bed and returned to the sitting room. Orphan was still in her room when a firm knock sounded at the door. It was thrust open before Thane could make a move toward it, and a group of Fæ servants entered. They wore simple robes of buttery yellow. Their soft slippers made no sound on the wooden floor.

Thane backed out of their way and walked over to stand by the fireplace. He took a small pastry from the plate on the little table and stuffed the whole thing into his mouth. He was still trying to swallow the lump of sweet bread when Orphan walked back into the room. She frowned at the parade of Færies who split apart, one group making for Thane's bedroom, the other for Orphan's.

Two of the Fæ carried clothing, two others hauled large shell-shaped tubs on their backs, and the last two each carried a large jug of water. Thane didn't believe the jugs would provide even enough water to cover the bottom of the large tubs.

"I guess the King really doesn't like how we smell!" Orphan said.

When he didn't answer, she turned toward him, took one look at his bulging cheeks, and burst out laughing.

"Wa? 'm 'unry," he pushed the words out around the food. Once he managed to swallow, he stuffed another pastry into his mouth.

Orphan rolled her eyes. "You're always hungry!" She grabbed a pastry as well but managed to exercise a little more self control while eating.

"That was really good!" she said as she wiped the last of the juice and crumbs off her lips with the tips of her fingers.

Thane turned away from the table, wiped his fingers on the side of his dirty breeches, and peeked toward the still open door of his room. Clean clothes had been stacked neatly at the end of the bed, and a Færie was tipping a steaming jug of water over the rim of the oval tub. There seemed to be no end to the supply of water cascading from the jug, it poured...and poured...and poured. He elbowed Orphan and pointed to her room where another servant was filling a tub for her. Once the tubs were full of water, the last of the Fæ left, and they were finally alone.

Thane grabbed a piece of meat before returning to his room, shutting the door behind him. He wasn't proud enough to refuse the offer of a warm bath and clean clothes. He was tired of his own stink, and his hair was so dirty it hurt to run his fingers through it.

He stripped off his filthy clothes and looked doubtfully down at the shell-shaped tub. It was about half as long and twice as wide as his body. An opalescent layer lined the inside of the tub, and the shell was so thin, he could almost see through it. Stepping hesitantly over the side, he slowly folded his long legs and lowered himself into the tub. With a sigh of contentment, he sunk gratefully into the warm water.

Chapter Sixteen

A City Under Ground

Thane had been waiting in the sitting room for nearly an hour before Orphan finally joined him. She had apparently been given the same new clothing he had. The unadorned cream-colored silk tunic fell to just below her knees. She had on leggings of the same material, and soft brown leather boots. She had washed and combed her hair as well. It was tucked behind her pointy ears and hung loose in soft red curls down the middle of her back. Thane hadn't seen it free of its braid since they were in Tír inna n-Óc and hadn't realized how much it had grown. She was beautiful.

She looked Thane up and down and smiled at him. "It feels wonderful to be clean doesn't it! Can you believe those tubs? I could have..."

"Not now. We have to go," Thane interrupted her before she could launch into a long description of her bath. Anxious about the meeting and eager to get it over with, he grabbed her hand and pulled her toward the door.

Brecc was still standing guard in the hall where they had left him. The Færie ran his eyes over their new clothes in obvious approval, but didn't say anything. With a nod to indicate they should follow, Brecc preceded them. He led them down hall after hall. Finally, after many turns, they passed through an enormous pair of gold doors.

The Throne Room was so vast that Thane had to squint to see the other end. Nine wide piers, bridged by pointed arches, lined both sides of the main room. Beyond the archways, Thane could see the upper galleries and the lower aisles that flanked the hall on either side of the room. At the far end of the room, staircases spiraled down from both galleries and ended on either side of a massive stone dais that held two thrones.

Thane and Orphan were ushered under the sturdy stone vaulted ceiling above their head. Thane looked up in awe at the thick folds of gold fabric that hung from each vault and fell in gentle waves to the floor. They walked past a large recessed area in the floor where a massive dark wooden table sat, flanked by dozens of empty gold chairs.

The King was seated on the throne to Thane's left, his elbows resting lightly on the golden arms of the ornate chair. His eyes were closed and his folded hands were held up so the tips of his fingers were just touching his lips. He looked as if he were in prayer. A beautiful Færie was seated on the equally elaborate chair next to him in robes spun from fine gold threads. Her hair fell around her shoulders like a sheet of silver silk.

The King opened his eyes and focused his startlingly pale gaze upon them. Their escort bowed toward the royal couple and left through one of the side arches. Thane and Orphan stood still, unsure of what was expected of them now.

"Nathaniel, Ceara, my wife, Queen Onagh." The King beckoned them forward as he made the brief introductions.

The Queen smiled at them. "Please, be at ease." She motioned to a pair of chairs that had been placed in front of the dais.

"Did you get enough to eat while you were in your rooms?" the Queen asked them when they were settled in front of her.

"Yes," Orphan replied.

"No," Thane said at the same time.

Thane and Orphan glanced at each other and laughed. It broke some of the tension that had been pressing down on their shoulders since they had first crossed into the underground city.

Queen Onagh smiled and said, "I will have more food brought to your rooms when we are done here. Also, you will be provided clothing more suited to the task ahead. If there is anything else you desire, please let Brecc know, and he will take care of it. He is here to serve you."

"Thank you," Orphan said. Thane nodded his head in agreement.

"I know that you must have your doubts about the wisdom and feasibility of this errand and your role in it," the King's voice drew their attention toward him. "I will not lie to you as I too have my doubts. It will not be an easy task to persuade Paiste to reveal to you the sword's location. He has been imprisoned for more than a millennia and will not be overjoyed to see you. He will be even less eager to negotiate with you."

"You make it sound like an impossible task," Thane said. He sat nervously on the edge of his seat.

"More improbable than impossible," the King's brows drew down in a frown, "as the Tuatha de Danann have refused to become involved, and other Fæ have been forbidden to render aid, you are on your own. Your Grandfather is a coward."

"He is not a..." Thane started to object when Orphan elbowed his arm nearest her. He snapped his teeth shut and looked down at the floor. She was right. It wouldn't do them any good to antagonize the King.

"The most direct route to the prison is through Formoire territory," the King ignored Thane's outburst and held a folded piece of parchment out to him. "I have acquired a map of the Paths from a captured Formoire. It is vague but to the best of my knowledge it is accurate."

Thane stood up and accepted the map from the King. He returned to his seat, unfolded it and leaned over to share it with Orphan. It was nothing more than vague squiggles and strange symbols. The only mark he could identify clearly was the Formoire Gate. He folded the map and slid it into his boot.

"Do not stray off the designated path as there are many creatures in their world who will be outraged at your presence. The Formoire will most likely sense you the instant you pass through the veil and will not hesitate to impede your progress. In the event you find yourself cornered or overrun, use the medallion."

"What do you mean 'use the medallion'? Use it for what? How?" Thane interrupted the King.

For the first time since they met, Finnbheara looked truly uncertain. "You do not know what it is that you carry? You have not been taught to use the medallion?"

Thane shook his head.

"Use the medallion how?" Orphan leaned forward and asked the question again. "Is it a weapon?"

"A weapon? No!" The King seemed almost insulted. "It is not only a Key that will open any Fæ Gateway, it holds the last hope of the mortals."

"It's what? Why do I have it then?" Thane asked.

"That you must ask Manannán mac Lir. We don't have time to train you in its use now."

"As your young friend back in the caves speculated, the sword is most likely hidden in the dragon's den. Once you reach the gaol, you will have to find a way to persuade Paiste to divulge its location to you. We must hope that his den has not yet been discovered by the mortals and his horde pillaged.

King Finnbheara stood up and held his hand out for his wife to join him. She stood beside him and said, "I suggest you get as much rest as you can. Food will be brought to you tonight and in the morning. Sleep well."

Brecc appeared silently behind them. He waited patiently as Thane and Orphan said their goodnights to the King and Queen, then preceded them through the throne room and back into the hallway. He led them silently back through the maze of halls. Orphan opened her mouth to say something, but Thane caught hold of her hand, gave it a quick squeeze, and shook his head. He jerked his head briefly toward their escort. He didn't want her to say anything in front of him that might be repeated to the King.

Orphan shut the door firmly behind them before collapsing with a sigh in one of the chairs by the fire. She leaned over and slowly began to untie her boots and pull off the thick wool stockings. He watched as she scooted her chair forward to wiggle her toes in the warmth of the fire.

A large tray of food and drinks had been left on the table near the fireplace. As hungry as Thane had felt earlier, the sweet smell of the breads now made his stomach clench. He wasn't sure he would be able to force the food past the lump in his throat.

Thane began to pace. His stomach hurt from a combination of too little food and plain old fear. He couldn't see how this was going to turn out well. He didn't know anything about dragons, let alone how he was going to talk one into giving him a Fæ sword.

"Tally wouldn't have let us come here alone if he didn't think we could do this." Orphan twisted around in the chair to watch him pace restlessly behind her. "Would you sit down! You're making me nervous."

She waited until he had pushed the second chair up closer to the fire, even with hers, and had thrown himself down in it before she spoke. "I have been thinking," she began, "there is something really suspicious going on. I can't imagine that of all the Fæ in this city, you...and I mean YOU...they don't really want me...are the only one who can retrieve the sword. If Finnbheara has known who had the sword all along, then why hasn't he found some other half-Færie get it."

"I don't know. We know we aren't the only half Fæ," Thane frowned. "Maybe it's my medallion."

"Why is everyone so interested in it?" Orphan squinted at Thane's chest as if she could see through his shirt to the questionable object within.

Thane reached into his shirt and pulled out the round gold pendant. He knew Orphan had seen it around his neck over the years, but he had never felt the need to let her examine it. He held it out to her and she leaned across the space between them to get a better look at it. The surface of the gem reflected the orange-yellow flames of the fireplace. The tiny carved dragon, dog, and horse looked almost alive in the dancing light of the flames.

"I've never really seen it up close. It's beautiful," she breathed. "It almost looks like it's alive. What's that swirling in the center of the stone? Some kind of liquid? Smoke?" She reached out a fingertip to touch the smooth surface of the stone then jerked her hand away with a sharp cry of pain.

"Ouch! It burned me!" She stuck the tip of her finger in her mouth and sucked on it.

"Burned you?" Thane said shocked. His eyes shifted from the medallion cradled in his hand, to the finger she still had stuck between her lips, then back to the medallion. What could have caused that to happen?

"How could it burn you? It's not hot," he said almost stupidly. It was warm to touch sometimes but never hot enough to burn. Frowning at her, he closed his hand around the medallion as if to protect it then shoved it briskly back into his shirt.

She stood up abruptly and backed away from him, her eyes riveted on the lump under his shirt.

"Get some sleep, Thane," she muttered around her finger as she left. Thane watched her until she shut her bedroom door softly behind her.

Thane sat for a bit longer staring at the flames. He almost longed for the days he had spent with the Reivers when he was just an orphaned stableboy. Back then, the medallion had been covered by a thick coating of hard mud and, as far as he had known, it was nothing more than a lumpy rock. He had not remembered who he really was at the time, but at least he had known exactly what was expected of him: keep the stables clean, care for the horses, stay out of the reach of Frammel's fists, and help Natty in the bakery. No one would have expected him to do anything as absurd as stealing a sword from a dragon.

He glanced at the uneaten food and hoped it would still be there in the morning. He stood up, stretched his back, and rolled his head around his neck trying unsuccessfully to ease the ache in his shoulders. Orphan was right. He needed to get some sleep. Tomorrow was going to be a very long day.

||||

Thane's eyes fluttered open, and for half of a minute he wasn't sure where he was. He sat up slowly. In the dim light of the room, he could just make out the strange leaf-shaped headboard and side railings of his bed.

He flopped back down, closed his eyes and snuggled into the soft, warm blankets. Despite the warmth and comfort of the bed, he hadn't slept well. His dreams were haunted by long, dark paths and spectral dragons. Maybe if he just lay here quietly, everyone would forget about him.

Soft noises were coming from the other room. Orphan must be awake. Resigning himself to the fact that if he didn't get up on his own, Orphan would be pounding on his door before long. He decided to get up. He rubbed a hand across his face, and drove his fingers back through his dark hair before sitting and swinging his legs out of bed.

A basin, a jug of water, and a cloth stood on a small table next to the bed. He poured out just enough water to wash his face and neck and ran the wet cloth quickly under his armpits for good measure. Someone had picked up his clothes from the floor. They had been replaced with sturdy black leather leggings and a dark gray, quilted tunic; his boots were shined and sitting on the floor next to them.

His stomach gave a little lurch of annoyance. It was not a pleasant feeling to know that someone had been walking around his room while he slept unaware. He would be lucky if that was the most uncomfortable thing that would happen to him today. He shook off his unease and dressed in the dark Fæ clothes.

He wandered out of his room to join Orphan in the common room. If he hadn't known how far underground they were, he would have thought the sun was shining in the little room, but there were no windows in here to let in sunlight nor a sun outside to shine on them. His eyes traveled around the room. He couldn't find the source of the light; the room was just bright. Orphan had moved the chairs back around the table and was eating off a tray of fresh fruit and cheese. A basket of bread sat in the middle of the table giving off the warm sweet smell of honey and almonds. He realized he was starving.

He grunted a greeting at Orphan as he slid into the chair across from her and reached for a piece of bread and cheese. They ate in silence, neither one wanting to discuss the day ahead.

"I'm ready to go when you are," Orphan said as she wiped her fingers on a linen cloth then dragged it impatiently across her mouth.

She was garbed in the same black and dark gray garments that he was wearing. Her hair was pulled back in its usual braid, her pointy ears tucked neatly beneath the red folds of her hair. She had evidently been awake for some time as her bag and weapons were already stacked neatly by the door.

"You needed the sleep," she answered his unspoken question. "I would have come in to wake you before much longer though. I think they are getting anxious for us to be going. Brecc has been here twice already to see if you were up."

"Give me a minute," Thane said, He returned to his room and threw his few belongings back into his bag. His Fæ hosts had left him a new black leather belt for his sword. He strapped it on, pleased to see that it fit snug on his waist as he hung his sword from it. He felt a tug of regret at leaving the bed behind, and with a last wistful look at its rumpled sheets, he left.

††††

Brecc had two stallions brought to the front of the castle for Thane and Orphan to ride. When Thane asked where Embarr was he was told that his horse would be well taken care of until his return. As soon as they were mounted on their horses, the Fæ led them back through the underground city, retracing the route they'd taken through the tall stone buildings the day before.

The city was awash in what, in any other place, Thane would have described as early morning light. The streets were busy with the

Daoine Sidhe going about their business much as they would have on any street in the human world. Thane squinted up into the canopy of light above but still couldn't see a ceiling. If he hadn't know better, he would have thought they were outside.

They dismounted and shouldered their weapons and packs. Brecc bowed to them and took the reigns of their horses. The stone door slid back and Thane and Orphan walked over the threshold to the Golden Tree.

King Finnbheara was waiting for them near the tree. Two Fæ warriors stood behind him. They were dressed for battle in tunics that were similar to the quilted ones Thane and Orphan were wearing, but the Fæ's clothing fitted to their bodies like armor. They carried burning torches. Long swords were strapped to their waists; the faint golden shimmer around the hilts marked the blades as Fæ. What would they need with weapons? Couldn't they use magic?

"Falius and Bræden will lead you to the veil of the Formoire Paths, but they can go no farther. From there you will have to find your own way through the veil and to the gaol of Paiste." The King stepped back from them and bowed, "Go with the Blessings of the Daoine Sidhe."

The King turned away and disappeared through the door that led back to the city. The Fæ soldiers adjusted their weapons and took up their positions, one guard to the front of them, one to the rear. Thane waved a hand to indicate that Orphan should precede him, then fell into step behind her, keenly aware of the tall Fæ following him. A heavy weight of dread and fear sat in equal measures upon his chest. Why did he feel like he was being led to his execution?

Chapter Seventeen

The Formoire Paths

The warriors escorted Thane and Orphan back through the long shell-lined tunnel. Thane looked up as they walked under one of the high domed ceilings. Light was streaming through the small hole at the center of the design at its apex, flooding the passageway with light. Thane was delighted to see that his guess had been correct. He wondered why people didn't fall into the hole. Was it enchanted?

The ground rose steadily beneath their feet until they reached the enormous circular chamber where they had first appeared in Cnoc Meadha the day before. Thane felt the hair stand up on his arms and the back of his neck as they crossed the center of the room.

"What is this place?" Thane turned to ask the Fæ behind him.

"The convergence point of nine Fæ paths," the warrior replied.

His short reply raised more questions in Thane's mind than it answered.

"Convergence?" Thane prodded him to continue.

"It is the point where three, six, or nine Fæ paths converge," the warrior fell silent again.

"What is it I feel here and when I am near a Fæ Gateway?" Thane felt like he was tugging every answer out of the warrior's throat.

"It is the pull of divine magic and ancient enchantments. Your powers will be at their strongest when you are near a convergence."

The Færies led them to the tunnel directly across from where they had just emerged.

"Where do these paths go?" Thane asked after they had been walking for a while.

"They connect cities, gateways, and other Fæ sites of power," the warrior in front of Orphan said as he pulled his sword free of its scabbard and signaled to the other to do the same. Thane understood that to mean that they weren't going to answer any more questions.

They traveled through a labyrinth of tunnels for hours in silence before they stopped for a short time to eat and rest. Orphan tried once more to engage their Fæ guides in conversation but was quickly discouraged by their one-word answers and lapsed into a brooding silence.

The afternoon's path took them farther and farther away from the meticulous streets and ornate hallways of the Daoine Sidhe. The green crystals no longer provided light. They had to rely solely on the two torches to light the way. The walls were now lined in broken bits of shells and coral. As they traveled deeper, the tunnels became much steeper and the ground rockier until eventually, the left wall dropped off completely to reveal a vast cavern below. They were left with only a narrow ledge to follow.

They were almost halfway around the edge of the open cavern when Thane's left foot came down on a soft section of rock and he felt the ground tilt out from underneath him. His arms pinwheeled, and for a heart-stopping moment he thought he had caught himself. Then time slowed down, and he realized that there was nothing he could do to stop his fall.

Thane scrambled his feet on the rough stone wall as he dropped off the path, his hands grasping at loose rocks and shells. He slid another ten feet before he was able to catch his boots on an outcropping of stone and halt his descent. He hid his face in his outstretched arms as rocks and dirt rained past him and fell down...down...down.

Orphan called his name frantically from above. He could just see the halo of her red hair silhouetted against the light of the torch over the edge of the path.

"I'm here. Give me a minute. I think I can climb back up," he shouted to her. "Just give me a moment to catch my breath." A cold sweat broke out over his body, his heart was pounding frantically in his chest, and he could barely breathe. He could feel blood dripping down his forearms, and they were on fire from where he had scraped them along the rough rock wall.

Thane didn't dare look down, so he tilted his head up to look at Orphan again. He could see many holes and cracks in the wall he was hanging from. If he was careful, he would be able to use them to climb the wall and get himself back up to the path. He took his time, and was relieved when he climbed back over the top edge without falling again. The two warriors watched as Orphan struggled to help Thane, but did not offer their help.

When Thane was steady on his feet again, he examined his bloody arms. The scrapes and bruises looked and felt much worse than they actually were. They would heal.

The Fæ turned away and continued on the path as if nothing had happened. Orphan looked around and grabbed Thane's hand to give it a brief squeeze. Thane was grateful for her presence.

It wasn't until much later that they stopped for a longer rest. The walls along the path had constricted to a narrow tunnel that was easy to defend. They made a small enchanted fire and settled around it to warm themselves. The Fæ took turns standing guard while Thane and Orphan slept. Thane closed his eyes, and even though he was exhausted by the long walk and his fall, he found he could not sleep.

𝍪

The unchanging torchlight made it impossible to tell day from night. Thane lost all sense of time in the tunnel. They walked, they ate, they slept, and then woke up to do it over again, all under the imposing silence of the Fæ. By his best reckoning, it took them three days to reach the Gate to the Formoire Paths. Thane was surprised that the only thing separating them from the Formoire lands was a veil of thick, amorphous vapor. It was similar to the fog they had encountered in the forest at Cnoc Meadha, only much more menacing.

Ancient, crumbling, stone pillars flanked an opening wide enough to march a dozen horses abreast through it. Its massive lintel was engraved with intricate swirling designs that were similar in form to the ones he remembered seeing in his grandfather's and Finnbheara's castles, only these were crudely cut images of thick, dark chains and fierce monsters.

"This is as far as we dare go," one of the Fæ warriors said. "The gaol is just over a day's travel from the Gate. May your journey be swift and rewarding."

Thane wanted to thank him by name but even after days of traveling with them, Thane found it hard to tell which was Falius and which was Bræden. He settled for a simple nod of thanks as one of them handed him a torch.

Their guides quickly retreated into the tunnel. Thane and Orphan watched them until they had completely disappeared into its dark depths.

"I guess we're on our own now." Orphan let out a long breath and turned to look uncertainly at Thane. "Where do we go from here?"

Thane thrust the torch at her, then pulled the map out from his bag and unfolded it. A thick, very crooked, black line was drawn from the bottom left corner of the parchment to the top right corner. Small markings indicated a turn here and there, but other than that, the parchment was blank.

Thane's heart sank. This wasn't going to be as straight forward as he had hoped. He rolled the map up and stuffed it into his boot where it would be easier to retrieve when he needed it.

Orphan stood in front of the Gate. Waves of malevolence and righteousness battled for dominance as a veil of dark mist undulated between the pillars, moving as if in a strong breeze, yet the air around them was stagnant and lifeless.

"It's not too late for you to turn back, Orphan. You don't have to do this. It is not you Zavior is chasing." Thane grabbed her arm and turned her around to face him. She looked scared. Her face was pale and drawn but her chin was thrust forward in determination.

"I said I would go with you, and that is what I'm gonna do. We're friends, aren't we? I won't leave you." Her green eyes looked sincerely into his. With determination, she reached back for her bow, nocked an arrow, and held it confidently in front of her. Thane pulled his sword from it's scabbard with his left hand and held the torch high with his right. They were about as ready as they were going to be. He took a deep breath, and turned to face the Gateway.

They stepped into the veil together. Thane felt his breath leave him in a rush of pain. The veil was not mist as he initially presumed. It was viscous and cold. Fear surged through his body.

He couldn't move; the veil held him as securely as a spider traps a fly. They struggled for a time, but their movements just seemed to tighten the bonds holding them. Thane felt his body getting colder as the temperature of the substance around them began to rapidly drop. The flame of the torch dimmed suddenly and they were left in nearly complete darkness.

Out of the corner of his eye, he saw a soft red glow. As it brightened, Thane began to feel the bonds thaw and loosen. When he could move, he turned his head toward the light. It was radiating from Orphan. The brighter her body shone, the more he was able to move until finally he had to close his eyes against the stinging glare of the light. He strained every muscle until he pulled himself forward, free of the veil. Orphan collapsed on the other side of him, gasping for breath. The torch burst into flame again as it clattered away from them, its light still glowing making the world seem to spin around them.

Thane rolled on his side toward Orphan. "Are you hurt?"

She shook her head, rolled to her back, and opened her eyes. Thane gasped softly. He was sure her eyes had glowed red for just an instant, then it was gone. He must have imagined it.

"What did you do?" he asked her as he forced himself to his feet. He rubbed his hands vigorously up and down his arms in an attempt to warm himself.

She grunted and shook her head. Thane decided not to press her for an explanation. She most likely didn't even understand what she had done.

He picked up the torch and Orphan's bow. He looked around for the arrow and found it still lodged securely in the veil.

"Uh...your arrow is stuck in the veil," Thane said hesitantly.

"I think we should leave it. I am not eager to stick even a finger in there ever again," Orphan said firmly as she sat up.

He reached out a hand and pulled her easily to her feet. She was shivering with cold, but Thane was happy to see that she was steady.

Orphan accepted the bow. She pulled another white-fletched arrow from her quiver and nocked it.

Thane held the torch high and looked around. This was a much smaller cave than the one they had left on the other side. It was darker and more primitive and smelled like rotten eggs and raw, putrid flesh. The walls were rough and wet, with no distinct edge where they met the floor. It looked more like an animal had burrowed the tunnel than an immortal.

Thane drew the map out of his boot and unfolded it. It was vague, and he was unsure whether they were supposed to follow the black line from the top down or from the bottom up. He asked Orphan her opinion, but she only glanced at it and shrugged.

"What difference does it make? Up or down, there is only one tunnel here," she observed as she pointed to the right.

They walked resolutely away from the veil. The further from the Gate they traveled, the narrower the tunnel became. As crude as it was, it was fairly straight. Thane avoided touching the walls when he noticed that there was a shiny, dark slime oozing from them.

They followed the tunnel for a few hours until they found themselves at the crossroads of three dark tunnels at the edge of a small lake. The water extended beyond the glow of their torchlight and disappeared into the darkness.

Thane pulled the rough map out of his boot again and studied the lines in the wavering light of the torch. He could see no markings to indicate a small body of water let alone a three-way split in the path. He crumpled the parchment up and flung it away from him in frustration. He watched as it bounced down the sloping rock, hit the surface of the water, and slowly began to float away. It didn't get far before it became wedged in a crevice between two rocks.

"What is wrong with you?" Orphan huffed and thumped him on the back with her bow. She scrambled after the scrunched up parchment. Ankle deep in the murky black water, her feet slid around a bit on the wet stone. Thane watched her use an arrow to unstick the map from between the rocks and pull it toward her. The map dripped nasty water on her as she tried to smooth out the wrinkles between her hands.

"It's useless!" He dropped down on the ground, careful not to lean back against the slime-covered rock wall behind him, and looked up at her. She was studying the map, twisting it this way and that.

"I think the King just scribbled a couple of lines on that parchment so we would feel like we had a chance of getting through the Formoire Paths on our own," he grumbled.

"And I think you were holding it upside down," she snickered.

He glared up at her, trying hard to resist the urge to kick her in the shins.

"I was not," he retorted. "Give it back!"

"No, really you were!" she laughed holding it just out of his reach as he made a quick grab for her. "I don't see anything I recognize either. Wait...what is this here?"

She dropped to her knees next to him and shoved the map under his nose pointing to the bottom of it. He squinted at it in the dim light of the torch. It was completely soaked, a blotch of what looked like red ink was bleeding up from the bottom of the parchment. The stain was working its way to the top, leaving strange red marks along the black line.

He looked up at Orphan to find her face just inches from his. He imagined he could almost smell the flowery soap she had used to wash with the morning they left the castle. He was so close, he could see specks of gold in her green eyes and each individual eyelash.

She blinked back at him, cocking her head to the side. "What?"

"Nothing," he muttered. Sometimes, like now, it still took him by surprise that she was a girl. He dropped his eyes to the map.

Thane was puzzled when he saw steam rising from between Orphan's fingers. Somehow she was using heat to dry the map out. As the parchment began to dry, the red symbols and marks began to disappear.

"Stop!" Thane ordered. "Look! The marks are disappearing. I think it has to be wet to show the real path. In some strange way, it makes sense. If the Formoire live in cities under the sea, then they might use the water to reveal their maps!"

Thane jumped to his feet and rushed to the pool. He took a couple steps into the water, quickly submerged the map and pulled it out swiftly. A thrill of excitement rushed through him as the red stain moved up the parchment again revealing the hidden paths and landmarks. Maybe this wouldn't be as hard as he initially believed.

No sooner had that thought entered Thane's mind than the water at his feet began to roil. He leapt quickly out of the lake and backed away staring in horror at what he saw. Dozens of pale skinned creatures with maggot-like bodies as long as Thane's arm, stared up at him with red eyes from just below the surface of the water. Small tentacles ringed their round mouths, wiggling and reaching out of the water as if they were trying to grab him and suck him back into the lake.

A high-pitched terrified scream pierced Thane's ears. Thane stared at Orphan shocked at the noise she was making. In all the years he had known Orphan, throughout all the things they had been through together, he had never heard her make a sound like that. He grimaced as her scream echoed through the dank underground.

Thane shoved the parchment back into his boot, grabbed Orphan's hand, and pulled her away from the lake. He could hear the creatures splashing around in the water and made the mistake of looking behind him. To his horror, he saw them pitching themselves out of the lake. The creatures began advancing on them. Even though their four short, spindly legs gave them an awkward waddle, they moved alarmingly fast.

Thane pulled out his sword as Orphan nocked an arrow. He wished he had a sparr as its reach was much longer than his sword, and he didn't want to get any closer to those things than necessary. He took a swing at the nearest one with his sword and sliced a long gash across the top of its head, lopping off several tentacles around its mouth in the process. White glutenous liquid gushed out of the wound, splattering Thane and Orphan. Everywhere it landed on their exposed skin, it burned.

Thane decapitated one as Orphan shot an arrow into the next. More creatures skittered toward them. Thane stabbed another and another, but he quickly realized that there would soon be too many for the two of them to handle alone. For every one they killed or wounded, two or three more appeared out of the water. Orphan was going to quickly run out of arrows and Thane could not fight them all with just his sword.

Thane grabbed Orphan's hand again. He picked a tunnel at random and started to run pulling her behind him.

The sucking sounds Thane could hear behind them made him want to move even faster, but the floor was not level, and the torch they held only illuminated a small distance in front of them. As it was, they stumbled numerous times but somehow managed to remain on their feet.

The tunnel split and they turned to the right. After a couple more turns, they found themselves in a small alcove. They came to an abrupt stop. It was a dead end; they were trapped.

Thane and Orphan spun around and pressed their backs flush against the slimy rock wall. Thane could still hear the wet noise of the creatures running toward them. Orphan was still shaking, but she seemed to have recovered most of her composure. Her feet were braced apart, and she had another arrow nocked. Thane jammed the torch into a crevice in the wall next to him to free his hand, then gripped his sword tightly in front of him with both hands. Their sprint had left his heart pounding and the blood racing in his veins.

The creatures appeared at the end of the narrow corridor. They crawled forward on spindly little legs, climbing and writhing over each other as they moved almost as one body. Their red eyes blinked rapidly in the glow of the torch as their long, fleshy tendrils searched the ground blindly in front of them.

Orphan shot the first two, killing one and wounding the other but that didn't stop the rest. The monsters just pushed their pale bodies over and around the their dying accomplices.

"What do we do now? We can't kill them all, there are too many!" she said, voicing his earlier fear.

Thane looked around the small alcove they were trapped in. The walls were smooth and wet, but just above his head, he could see what looked like a rock ledge.

"Up! Let's go up!" Thane pointed to the ledge. "It doesn't look like those things will be able to climb the walls."

Thane crammed his sword back into it's sheath, grabbed the torch and flung it up and over the protrusion. He realized his mistake a moment later when they were plunged into complete darkness.

Orphan mumbled and instantly a small ball of blue flame hovered just above the floor in the middle of the alcove. She shoved him, urging him to move.

"Quick, stick your foot here and I'll boost you up," Thane said as he bent and cupped his hands in front of her. "Don't glare at me! I know you can do it yourself, but you won't be able to reach the top."

Even with the boost she had a hard time lifting herself the rest of the way. Thane shoved at the bottom of her feet until she disappeared over the rim, then he grabbed the ledge with his hands, pulled himself up the wall, and scrambled over the edge after her.

They peered over the side. The writhing mass of squirming white bodies had just entered the alcove. They couldn't quite crawl up the walls, but they were starting to crawl over each other, building a mound with their bodies. There were so many of them that it wasn't going to be long before they could reach the ledge.

Thane looked around desperately. The only escape he could find was a small opening at the base of the wall behind them.

"Keep watching those things," Thane ordered Orphan. "There's an opening here."

He dropped to his knees and tried to look into the hole. It was too dark to see anything beyond the entrance. He groped around on the floor until he found the torch and thrust it toward Orphan.

"Here! Light this!" Within seconds, she had it glowing and had thrust it back at him.

He lay flat on the ground and held the torch in the opening. The tunnel wasn't long. He thought he could see the end of it. He had no idea where it led but figured anywhere had to be better than staying here.

"It looks like a short tunnel, but if we have any hope of fitting through it, we are going to have to remove our packs and weapons and push them ahead of us," he said to Orphan as he shook his pack off his back, and unbelted his sword.

"I am going to push the torch into the mouth of the tunnel first so that I can see where I'm going. I think I can use magic to hold it out in front of me. Make another light and do the same thing or else I don't think you will be able to see behind me."

She nodded hesitantly.

"Just don't burn my feet all right! I need them," he tried to make her smile but his joke fell a bit flat. She was in no mood to fool around.

"Go!" she pushed him.

Thane lowered himself to his stomach again and began to crawl forward on his belly, shoving his sword and pack in front of him. The torch stayed in front of him, lighting the narrow tunnel just enough for him to see by.

"Hurry, they have almost reached the ledge," Orphan's frantic voice called from behind him as she too entered the tunnel.

They crawled as fast as they dared. Thane had a moment of panic when he couldn't squeeze his shoulders through a narrow section of the tunnel. After twisting and turning futilely for a few moments, he managed to fold his shoulders painfully up around his ears. His fingers found ridges on the sides of the tunnel walls to grip, and he pulled himself slowly forward.

Thane heard his sword and pack hit the ground not far from where he'd gotten stuck. He tumbled hands first out of the tunnel. He rolled out of the way and hollered a warning to Orphan as her flame tumbled from the hole and extinguished. Orphan's pack, bow and quiver fell out next. Even with his warning, there was no graceful way to get out of the narrow tunnel. Thane tried to catch her as she fell out, head first but she came out too fast. Her momentum landed them both on the ground. They untangled themselves and scrambled quickly to their feet.

They could hear the wet sucking sounds of the maggoty creatures echo through the tunnel. They must have climbed over the ledge back in the alcove.

"We have to find some way to seal the tunnel!" Orphan panted.

They were in a large rectangular-shaped cave that was much like the ones they stayed in with the gallóglaigh. Hundreds of spikes hung from the ceiling and the ground was littered with sharp broken pieces of rock.

"Help me. We can shift these rocks and stuff them into the tunnel. That should stop them," Thane said as he bent down and began to shove rocks through the opening.

Thane and Orphan used magic to push the rocks deeper into the tunnel. Since the rocks were not very heavy, they had to use dozens of them before they were satisfied that nothing would be able to get through.

Thane was surprised at how exhausted he felt when they were done, but he knew they shouldn't stop to rest. There was no guarantee the creatures would not know another way around their blockade.

Chapter Eighteen

Captured

The cave only had one exit. They gathered up their belongings and ran. They hadn't gone very far when they turned a blind corner and Thane smashed his shins into an unseen step in the tunnel floor. He lost his balance and fell forward on to his hands and knees. The torch flew out of his hand with a clatter, and spun away from him making the light swivel around in circles on the walls. Orphan barely stopped herself from falling on top of him, but she still managed to get her legs tangled with his. Thane pulled himself away from her and scrambled up to sit on the ledge with a groan.

"Do you think we can stop running now?" he panted.

"I hope so!" Orphan sank down beside him obviously out of breath as well. "We should be able to hear them if they break through the rocks."

"Did you get burned by the splattered blood?" Thane held his hands out in front of him. Angry red welts marked his exposed skin and he could feel small patches of skin burning on his face.

"Yes, some," she looked down at her own hands. "It burns, but I don't think it's poisoned like my Roki wound. She pulled off her pack and rummaged around in it until she found a cloth. She gingerly wiped the dried blood and gore off her face and arms and handed the cloth to Thane. When he was done, she took it back, folded it, and stuffed it back in her pack.

"We should try to figure out where we are," Thane suggested as he reached down and pulled the parchment out of is boot. It still felt damp but the red markings were beginning to fade.

Thane held the parchment between them so Orphan could examine it as well. She was much better at deciphering the images than he was.

"I think this is the lake with those maggoty monsters," she said. She had placed her finger next to a circle that appeared to be the cave they had been in. It had four thick lines coming off of it and an irregularly shaped area on the other side. Inside that area, dozens of little tiny dashes were drawn. Each dash had even smaller marks drawn on them that made the dashes look as if they were creatures with little legs. There was another tunnel coming off of the far side of the lake. Thane was grateful to see that it led off the map, because even if it led right to the dragon's gaol, he would have been hard pressed to persuade Orphan to cross that lake.

Thane watched Orphan's finger trace each line to its end. The lower tunnel led straight off the bottom of the map. That was probably the tunnel they had used to enter the cave. The three remaining lines were grouped near the top right of the cave. The first of the three wove and twisted past smaller tunnels until it ended in the upper right corner, which was marked with a small line drawing of a dragon. The bottom one disappeared off the right side of the map. The middle line led to a network of tunnels that connected the other two.

Orphan pointed to the middle tunnel. "This is the one we took. See here, how it is the only one that has such a small alcove close to the lake. This short, thin line must be the little tunnel we crawled through and this rectangle is the cave we just left." Thane was impressed that she was able to make sense out of the strange symbols.

"That would mean we are here," Thane said as he moved her finger to the side and pointed to the bend in the line. Thane could see now that they had been working their way toward the right, when they should really been going toward the left to intersect with the top tunnel again.

"Yes, and we need to be here," she said. They had managed to run down the wrong tunnel; instead of going toward the dragon's gaol they were moving in the opposite direction.

"We'll get there, it is just going to take us longer," he tried to be encouraging. "We need to eat and rest before we try to head over to the other path."

"There's a couple places we can stop. This one has only one way in and out," Orphan pointed at what looked like an alcove cut into the side of the tunnel just a little further up the path, "but this one has three exits. I think we should stop there. I don't think I want to get cornered by anything again," Orphan said.

"That makes sense. Let's move up to there," Thane said. "We can eat and take turns at watch. Maybe we'll be able to get some sleep too. At least if anything sneaks up on us in there we won't be trapped."

Thane stood up. He pulled out his sword and Orphan nocked an arrow. They had already discovered they were not alone, and they were determined not to be caught off guard again. Thane held the torch high as Orphan directed them through the tunnels.

The large room was exactly where the map said it would be. It was much smaller than the room with the lake, but there was a wide wall with a stretch of dry, flat ground in front of it that would make a comfortable rest area. They dropped their packs and weapons on the ground next to the wall and sat side by side facing into the room.

"We'll have to be careful to conserve as much of this as we can," Orphan warned as she dug into the packs of food the Fæ had given them. She gave them each a small scone and an apple and passed the leather bag of honeyed mead to Thane with a warning to only have a sip. "I know the Fæ said it was a little more than a day's travel, but there's really no way of telling how long we'll be wandering around down here. We can't run out of food."

Thane frowned at her as he took a bite out of the scone. He was already starving. Disgruntled by the thought of spending days down here with little nourishment, he thrust the leather bag back at her and mumbled, "Which watch do you want?"

Orphan took the torch and thrust it into a soft spot on the ground. "I'll take the first watch. I want to study the map while it's still wet before I sleep. I'll try to plot a path for us to the dragon's gaol."

"Don't let me sleep long." Thane wrapped his cloak around himself for warmth, slid down the wall, and turned away from her to curl up on his side with his sword clutched tightly in both hands. He put his head on his pack and closed his eyes. The ground was hard, but he was exhausted. He fell asleep to the sound of Orphan murmuring as she examined the rapidly fading marks on the map.

His last thought before he fell asleep was that they would need to find more food. If the marks on the map faded and they got lost in the caves, he didn't want to starve.

⊞

"THAAANE!"

Thane's eyes flew open, and his body jerked as fear jolted through him. He turned his head to see what had made Orphan scream. She was on her feet, bow nocked, and facing away from him. Four huge Formoire warriors were standing at the mouth of one of the tunnels that opened up into the cave. The Formoire looked just as surprised to see Thane and Orphan as Thane and Orphan were to see the Formoire.

Thane struggled to sit up, but his feet became tangled in his cloak. By the time he freed himself, the warriors had recovered from their surprise and were charging at them. Thane leapt to his feet and brought his sword up defensively in front of him just as Orphan loosed an arrow at the nearest Formoire. The arrow hit him in the neck and the warrior stumbled with a bellow that shook the walls. She must have hit just the right place because the Formoire imploded before it could take another step forward.

Thane swung his sword up to meet the descending strike of the next Formoire's blade. The force of the blow drove Thane painfully to his knees. He threw himself to the ground behind the warrior and rolled. He brought his sword around to swing at the back of the warrior's legs and sliced him across the back of the knees. The Formoire dropped to the ground with an agonizing wail of pain. Orphan shot an arrow at him and, although the warrior didn't implode, Thane could tell it wouldn't be going anywhere soon.

One of the last two warriors knocked the bow out of Orphan's hand, grabbed her around the waist, and threw her over his shoulder. He had Orphan's body wrapped around his neck like a cape, her left wrist and left ankle gripped tightly in his hands. He shouted something at the last standing Formoire before moving back toward the tunnel with Orphan. Her red hair had pulled free from its braid and hair fell across her face as she struggled and kicked. She couldn't get loose. Her blows were having no effect on the Formoire. She might as well have been a small child.

Thane struggled to his feet and moved away from the wounded Formoire who was still rolling around on the ground. Thane took a stumbling step toward where the warrior was headed with Orphan, but to his horror, he felt something grab him from behind. Thane's sword was pulled out of his hand as he was roughly lifted and thrown over the neck of the last warrior just as Orphan had been.

Thane tried to tug his right arm and leg free from the biting grip of the Formoire's hands, but he couldn't do more than beat the Formoire's side with his free fist and foot. Thane remembered the knife in his boot and brought his knee up along the warrior's back. He stretched his hand down and pulled his foot forward until he could reach the knife. It took him two tries before he could get it free.

Thane grabbed the knife in his left hand and plunged it as hard as he could into the side of the Formoire's chest. The warrior let go of him instantly, and Thane hit the ground hard. To his horror, the Formoire fell on top of him a second later

As Thane struggled to push him off, he heard Orphan scream again. Thane looked up just in time to see the flash of her red hair as they disappeared into the tunnel.

"Orphaaaan!" Thane screamed. He reached his arm out futilely toward her. "Orphaaaan!"

Panic seized him. He redoubled his effort to get the moaning Formoire off of him, but the beast was huge and heavy. Thane had a sudden realization that he wasn't powerless. He stopped struggling, closed his eyes, and focused all his powers into a tight ball of energy in his chest. He threw it out in a wave of pulsing blue light. The Formoire warrior was lifted off of Thane. His body flew across the room and smashed into the cave wall.

Thane stood up and looked desperately around the cave. The two remaining Formoire were badly wounded, but since they had not imploded, he knew they were not dead. It wouldn't be long before they would recover and come after him.

All of their belongings were scattered across the cave. He didn't dare take the time to gather them, so he just grabbed the flaming torch and picked up his sword from the ground. He took a moment to pull the knife out of the Formoire at his feet. He wiped it clean on his sleeve, shoved it back into his boot, then bolted down the tunnel after Orphan.

†††††

Thane ran until he reached a fork in the tunnel. He hesitated. Thane assumed that the large path that led to the left would eventually take him toward the dragon. He remembered that the tunnels that went to the right led mostly off the map and took a guess that the Formoire would want to head in that direction. Thane hoped for the best, turned right, and ran down the tunnel.

Relief flooded through Thane as he heard yelling coming from further up the tunnel in front of him. Orphan was screaming furiously at the Formoire to put her down. Thane knew that if she had the strength to scream, then she probably wasn't badly hurt.

He ran forward cautiously until he reached another split in the tunnel. He followed Orphan's voice to the left and slowed as her yells got louder.

He was close enough now to see a hint of light at a bend in the tunnel. Orphan screamed and Thane heard a loud thump as if something heavy had been dropped to the ground. The tunnel fell silent.

Thane extinguished the torch under the toe of his boot and slowly crept forward, afraid of what he might see. He stepped around a bend in the rock wall and found himself looking into a large cave that was lit by several torches hanging from the walls. The Formoire was in the center of the cave with his back toward the tunnel where Thane stood.

Orphan was lying at the feet of her Formoire captor facing Thane. She wasn't moving. The warrior was bent over her, tying her hands together with a short length of leather. Thane started to rush forward when he noticed her eyes were open and she was looking right at him. Relief washed over her face and she quickly glanced away so as not to draw attention to him.

Thane stepped back into the shadows of the tunnel. She was all right. He would have to disable the warrior if they had any chance of getting away.

Thane gripped his sword and moved back into the cave. The Formoire heard him this time. He stood up and spun around to face Thane, his sword raised, ready to fight.

Thane rushed forward with a yell. He swung his sword down from the right and was met with a block from the Formoire's blade. Thane lunged forward again. He swung and was blocked again. The Formoire defended himself but didn't seem to want to attack Thane. He just used his sword to block Thane's strikes. Thane realized with a sudden burst of insight, that the Formoire must have orders to capture them but not hurt them.

Thane attacked the Formoire again. He swung his sword low, then immediately brought it back along his opponent's mid section. Thane missed but it forced the warrior to back up toward Orphan. Orphan lifted both her legs and kicked him hard behind the knees. The warrior fell forward and Thane swung his sword around one last time. The Formoire imploded as Thane's sword passed through it's neck.

Thane flung himself through the falling dust to Orphan's side. He used his sword to cut through the leather ties at her wrist. She threw her arms around his waist. She was shaking and, as he held her tightly, he realized that he was shaking too. He had almost lost her. He should never have agreed to let her come with him because he would never forgive himself if anything happened to her.

"Did he hurt you?" Thane pulled away long enough to ask.

She just shook her head and buried her face in his neck again.

Thane held her until they both were calmer then stood, pulling her to her feet.

"We need to move on," he said softly to her.

"I know. I'm sorry. I didn't...they just...suddenly they were there. I'm sorry," she babbled at the floor. "It was my watch, I should have heard them coming sooner. I should have been able to get us out of there before they arrived."

"It's not your fault. They are surprisingly quiet for such big creatures," Thane tried to reassure her. "I don't think they expected to find us there either," Thane continued. "Their hesitation gave us a chance to fight back, and we did. We got away."

She nodded and let go of his hand, but he could tell she didn't believe him. She moved away from him and looked around the cave. Dust from the Formoire was spread out on the ground under their feet. Orphan took a few steps back until she was out of the worst of it.

"Where are our bags?" she asked.

"I didn't have time to grab them. I didn't want to lose you, so I just grabbed my sword and ran. We can't go back for them either. The other two Formoire were only wounded. They may still be there, and I don't think we should try to fight them again," Thane explained. "I don't even have the map."

"You slept for at least a couple hours, so I had plenty of time to study it before it dried out. I think I can figure out where we are." She gazed around the cave for a moment.

"There was only one cave with four entrances. If that tunnel is the one that led from the cave we were resting in," she pointed to the one Thane had come out of, "then this tunnel is the one that should take us toward the dragon's path." She turned and pointed to the tunnel behind her.

Thane nodded. He ran back to fetch the torch he'd left in the tunnel, gave it to Orphan to light and said, "I'll follow you."

𝍸

Thane and Orphan decided to walk side by side whenever they could. Orphan held the torch and Thane's knife since she had lost her bow in the cave. Thane kept his sword out, ready to fight in case they came upon any more creatures or Formoire.

They had been walking in silence for at least an hour before they reached a small cave. Orphan became increasingly excited as she counted how many exits the room had.

"One, two, three, four, five, six and the one we just came out of makes seven. Perfect! I know exactly where we are; I saw this cave on the map. I think we are almost there. Come on!" She followed the wall on her left and turned into the very next tunnel.

It was another hour before a narrow path intersected theirs at right angles. Thane kept walking when Orphan turned to the right.

"This way," she whispered when she realized that Thane hadn't followed her.

"You sure?" Every tunnel looked the same to Thane, and he was so turned around, they could have been heading back to the veil for all he knew. "It's so narrow."

"Yes! I told you, I recognized the last cave. After the cave with seven tunnels, we need to turn right. This tunnel should lead us straight to the gaol." She sounded a little annoyed that he was questioning her judgement. She stood with her feet braced apart and her hand on her hip as she waited for him to agree with her.

"I have no idea where we are, but I trust you Orphan. Let's go then." His words seemed to satisfy her because she lifted the torch and walked deeper into the narrow tunnel.

It took much longer to reach the end of the tunnel than Thane had anticipated. He was not sure what he was expecting to find, but a dead end with a hole in the wall was not it.

The hole was as high as Thane's chin. He took the torch from Orphan and held it into the opening. It was larger than the one they had used to escape Orphan's maggot monsters, but not by much. He could only see a short way into it because it curved to the right. There was a familiar pleasant smell coming from inside the hole.

"I can smell the loch," he whispered to Orphan. "This is it."

Thane sheathed his sword. There would be no room to maneuver it in the narrow tunnel. If they were attacked again, he could throw the torch at the creatures and hope they could retreat.

Thane hoisted himself up with his arms. The toes of his boots scrabbled on the walls until they found purchase on small crevices stippling the wall. The opening was just tall enough for him to sit up in. He reached down for the torch, then held his free hand out to help Orphan over the lip of the opening.

As soon as she was up, Thane crawled forward on his elbows and knees. His back brushed the top of the passage and his tunic caught on a projection. He had to back up and wait while Orphan fiddled with it until he was free to move forward again.

He followed a sharp bend in the tunnel and almost fell out of the narrow exit. He stared out into an immense cavern that was dimly lit by dozens of enchanted torches. The torch light glittered and danced on the smooth glasslike surface of the cave. A huge wall of water formed one side of the cavern, yet no water seemed to be falling into the cave; the floor was dry. Thane could see fish through the curtain of water.

The gaol was in the center of the cave. Dozens of iron bars as thick as Thane's forearm arched over a sleeping dragon like the bare ribs of a giant animal.

Orphan poked him in his back with the tip of her finger. "What's the matter? Move out of the way," she whispered.

Thane swung his legs forward, rolled onto his belly, and dropped down into the cave as quietly as he could. He moved aside to give Orphan room to scramble down after him. They stood together staring at the huge iron cage.

Chapter Nineteen

The Gaol of Paiste

"That's a *small* dragon?" Orphan squeaked in horror.

The enormous dragon opened an eye and looked right at them. He appeared old and decrepit, almost emaciated. Faded, dull black scales covered most of its long body; many of the scales were chipped or peeling off. His head was a little more than half as long as Thane was tall. His narrow jaw was lined with wickedly sharp teeth. Two boney ridges ran along the top of his nostrils, up between his eyes and ended in a crown of spikes that fanned across the back of his head. Similar spikes followed his spine along his neck, lower back, and tail. His black wings were parchment thin, and were folded around his body as if he were trying to keep himself warm.

Who are you to dare disturb my captivity? Have you come to gloat...after all these years?

A deep, gravely voice intruded on Thane's thoughts. It took him a moment to realize that the dragon was speaking to him inside his head.

"Uh, we were hoping you could help us...uhh...we are looking for a sword and...we think you may have had it...a long time ago," Thane blurted out badly. He hadn't stopped to consider how they would communicate with Paiste or what he was going to say to him.

Man and Fæ have taken everything from me. I will not so easily reveal to you the location of my most valued treasures, the dragon's voice echoed again inside Thane's head.

"But that wasn't us," Thane tried to reason with him. "We didn't take anything from you."

You are of them. The dragon growled low in his throat.

Do you remember this?

A sudden assault of images pounded into Thane's skull. Thane was reliving the dragon's memories, seeing what he had seen, and feeling his emotions.

Thane was a baby dragon, sitting in a large nest tucked deep into the back of a cave. A brown and red dragon licked lovingly at the scales around his neck. He felt a baby's comfort and love as the mother dragon tucked him securely under the warmth of her belly. Thane's heart hurt as his own memories of his dead mother mixed with the images the dragon was sending him.

Pure joy shot through Thane's body as the image changed. He watched the most frightening visions of land and sea pass below him while he soared through the air. He flew during the brightest of hours of the day and in the darkest hours of the night, reveling in the euphoric sense of freedom he felt as his wings pushed against the air to lift him high.

Then, confusion spun through Thane as he saw dozens of dragons and Fæ and heard them as they spoke of leaving their home. He felt the young dragon's refusal to leave and his anger at those who had left him behind.

Thane felt the desperation of the dragon as he stole sheep and cattle to appease the burning pains in his gut and the fear that drove him to retaliate against the humans who hunted and tried to kill him.

The dragon's hate filled him as he remembered the human in dark brown robes who had tricked him. Thane felt burning pain sear his body when the iron bars where placed across his back and he was lowered into the underwater gaol by the deceitful monk, King Finnbheara, and two other Fæ.

Finally, the loneliness of a millennia of solitude seeped into Thane's being until he thought he might die from the pain of it.

Paiste released Thane's mind with a brutal thrust of anger.

Thane stood shivering from the strength and range of emotions he had been dragged through. He turned to Orphan.

She was staring at the caged dragon with tears streaming from her eyes. Orphan crumpled to the ground, holding her head between her hands as if it were bursting with pain.

"Thane! Can you hear him? Can you feel it?" she cried. "He's so lonely...an agony of loneliness...and sooo cold."

You dare mock me. I will roast you where you stand!

The dragon opened his mouth, his long black tongue looked dry and brittle. He inhaled sharply, a deep rattling breath that shook his whole body.

Thane pulled at Orphan, but he couldn't get her to stand. He threw himself to his knees, wrapped his arms around her, and bent his body over her in a foolhardy attempt to shield her from the blast of flames.

Paiste coughed and spit a mouthful of sparks in their direction. Smoke curled harmlessly out of his nostrils and leaked from between his long gray teeth.

A wave of the dragon's hopeless agony washed over Thane. The dragon had nothing left with which to fight...no air filled his bellows...no fuel to feed the flames.

He heard Orphan's low moan against his chest and knew that she felt it too, that she had seen and felt everything he had.

Orphan tore herself out from under Thane's protective embrace and ran towards the dragon's prison. Before Thane realized her intention, she had squeezed herself through one of the gaps between the iron bars and dropped to her knees at the dragon's head. She looked tiny and vulnerable next to its towering mass.

Thane tried to follow her but his shoulders were too wide to fit through the narrow spaces between the bars. He gripped a bar in each hand and tried to persuade her to come out.

"Orphan, what are you doing? Get out of there!" He yelled, tugging violently on the bars.

"Orphan! Please!" He screamed. "You're going to get yourself killed! Get out of there!"

Orphan was so focused on the dragon, she didn't seem to hear his pleas. Thane watched helplessly as she laid a hand on either side of the dragon's scaly face and closed her eyes. Fire lit the palms of her hands. The flames spread across his nose and washed over the blackened head. It ran up his neck then along the immense body in front of her. Paiste's flanks shivered as wave after wave of rippling heat shot over his scales, leaving a path of deep glistening red in its wake. What had she done?

The flames suddenly went out and Orphan abruptly let go of his head. Eyes still closed, she crumpled forward onto her hands and knees in front of the dragon.

Thane could feel Paiste's intense relief as warmth spread throughout the dragon's body from Orphan's touch.

Paiste growled deep in his throat and inhaled sharply. When he lifted his head and opened his mouth, an inferno poured out. Orphan tucked her head down between her arms as he sprayed fire above her until the wall beyond the cage behind her glowed red.

"Orphan!" Thane screamed at her again.

Frantic now, he grasped the bars of the cage again and pulled. He was strong but not strong enough to bend iron so he focused all his energy on bending the bars apart with magic. This time when he pulled, the bars gave under his hands until he had made an opening big enough for him to fit through. He ducked through the opening and fell to his knees next to her.

Thane was shocked to find the fire hadn't burned even one hair on Orphan's head. It hadn't even damaged her clothes. He grabbed her under the arms and dragged her away from the dragon. Thane collapsed on the ground with his back against one of the iron bars of the prison, Orphan between his knees. She leaned back against him with a groan.

Thane eyed Paiste warily. The dragon was ignoring them for the moment. He was intently licking the scales on his side that had been transformed into the deep red color of wine.

"What did you do to him?" Thane whispered in her ear.

"I don't know." Her voice was so low he could barely hear her.

"How did he not roast you in that blaze?" he asked in amazement.

Thane didn't understand it. The fire went straight over her. Even if it hadn't touched her, which it did, the heat from the flames should have baked her where she sat. Did she absorb the heat?

She didn't reply. They sat tucked together for a long time, watching the dragon. He looked like a cat, curled up around himself, licking every scale he could reach until he glowed. When he finished, he swished his barbed tail from side to side, then sent another stream of fire toward the ceiling with a roar of joy before turning his great golden eyes on them.

Thane began to feel a cool wetness seep along the underside of his legs where they touched the floor of the cave. Afraid for a moment that he had wet himself, he looked down. He was shocked to see a rivet of water hitting his right leg. His body was acting like a damn. The water rushed against him and split in two streams, one ran toward his boots and the other around his back.

Thane rose swiftly to his feet, lifting Orphan up with him. He followed the rivet of water to its source and was shocked to see the wall of water that was holding back the lake had long fissures in it. Water was shooting out of the cracks in hard streams.

The dragon swung his head toward the lake as well. He reared up on his hind legs and bellowed frantically.

Thane grabbed Orphan's hand and tried to pull her out of the iron prison, but she resisted him. Although, Thane wasn't sure they would be able to get far enough away from the dragon to be safe now that Orphan seemed to have restored his ability to make fire.

You have broken the enchantment of the cave by breaking through the iron bars. The gaol will not last long now. It will flood and I will be imprisoned in its depths to drown and yet to be unable to die. Paiste let out another stream of fire at the ceiling.

"We could set you free," Orphan offered recklessly. Thane glanced at her in surprise. What was she thinking? They couldn't set a dragon free on the world, could they?

The dragon was silent, his eyes unblinking as he gazed steadily at them waiting for her to continue.

"If you tell us where the Fæ sword you stole from the Formoire Gronsin is, then we will get you out of here," Thane offered.

And if I do not confide in you, will you leave me here in this gaol to be tortured?

"Yes," Thane threatened.

"No!" Orphan shouted over Thane's voice.

"Will you give us your word," she asked, "that you will take us to your horde and give us the sword?"

It is mine by right of possession, he growled as he backed up and raised himself to stand on his hind legs. His wings unfurled to their fullest length; the iron bars across the top of the cage were just feet from the tips of his flared wings.

Why is it you are searching for this sword?

"Zavior, an evil Færie, is determined to lead the Formoire in a rebellion against the mortals and intends to reclaim Inis Fáil. He needs the sword to ensure his rule over both mortals and Fæ. We will do anything to prevent that from happening," Thane explained in a rush. He didn't dare take his eyes off the dragon to look at the lake wall, but could feel the water beginning to move over the toes of his boots. The cave was filling fast.

Zavior, son of Lugh Lámhfada? This Fæ I know well. He fought the Fæ council to keep dragons here in the mortal world. What are you insinuating? He was not evil. He was a friend.

"Zavior killed my parents and many other innocent people!" Thane felt anger replacing his fear of the dragon and stood his ground as the dragon in front of him blustered. "He is not the same Fæ you remember."

Could he be no better now than the rest of them?

I was the last dragon born of the fires of the Earth. There was a time when mortals, dragons, and the Færies lived in peace together. Then the Fæ chose to retreat to their haven in Tír inna n-Óc; they deserted me, left me to fend for myself. I was punished for trying to survive. The Fæ betrayed me! Trapped me here, under water, in the cold.

None came to free me. For years, I tried to melt the enchanted iron but only managed to vitrify the walls of my gaol until they turned to glass. Oh, how those walls have mocked me! Paiste lamented. *I have been guarded by the imprisoned reflection of my immortal body for a thousand years.*

Paiste folded his wings in front of his body as if he was drawing a cape up under his chin. Thane noticed the last joint in his wings had three claws that he moved in conjunction with the ends of his wings. It gave him the appearance of having extremely long, misshapen fingers.

Why should I lend my aid to them now?

It shocked Thane to realized Paiste was pouting.

"There is no reason we could give you that would make up for the years you have spent here, but we need your help," Orphan begged him.

The sword is hidden high atop a mountain. I will not tell you how to find it, but I might be persuaded to take you there.

"How do we know we can trust you? How do we know that once you are free, you won't kill us or desert us down here?" Thane demanded. He knew that if they set the dragon free, they would have no control over him.

"I believe him. I don't believe he will betray us." Orphan walked back to Paiste and put her hand on his front leg. Paiste grumbled at her but didn't pull away.

Thane looked skeptically at them. The dragon wanted freedom and would probably say anything to achieve it. Thane didn't trust Paiste and couldn't understand why Orphan was so enthralled with him. She was beginning to act as if the dragon was her pet.

Thane reluctantly acquiesced, because Orphan was right, they couldn't leave him here. Even if he were immortal, he could still be killed or worse as Paiste had suggested, not die and have to live in endless pain and fear, drowning over and over but never really dying.

"Do you have any idea how we can get you out of here?" Thane asked.

The iron bars of the prison must be destroyed. Is that within your power?

Thane looked up at the bars around him. He had parted them enough to slip his own body through, but the dragon was much bigger. He shrugged.

"I believe it will be. With Orphan's help we may be able to make a hole big enough for you to slide through."

Once you break the iron bars, the enchantments on the prison will fail. We will have very little time before the cave floods completely, his voice rumbled.

Orphan waded through the knee deep water to stand beside Thane.

"Tell us what to do," she said.

The dragon bent his scaly body low to the ground and folded his wings up tight to his body.

Climb on my shoulders, and hold tight to my neck. I will take us to the surface.

A rumbling growl sounded low in the dragon's throat as Orphan stepped on his bent rear leg and hoisted herself up. She shimmied up his body and sat astride him in the crook between his neck and back. She pulled herself up tight to the spike in front of her, leaving a small space behind her. Settled, she looked expectantly down at Thane.

Thane hesitated. The water was now lapping at his knees. He knew they couldn't reach the opening of the tunnel to go back the way they had come, he didn't see any other passageways, and it was just a matter of time before the cave was totally filled with water.

Thane reluctantly approached the dragon. Once he was close to the dragon's belly, he could see that it was completely covered in overlapping black scales similar to those on a fish, only they were much thicker and they were larger as they spread up and around his body. The ones on Paiste's back were about the size of Thane's open hand and were no longer the dull black they had been before Orphan had shared her fire with him. Now they were the deep red color of the roses he remembered his mother growing in her garden at the back of the castle.

Thane put his hands on the dragon's back leg and slowly pulled himself up out of the cold water. He was surprised at how warm and smooth the dragon's body felt, like glass windows warmed by a summer sun.

Thane climbed slowly up the dragon's back and sat behind Orphan in the space between her body and the last spike at the base of his neck, with a leg on either side of her. The scales across the dragon's shoulders dug into the back of his legs and the ridge that ran down the dragon's back made for a very uncomfortable seat. He eyed the sharp spike in front of Orphan. He worried that she could be thrown into it, but didn't see any other way that they could sit.

"I am going to bend the top three bars toward the back. Can you bend those toward the front?" he said as he pointed at the iron bars above their heads. "If we can peel those bars back, we may be able to squeeze through the hole."

They worked silently for a few moments. Each looking up at the bars in concentration. The iron began to groan as the bars slowly peeled away from the center leaving a sizable hole in the top of the gaol.

The dragon stretched up to it's full height and leapt up to grab the bars on either side of the opening with the claws on his front legs. He howled in pain as the iron burned, but he didn't let go. He slid through the bars, careful not to dislodge Orphan and Thane. They continued to pry open the bars as Paiste maneuvered his bulk through the opening.

Paiste froze with half of his body out of the cage as a sudden loud crack shook the cave around them. Swinging his head around, Thane was shocked to see the massive wall of water bulging inward. The further apart they stretched the bars, the more the wall bulged.

We must clear the iron before the wall breaks or all will be lost, Paiste said.

With one last push and a roar of triumph, the dragon burst through the bars. His victory was short lived as the enchantment broke and the immense wall of water rushed into the cave.

Chapter Twenty

Freedom

Thane had just enough time to take a deep breath before the flood of ice cold water washed over them. He tucked his arms around Orphan and clutched the spike in front of them, trapping her between his body and the dragon's neck. It took all of Thane's strength to hold them there and keep them from being pulled off the dragon's back.

They were completely at the mercy of the dragon. Thane could feel the strong drag of the water on his body and sword as Paiste struggled to swim out of the cave opening. He opened his eyes to peer through the water; there was nothing but darkness, so he shut them again and hung on tightly. His lungs felt like they were on fire, and he wasn't sure how much longer he would be able to hold his breath.

Just when he was beginning to get lightheaded, sure he was going to lose consciousness, they burst through the water into the sky. Thane took a huge gulp of air. He could feel Orphan's body convulsing as she coughed in front of him and felt what he hoped was only warm water running over his hands. He wasn't sure he wanted to know what Orphan had just thrown up on him.

Paiste flew straight up in the air then banked to the right. Thane gripped the dragon with his legs until his thighs were quivering with the effort of trying to keep his seat. He could feel Orphan trying to pull her weight off of him. They were in real danger of dropping off the dragon's back, a thousand feet in the air.

As if suddenly remembering he had riders, Paiste abruptly pitched forward and leveled off. This time, Thane was thrown forward on top of Orphan, smashing her head against the spike in front of her and jamming his fingers between the spike and her body. To make things even more uncomfortable, the long wet stands of her hair, which had come loose from its braid earlier, were whipping him in the face.

Paiste circled the loch, his head held high, his wings stretched wide. Thane could feel the dragon's unadulterated joy pulsing through his own body. He found himself relaxing enough to look eagerly around at the view below.

They were flying above the lake underneath a brilliant golden sun. He should have been petrified, but he wasn't; he was exhilarated. It was just as it had been in Paiste's memory only it was better; it was real.

They banked right over the lake and flew along a landscape spread out below them that was every hue and shade of green imaginable. Ribbons of water crossed the flat, verdant pastures and rises of thick, forested lands. Paiste must have known precisely where he was going because he didn't hesitate. He flew steadily toward the west until he reached the coast, then turned to the south to follow the rugged line of cliffs.

Having felt the pain of the dragon's confinement, Thane was hesitant to ask him to end their flight. They had been in the air for hours. They needed to land soon. Thane could no longer feel his limbs from sitting in the same position for so long, and even though the heat from the dragon's body was keeping them reasonably warm, he could feel Orphan shivering in front of him.

Thane tried to call out to the dragon to ask him to land, but his voice was just thrown back in his face. He thought about how Paiste could speak in his mind and wondered if it would work in reverse. He closed his eyes and imagined shouting out in his mind, *Paiste!*

Orphan jumped in front and threw her hands up to cover her ears. She twisted around and yelled, "Don't scream in my ear!"

Thane's mouth dropped open. He sent a tentative thought out, *You can hear me?*

She nodded tiredly, her face pale, her lips blue from the cold. Her eyebrows rose suddenly; she just realized his lips hadn't moved. "I can hear you in my mind!" she yelled.

Paiste interrupted them with a derisive snicker. *Of course she can hear you. What kind of Færie are you that you cannot communicate without the use of your mouths.*

Will you find a place to land please? Thane ignored the dragon's rude comment.

We will be at my home in moments. Can you manage to hold on a bit longer?

Birds scattered as they flew over a cliff. Paiste flared his wings to catch the air and lowered his legs. His claws clattered on the stones as he landed awkwardly on the rough rock wall just beneath the summit of the cliff.

Thane didn't see anything that looked like the opening of a cave, but from his past experience with the gallóglaigh, he was not surprised that it was well hidden. Paiste leapt onto a stone ledge and dug the claws of one of his front legs into the stone cliff. He used the claws on the last joint of his wings to anchor himself to the face of the cliff as he pried out a large stone. A gap half as tall and just as wide as the dragon was opened up before them. He ducked inside.

As soon as Paiste crouched down, Thane slid eagerly off his back. Thane had no feeling left in his legs, and they buckled underneath him. Orphan didn't seem to be fairing much better as she landed in a heap on the ground next to him.

Paiste swiveled his head around to survey them.

Come young ones, it is my turn to aid you, he said as he stomped off.

Thane and Orphan followed him cautiously into the dark cave. Paiste sent a blast of fire skidding across the roof of the cave. For a moment Thane caught a glimpse of an immense room before it was thrown into darkness again. Strange shuffling and clinking sounds rang through the cave before a fire burst to life against the back wall.

Come, warm yourselves.

Orphan didn't hesitate. Before Thane could question the wisdom of going further into the dragon's den, she had stumbled across the open floor and dropped down as close as she could get to the fire.

Thane followed and stood next to her making sure to keep the dragon in sight. As much of a relief as the warmth was, Thane desperately wished he could get out of his cold, soggy clothes and lie down for a few hours. He also realized how hungry he was.

Orphan rubbed her hands together in front of the blaze. Thane could see that her eye was turning black and blue where she had hit it against the dragon's spike, and she looked like she was going to fall asleep where she sat.

Paiste was stomping around the cave, poking at piles of rocks in the darkened recesses of the cave and mumbling to himself.

As Thane's eyes began to adjust to the dim light, he realized that what he thought were piles of rocks were actually piles of coins, gold and silver artifacts, gems of all colors and metals in all shapes and sizes. Paiste was shoving the treasures aside with his front legs and the tips of his wings with little regard for their worth.

The dragon swung around suddenly and rushed over to them. His huge feet pounded into the stone floor making the ground shake.

Thane reached for the pommel of his sword, unsure of the dragon's intentions.

Is this the treasure you desire young Fæ? Hanging from the claws of his right wing was a sword belt, scabbard and sword.

Orphan lifted her head and turned to stare at the dragon. She stood slowly as Paiste stumped his way toward the fire. He threw the sword at Thane's feet and stomped off to lay down with his tail curled tightly around his legs and his head resting on his wing.

Thane and Orphan remained motionless staring down at the shimmering sword on the floor in front of them. Thane bent to pick it up carefully with both hands. He held it out for both of them to examine.

The scabbard was solid gold and encrusted with jewels. He could feel the power rippling off the weapon. The belt was made of pounded gold discs and clinked musically as it swung back and forth beneath his hands.

Orphan reached out, grasped the hilt, and slowly pulled the glowing sword from the scabbard. It was even longer than the sword Thane carried. The blade was flawless, not a blemish was on it even after a millennia of being hidden away in the cave. The familiar swirling interwoven circles and scrolling designs of the Fæ were etched into the blade around an ancient script Thane couldn't read.

Thane grabbed Orphan's hand and slammed the blade back into the scabbard. He looked into Orphan's eyes and nodded. This was Fragarach. He was sure of it. He handed the sword to Orphan and turned back to the dragon.

Paiste seemed unconcerned with them now. He appeared to be sleeping, but Thane wasn't fooled. He could feel the dragon's alertness. They were being watched, and watched closely. They were not going to be allowed to just walk out of the cave with the sword.

"What do you want in return for the sword?" Thane asked.

Paiste opened his eyes and stared intently at Thane.

I want my family back, I want to be free to fly the skies, and I want to roam the lands at will, free from fear of attack. The dragon sighed and closed his eyes again. *I want a mate.*

Yet, what I want or do not want is not relevant as it is not possible for you to give me these things, is it.

"We can't let you roam free here. You will only be caught again or worse, killed," Thane said, "but I can promise you safe passage to Tír inna n-Óc. That is where the rest of the dragons went, is it not? That is where you can find your family and...your mate. You would be safe from mortals there."

I don't believe you, Paiste growled. *I was told the Gates would be closed to me and all immortal creatures like me if I didn't leave with the rest. How is it you, a mere boy, can get me through the Gate.*

Thane hesitated to trust Paiste with the knowledge of what he carried, but he could see no other way around it. The dragon would learn about the medallion as soon as they reached the Gateway anyway. He reached a cold, numb hand into his tunic and pulled out the warm medallion. Thane walked closer to Paiste and held it out for him to examine.

"I have a key," Thane explained simply. "I can get us across any Fæ Gateway." Thane felt Orphan come up next to him.

"He's telling the truth," Orphan reiterated.

Thane couldn't believe they had gotten as far as they had with the dragon. Success was within reach, if he could just find the words to persuade the dragon to trust them. Thane took a step closer to the dragon and was about to say something about how honest they had been with him, when the dragon let out a bellow and cried out in their minds.

What is that mark on your finger? Are you trying to deceive me? You tell tales of Zavior's foul deeds, yet you are one of his young! Tendrils of black smoke curled out of his nostrils as he stood up on all four feet and lifted his head high above them.

"What are you saying?" Thane asked, stunned by the dragon's accusations.

The crescent-shaped mark on her finger...the Fæ don't scar. That is a mark of birth! Zavior carries the same mark on his thumb, just as his mother before him, and her father before her. I knew them all.

Thane spun around. Orphan was clutching the Fæ sword to her chest. He stared at the small crescent scar on the back of Orphan's left thumb in shock. She had told him she didn't know what it was from. She had sworn to him that she didn't know who her parents were.

"What?" Orphan croaked.

"Her father?" Thane took a step back from her. His thoughts tumbled around in his head, each fighting to be realized.

Of course she was Zavior's daughter….It all made sense now…Zavior's son is her brother…that's why Iagan looked so familiar when they saw him at the castle…and her dislike of water…her affinity with fire...the red spark in her eyes at the veil. Why hadn't he seen it before? It was so obvious!

Thane looked at Orphan again. All the color had drained out of her face. She was staring in horror at the dragon, shaking her head in denial. She dropped the sword and backed away from them both.

"No. You're lying!" she stammered. "Why would you lie?"

You didn't know? Paiste's deep voice rumbled in their minds.

He lowered his head, swinging it back and forth between them. His anger seemed to have dissipated with their obvious ignorance of her true parentage.

Humph...Well, this changes nothing. You have promised me safe passage through the Gates to Tír inna n-Óc. Rest now. We will head to the Færie Gate when we have rested and I have had a chance to gather some treasure to take with me.

With one last look at Orphan, Paiste stomped across the cave. He curled up like a cat on top of a mound of gold and jewels and folded his wings in front of his chest. He put his head down on his wings, closed his eyes, and ignored the storm he had let loose between Thane and Orphan.

Thane was furious, his sense of betrayal acute. His stomach hurt and he couldn't think past the fact that Orphan's father was the monster who had killed his parents, Martha, Natty, Marcus...

Thane turned his back on Orphan without saying another word, scooped Fragarach from the ground where she had dropped it, and stomped around to the other side of the blazing fire. He dropped to the hard ground and lay down.

"Thane..." Orphan whimpered. "I didn't know."

Thane couldn't push his voice past the lump in his throat to answer her. He turned his back to her and lay facing away from the fire. He put his head on his arms and squeezed his eyes shut.

Thane listened to Orphan moving around on the other side of the fire. Her breathing was ragged, but he didn't make a move to comfort her. He knew it was wrong to be mad at her when she obviously hadn't known either, but he couldn't help it. How many more secrets were there? How many more times would his world be shattered by the discovery of things that had been deliberately hidden from him.

Thane lay on the hard stone floor and thought back to all the conversations they had had with Tally about Zavior and about Orphan's mother and her decision to leave Orphan with the mortals when she was a child. He wondered if Tally had been aware of Orphan's parentage. Tally had never once hinted that he knew, and yet he had always been very evasive when asked about her past.

Hurt, exhaustion, and numbing cold took their toll on Thane. Sleep finally pulled him under.

Chapter Twenty-One

Good-bye

The tinkling and clanking of tiny bells woke Thane. He opened his eyes and, for a brief moment, with the light of the fire reflecting off the stone walls, he thought he was still in the caves with the gallóglaigh. Then he caught sight of the dragon moving around the dim cave happily digging through the piles of gold. The dragon ignored him as he sat up and stretched the kinks out of his back.

Thane spotted Orphan sitting on the other side of the fire with her arms wrapped tightly around her knees staring into the flames. She looked like she hadn't slept much, if at all. She didn't acknowledge Thane's presence and he felt a twinge of guilt when he noticed that her eyes were puffy and rimmed in red. A part of him wanted to say something to comfort her, but he was still too angry and confused. He couldn't find the words to tell her how he felt, so he didn't say anything.

Thane turned his attention toward the clamor coming from the other side of the cave. He stood up and moved a little closer to get a better look at what the dragon was doing. Paiste was up to his scaly knees in treasures, digging through them with his claws.

Thane backed up a couple steps when the dragon growled low in his throat and hurdled a golden goblet and some coins across the cave. They flew past Thane, hitting the stone floor with the sound of a hundred tiny bells before rolling off into a darkened corner.

A lifetime of treasures. How do you expect me to leave them? Paiste groused at Thane. He stretched out his long neck and let out a roar that rained dust and small stones down on their heads.

Thane looked at the mounds of jewels and precious metals that surrounded them and shook his head. There was too much here to move. It would take a dozen wagons to move this much treasure and even if they could get it to the Fæ Gateway, they wouldn't be able to carry it across.

"I'm sorry," Thane said sincerely. "Maybe we can carry a few of your favorites."

Favorites! They are all my favorites, Paiste whined. "How can I choose..."

The dragon buried his head in a pile of treasures and when he straightened up, he had three thick gold chains swinging from his neck. He waddled over to a different pile and hooked two cups and a jewel-encrusted gold crown with the claw of his right wing.

Thane watched him stomp across the cave and dig out a quiver full of gold fletched arrows and a black and gold bow. The quiver was covered by the finest chain mail formed from tiny interlocking rings of gold. The bow was made of a thin black wood. It was inlaid with golden images of dragons and was tipped with gold points. He stomped over and dropped them on Orphan's lap.

For you, in thanks for your gift of fire.

Orphan held the weapons close to her chest and stared stupidly up at the dragon.

"Thank you," she whispered.

Paiste turned to Thane and said, *The Færie Gate is not far inland. You are confident in the ability of your key?*

Thane was just repeating what King Finnbheara had said. He had never tried to use the key on his own, so if he was honest, he would have told the dragon 'no'. He had only crossed the Fæ Gates while riding Embarr, so he couldn't be absolutely sure whether it was Embarr or the medallion that had allowed him safe passage.

"That is what I've been told. If I am riding you, we should be able to fly through the Gateway together. I believe we will need to be there at gloaming for it to work properly though," Thane said with more confidence than he felt. "Is that possible?"

We must leave now if we are to make it to the Gateway before the next gloaming.

"We are ready," Thane said. He didn't want to spend another night in the cave. He was eager to get the sword to Tír inna n-Óc, and he was starving. He was sure they would be able to get some tasty food at his Grandfather's castle. Thane's mouth began to water just at the thought of it.

Paiste took one last look around the cave then dropped to his knees in front of them.

If you are quite ready, climb back upon my shoulders.

Orphan put her arm through the gold linked strap of her new quiver and slipped it over her head. The bow went over her head next. She took another couple of minutes adjusting them so the strap and bowstring rested comfortably across the front of her chest.

Without even a glance in Thane's direction, she climbed Paiste's scaly leg and crawled up his back. She settled herself into the same crook at the back of Paiste's neck where she had sat for their flight to the cave.

Thane wrapped both sword belts around his waist and scrambled clumsily up the dragon's tail on his hands and knees. This time, when he dropped himself down on Paiste's neck, he was careful to keep the last spike between Orphan and himself. He wrapped his hands around the spike in front of him, painfully conscious of his irrational desire to not touch her.

The moment Thane indicated that he was ready, Paiste slid his body through the narrow exit and rolled the rock back into place. Thane and Orphan clung precariously to the dragon's back as he scratched for a secure grip on the rock face of the cliff with the claws on his feet and the jointed claws of his wings.

Without warning, the dragon pushed himself off the wall, unfurled his wings to their fullest extension, and lunged into the sky.

Thane's stomach lurched as Paiste's enormous wings caught the air and lifted them violently skyward.

They soared over the open ocean. The sun was low in the sky and lit the large expanse of the ocean in glistening greens and blues. The dragon glided to the left and circled around to head back toward the cliffs.

They followed the ragged line of the cliffs briefly before heading inland. Thane looked down. The ground below them was a blur of dark greens and black. He had no idea where they were. Everything looked so different from up here.

Thane gripped the spike in front of him until his hands hurt as Paiste angled briefly up toward the darkening sky before twisting downward and heading across a valley. He skimmed over a long dark lake nestled between the jagged slopes of two mountains.

Paiste fell into a sharp dive and Thane and Orphan fought to hold on as the wind tried to rip them off the dragon's back. They landed on a shallow stretch of rocky shore between the lake and the forest.

Thane swung his leg over the spike in front of him and tumbled gratefully to the ground. He squinted through the fading light at the dense trees around them. A small stream cut through the trees and emptied into the lake.

"Where are we?" Thane asked out loud.

Several Fæ Paths converge here. Can you not feel it? Paiste raised his long snout and sniffed the air.

Thane shrugged as he watched Orphan climb down off the dragon's back. The prickly sensation told him he was close to something Fæ, something not of this world, but there was no waterfall or mist here, nothing to indicate they were near a Fæ Gateway.

"Where is the Gateway?"

The Gateway is not far. We must walk from here. I cannot fly through the dense forest...although it will be no easy task to squeeze myself between the trees either. Paiste's chest rumbled in what Thane assumed was the dragon's idea of a chuckle. He turned toward the stream.

Paiste folded his wings in close to his body and forced his girth through the first few trees. Thane followed him without waiting for Orphan.

The forest was dense and had a thick canopy of leaves overhead. Thane could see why Paiste was reluctant to fly here. It was hard to see more than a few feet around them in any given direction. Paiste cleared a path between the trees with his body, stomping down the undergrowth with his massive feet, and pushing over small trees with his shoulders.

The farther into the forest they went, the warmer the medallion felt under Thane's shirt. They followed the stream until it stopped at a glade next to a small body of water at the base of a coarse rock wall.

The sun was now below the horizon, and stars were beginning to appear in the East. The rock wall began to shimmer and blur. The medallion felt like it had been set on fire against

Thane's chest as a waterfall suddenly appeared before them. Thane recognized it now. It was the same waterfall they had come through when they had left Tír inna n-Oc months ago.

Thane thought he saw movement in the trees in the corner of his eye and spun quickly to the left. He couldn't see anything unusual, but the silence was unnerving. Something was not right; not even the smallest of creatures were making noise in the forest.

Paiste turned to look at Thane. *It is the gloaming.*

"I think that we will need to be riding you for all of us to pass through the Gate. At least, that is how Orphan and I left Tír inna n-Óc with Embarr." Thane looked back at Orphan for the first time since they had entered the glade. She was still standing within the shelter of the trees.

"I am not going with you," she said without looking at Thane.

"What do you mean you're not going?" Thane was taken aback. "Don't be ridiculous. You can't stay here, and it's not like you have anywhere else..."

Thane stopped in mid-sentence as another shifting shadow caught his eye. He squinted into the darkness, certain now that something was moving in the trees.

"What's wrong?" Orphan asked, her gaze followed his to the darkening forest.

"There's something out there," Thane whispered.

"I don't see anything," she said as she glanced at Thane. "I am not going with you to Tír inna n-Óc. I am not wanted there.

Don't you see? That's why your medallion burns me. I'm not meant to cross the Gate."

"That's stupid. You've crossed with me before. I'm not leaving you here," Thane was beginning to get desperate as she turned away from him.

"You don't have a choice," she insisted.

Paiste's painful bellow interrupted their argument as arrows began to fly out of the surrounding shadows and one tore through the thin membrane of his right wing. He opened his maw and shot a stream of flames toward the tree line.

Færie, we must leave now.

Thane turned toward Orphan again. She was gone. She had already slipped into the surrounding forest and disappeared. He made a move to search for her when the dragon cried out again.

She must find her own way. Let her go. The gloaming is upon us, we must leave now.

Thane hesitated. As angry as he was, he couldn't leave without Orphan.

Thane hesitated a moment too long. A volley of arrows erupted from all around them as Zavior's son, Iagan, and a dozen misshapen Formoire warriors burst through the forest on the opposite side of the waterfall. Thane could see warriors on the cliffs above the waterfall and more Formoire were charging toward him from the forest on his side of the water.

Thane pulled his sword from its sheath and prepared to defend himself. The first Formoire attacked with a ferociousness that rivaled the gallóglaigh. Thane blocked blow after blow before he realized that, just like the Formoire in the tunnel, this one was just engaging him; he was not trying to kill him. The warrior was pulling his swings back at the last moment so as not to deliver a lethal blow.

Thane switched his sword to his left hand in an attempt to confuse the Formoire and throw him off his balance. It worked. The Formoire stumbled back as Thane drove his sword into the warrior's groin. The massive creature stumbled, and fell backward into the pool at the base of the waterfall. Thane gripped the sword with both hands and spun to find another Formoire at his back. Before he could bring his sword up again, the warrior fell forward. He crashed onto the ground at Thane's feet with an arrow in his back...an arrow with golden feather fletchings! Orphan was still here!

Thane looked frantically around for her but couldn't find her. He saw another one of her arrows fly out of the forest. He followed it's line of flight until it impaled another Formoire.

A searing pain tore through Thane's left shoulder. The force of the blow spun him around and knocked him off his feet. He lay flat on his back. He looked up and found the sky suddenly filled with flame. The ground under Thane shook as Paiste came charging toward him bellowing, gold chains swinging back and forth from his neck as he shot fire at the attacking Formoire.

Thane glanced down at his chest and was shocked to see a black arrow sticking out of his shoulder. He could tell by the shortened length of the shaft that the arrow had gone fairly deep. It would not be easy to remove.

A shadow fell over Thane as Paiste stood protectively over him. The dragon had his wings tucked up close to his body to keep them from being torn to shreds by the flying arrows. Thane could hear the ping of arrows ricocheting off of the dragon's hard scales as the Formoire loosed more arrows at them. Battle cries were coming from the cover of the trees as Iagan shouted directions at his warriors. It was becoming apparent to Thane that the Formoire were terrified of the dragon's flames.

Thane screamed as Paiste lowered his head and, without warning, used his teeth to break the arrow off close to Thane's shoulder. Blackness threatened to engulf him as a wave of pain raced through his body.

Paiste swept the area around them with another wave of flame. It was keeping the Formoire warriors on the ground back but they were still raining arrows down on them from above.

We must go. I cannot hold them at bay for much longer. Can you climb up on me?

Thane didn't answer.

The dragon lowered his head and shoved the length of his snout across Thane's body.

Wrap your arm around my head! Paiste ordered.

Thane managed to sheath his sword, then forced himself to lift his right arm up and grasped the nearest spike. The dragon lifted his head and pulled Thane's body up with him. Thane's left arm hung uselessly at his side.

Swing your legs around my neck and hold on tightly!

Paiste was able to twist his head back just enough to enable Thane to swing his leg across Paiste's neck.

Paiste was spiraling up into the air almost before Thane had a chance to secure himself between the dragon's spikes. Thane grabbed the spike in front of him with his right hand and desperately tried to hold on.

"Aim for the dragon's wings, the wings," Iagan screamed from below them. "Don't let them get through that Gate."

Thane looked down as Zavior's son took aim at them with another arrow. Thane tucked his body closer to the dragon's neck as the arrow shot by his ear and flew harmlessly away.

Go through the waterfall. Trust me! Don't stop! Thane screamed at the dragon, desperately trying to get Paiste to hear him.

Thane felt scales ripple under his legs as Paiste's body tensed beneath him. They dove straight toward the waterfall, the medallion was so hot against Thane's skin that he was sure it was going to leave a wound. He fervently hoped that he was correct in his belief that he could get them both through. Otherwise, it was going to be a short trip.

Thane felt Orphan's thoughts brush against his mind as Paiste dove headfirst into the waterfall.

Good-bye, Thane.

Pronunciation Guide

gh - as in ugly   ch - as in lock

Balór – **Ba**-lor

Brecc – Brehk

Buarainech – **Boo**-ar-an-ach

Cianán – **Kee**-a-nan

Ceara – **Keh**-ra

Claidheamh mór – **Kleye**-mor (Claymore)

Cnoc Meadha – Cnock me-a

Cúchonnacht – Koo-**Cho**-nacht

Cú Chulainn – **Koo** -hull-in

Daoine Sidhe – **Da-uh-ee**-na Shee

Dian Cécht – **Jee**-an Kecht

Dùn Scàith – **Doon** Ska-ee

Eoin – **Eh-oh**-een

Fir Manach – Feer **ma**-nach (Fermanah)

Fragarach – **Freh**-ka-rach

Finnbheara – Fee-yon **veh**-ra

Formoire – fo-**mo**-ruh

Gallóglaigh – ga-owl **ok**-leech (Galloglass - plural)

Gallóglach – ga-owl **ok** - lach -(Galloglass- singular)

Gráinne – Graw-nya (Grace)

Granuaile – Graw nya wail

Iagan – **Ee** gan

Inis Ceithleann – **Ee**-neesh Cay-lan - (Enniskillen)

Inis Fáil – Ee-neesh Fail (Ireland)

Lugh – Loo<u>gh</u>

Maighréad – My-raid (variation Margaret)

Manannán mac Lir – **Man**-nan-an mac Leer

Mag Uidhir – Ma-Guier (McGuire)

MacLeòid – Mac Laawtch (MacLeod)

Muirghein – **Mur**-ghyen

Ní Mháille – Nee Vall-uh (O'Malley)

Pádraig – **Paa**-treek

Rian – **Ree**-an (Ryan)

Sorcha – **So**-ra-<u>ch</u>a

Seanchaidh – **Shen**-a-chee

Taliesin – Tally-**ess**-in

Tír inna n-Óc – **Cheer**-na-nok

Tuatha de Danann – Tooah Day Danaan

Uí Néill – Ohee Nyayl (O'Neill)

AUTHOR'S NOTE

Margaret D'Agostino won the privilege of naming one of the characters in this book. I named Rian Mag Uidhir in honor of Ryan Lopynski at her request and Maighréad in honor of her.

I want to acknowledge the Ryan Lopynski Big Heart Foundation. The foundation was started to honor the memory of Ryan Lopynski who died without warning at the age of eighteen of unknown causes. They are working to prevent and foster awareness of sudden cardiac arrest in young adults. Please visit their website www.ryanlopynski.org for more information on what you can do to help.

For the latest information on
The Fæ Prince of Fir Manach Series:
Facebook at www.facebook.com/KRFlanagan
Pinterest at www.pinterest.com/TheFlanaganPin
Twitter @KRFlanagan

Made in the USA
San Bernardino, CA
17 January 2013